Anima Mundi

ANIMA MUNDI

△▽△

by Susanna Tamaro

translated by Cinzia Sartini Blum
& Russell Scott Valentino

*Æ*B

Autumn Hill Books
Iowa City, Iowa

ÆB

http://www.autumnhillbooks.org

Autumn Hill Books, Inc.
P.O. Box 22
Iowa City, IA 52244
© 2007 by Autumn Hill Books
All Right Reserved. Published 2007
Printed in the United States of America

Originally Published as Anima Mundi
© 1997 Susanna Tamaro

Typeset in ITC Berkeley Oldstyle Std

Library of Congress Control Number: 2007932339

Autumn Hill Books ISBN - 13 : 978 - 0 - 9754444 - 4 - 3
Autumn Hill Books ISBN - 10 : 0 - 9754444 - 4 - 1

CONTENTS

Marvel not that I said unto thee, Ye must be born again. The wind bloweth where it listeth, and thou hearest sound thereof, but canst not tell whence it cometh, or whither it goeth: so is every one that is born of the Spirit.

John 3:7-8

FIRE

I

In the beginning was the void. Then the void contracted, becoming smaller than the head of a pin. Was it by its own will or did something force it? No one can know. What is too compressed, in the end, explodes with furious rage. An intolerable glare came forth from the void, dispersing into space, so that there was no longer darkness above but light. From the light the universe gushed forth in crazed splinters of energy projected into space and time. Racing on and on, they formed the stars and the planets. Fire and matter. This could have been enough but it wasn't. The molecules of amino acids continued on, millennium after millennium, transforming themselves until life was born: microscopic unicellular beings that, in order to breath, needed bacteria. From there, from those primordial pools, with a progressively ordering movement, each living form had its origin: the large cetaceans of the depths and the butterflies, the butterflies and the flowers that host their larvae. And man, who stands upright instead of walking on all fours. From four to two things change. The sky is closer; the hands are unencumbered; four movable fingers and an opposable thumb can take hold of anything. And then freedom, dominion over space, action, movement, the possibility of creating order and disorder. Meanwhile, the universe opens and the stars grow ever more distant, racing to the edge like balls on a billiard table. Was all this the work of someone or did it go forth by itself, with the inertia of an avalanche? It's said matter has laws—at that temperature, under those conditions, it could not have made anything other than this, the universe. The universe and the miniscule galaxy containing, suspended, the flowering garden of the earth. Some hundred species of plants and animals would have been more than sufficient to transform our planet into something different from the others. Instead, there are tens upon tens of thousands of different forms of existence. No one person in a single life could learn to recognize them all. Waste or wealth? If matter has its laws, who then made the laws of matter? Who put things in order? No one? A god of light? A god of shadow? What spirit nourishes that which, programming the life of a thing, also programs its death? And what importance can it have? We're in the middle, constantly pressed between the two principles. A fleeting form of order, cells aggregate into our body, into our face. Our face has a name. Our name a destiny. The end of the journey is the same for everyone. Order becomes sporadic, turning to disorder. Enzymes depart with their messages and find no one to welcome them. Messengers of an army that no longer exists. All around is only the deaf silence of death.

Order, disorder, life, death, light, shadow. From the

moment in which I became aware of my existence, I did nothing but ask myself questions, questions no one could answer. Perhaps wisdom means simply not asking yourself anything. I am not wise and never have been. My element is not quartz but mercury. Unstable, mobile, feverish matter. The quick silver forever destined to move. And always in disorder.

Such were my thoughts as I leaned against the gate of the cemetery, waiting for my father's corpse. It was cold, windy. The only birds able to brave it were the crows.

The city services van arrived late, shrouded in a black cloud of diesel fumes. "Where's the priest?" they asked as they unloaded it. "The priest isn't coming," I answered.

Everything happened quickly. The loculus was already open. The men hoisted up the coffin and slid it inside, then sealed it with a white marble slab. They used a drill to fasten it shut. That and the cawing of the crows were the only sounds.

Instead of making a speech, his three friends — the only ones still living — started singing something that sounded like the "Communist International." They sang faintly, as very old people do. The wind blew in short bursts, ripping away the notes as soon as they sounded. I watched them and they did not watch me. They carried three red carnations in their hands, holding them with awkward shyness like children who don't know to whom to give them. There was a small vase outside the loculus, but it was too high to reach. They looked around, hesitating, then opened their fingers and let them fall to the ground. It had rained during the night. The mud on the ground soaked the petals. They were no longer flowers but refuse.

13

We left, one by one, our eyes on the ground. In front of the cemetery gate, I gave a tip to the sextons and without saying a word shook hands with his friends. To the south, the leaden color of the sky was breaking into a lighter streak. Everything was over, closed. Forever.

My father was over six feet tall and weighed some two hundred pounds. He wore enormous shoes. As a child I would put my feet inside them. For me they were Polynesian pirogues, not shoes, and with the carpet beater as an oar I'd make circles around the room.

He was born a few years after the Great War. He'd lived with his massive body through the majority of the century. Along with him went his gastric juices, his cerebral neurons with their branching dendrites, his heart with its ventricles and auricles, the come-and-go of his arterial and venous blood, his bones and tendons, the spongy walls of his lungs, and the smooth, slick sides of his intestines. For eighty years that ensemble of functions that responded to the name Renzo had moved in time and space. It had fought for some things, against others, it had screamed and shouted, and it had consumed an unspecified number of gallons of alcohol. It had made my mother live in terror and entertained friends at the local bar; it had put a son into the world. And that very son, that very morning, had buried it, with a tip for the sextons. The son was not sad but bewildered. Maybe it's always like that when the last parent passes on. All of a sudden you're alone, and in that solitude a lot changes. You're no longer a child. There's no longer anyone to rebel against. The end that, in the order of things, looms on the horizon is yours.

My mother used to say the world was made by God. My father maintained that God had been invented by the priests in order to keep people in line. Up to a point, I preferred thinking of something simpler, a conjurer for instance. One day I'd seen a show in which a man had pulled a rabbit out of hat with the wave of a wand. After that, with the same wand, he had reassembled the fragments of a broken glass. With a wand, then, you could do a lot. Band directors used a wand. Waving it in the air, they transformed the confused black scribbles on paper into music that could make you weep.

I believed in the conjurer for quite a while. Then, from one day to the next, I stopped believing in anything. It happened when a classmate of mine died. He was riding his bike to get cigarettes for his mother. It was twilight and hard to see. A car struck him and he was caught underneath. We weren't especially good friends. It's just that the day before, he'd let me use his eraser. All of a sudden his desk was empty and the eraser was at the bottom of my satchel. There was no one to give it back to anymore. That's it. First there was Damiano. Then, in his place, the void.

We'd gone to the funeral in our school smocks and ties, the oldest two boys carrying a large wreath. We passed in front of his house on the way to the cemetery. His mother had forgotten to bring in the laundry. His pants and shirts were still there on the line, whipped by the wind like the flag of a vanished country. When the priest said, "We are thinking of your little smile up there, in the pastures of the sky," I broke into tears. I wasn't crying because I was moved but because I was angry. Why were they kidding us, I asked myself? He's no longer anywhere. The eraser is cold in my pocket.

That day I realized I was like one of those fakirs in India, who live for years perched on top of a pole. I was alone, sitting on a pole, surrounded by the void. In my head, thoughts. Others were probably like this too. They just didn't seem aware of it.

Once our teacher had explained to us that saprophytes were one of the foundations on which our existence rested. They could be vegetable or animal. Their function was to decompose all that had once had a life of its own. They broke down complex molecules into simple molecules. The ammonia, nitrates, and carbon monoxide of our bodies helped plants grow. Animals ate the plants, and we ate both the animals and the plants. The squaring of the circle. Before the absolute void were these tiny creatures, humble transformers.

While my father's friends mumbled the International, it was of them I was thinking. I watched the three old men and wondered if they felt that anxious seething beneath their feet. They too in the end were nothing but fodder for the saprophytes, and deep down they knew it. It wasn't appropriate or nice of me to think this, but I couldn't get it out of my head. More than twenty years had passed, but here again were all my childhood fantasies about death.

When my grandmother passed on, my mother had explained to me that death was a kind of sham because you never die forever. "One day," she said, "the trumpet of judgment will sound, and there will be a kind of great revelry. Then everyone will come out of their tombs." I was troubled. I already knew about the existence of paradise, purgatory, and hell. So I wondered how such a thing was possible. When you died, you went up or down or you stopped for a while half way in between. It depended on whether you'd been good or not. What did opened sarcophaguses have to do with it? There couldn't be anything inside anymore. I couldn't see any reason why at some point you would need to rush back into your tomb as if forming up for review. Thinking about such a thing made me recall the mornings when, though awake, I'd pretended to be asleep. I liked being awakened by my mother, so as soon as I heard her step, I'd close my eyes again. It was a kind of game. Maybe one day, to please God, all the dead people were just going to pretend to be dead. At a pre-arranged sign, from hell, paradise, and purgatory, in a great stampede they would all rush to the place they'd been buried.

But even if that were the case, there were still practically insurmountable problems. I saw how they'd sealed up Grandma, and I knew how small she was. How would she ever be able to get that cover off? For her even a toothpick would have been too heavy. And what about all those poor men who'd been blown to pieces on battle fields, the bodies of Pyrrus's and Hannibal's soldiers mingled with the enormous bodies of their elephants? How was it possible that, at the blast of a trumpet, everyone would be able to find his own parts? What if, in the rush, someone grabbed the leg of an enemy or an elephant rotula by mistake? Then

17

what? Would he present himself to God like that? And what about the inhabitants of India, whom no one had warned about this, and who continued to cremate themselves? Could the ashes be resurrected too?

I got home after the funeral with these thoughts in my head and immediately looked for something to drink. There was only a half-bottle of sweet liqueur, which my mother used to use for cakes. It no longer had any aroma, but there was still alcohol in it. I drank it from the bottle. I would have liked to lie down, but it wasn't possible. There was just a skimpy vinyl couch.

I was sitting in the very same place, my feet dangling above the floor, when I had asked my mother, "Does the devil exist?" She'd been washing the dishes, and I could see her back with the apron tied at the waist. "What's got into you?" had been her vaguely surprised answer. My question had been neutralized by another question. "Nothing," I'd said, shrugging.

A few days later, I had repeated the same question to my father. He broke into laughter. "Of course he does," was his response. "The fascists are the devil." It became clear to me then that none of them would be able to give me an answer.

I often thought about that skeleton holding a scythe, which was painted on the walls of the church. It was mowing hay, and hay was our life. If God was good, as they said, who had invented that skeleton? Maybe God was not so good. Or maybe he was good but distracted. Or maybe he'd had a bad day and on that day created the devil. The devil and death.

When my mother saw me pensive, she'd say, "Why don't you go outside and play with the others?"

Now no one said anything to me anymore. I had come back home. The house was empty, and I was grown up. The questions I asked myself were the same as those I'd asked when my feet didn't reach the floor from the couch.

Once, at the Sunday movies, I'd seen *Moby Dick*. A fraction of a second before the white whale burst forth from the water, the projector had caught fire. There'd been a flare up and, immediately after, in the darkness of the hall, the white sheet had become visible again.

The scene came back to me as I thought about my past. What had happened in all those years?

I had escaped, run far away. In that flight I'd deluded myself into thinking I could make a new life. Then I'd come back. Like a good son, I had buried my father and tipped the sextons. And with that tip I'd realized that behind me there were only burned film frames. The leviathan had neither died nor disappeared. It was still there, just beneath the water's surface. Walking through the empty rooms, I could glimpse its silhouette—ominous, gray, silent, ready at any moment to leap out and destroy all.

19

II

The house where I was born is a small, three-storey building from the early fifties. Gray cement outside, bleakness inside, nothing to make it pleasant. The kitchen windows overlook the street, the bedroom windows open onto the courtyard. A courtyard where no flowers grow, only car junk. The plastic blinds, once blue, are now of indeterminate color. There's a strong mustiness in the stairwell, mixed with the stench of cat piss. At first only my mother lived here. Then when she got married, my father moved in too.

Even though on the credenza there's a picture of the two of them with me as a baby in their arms, and even though they're smiling in it, I can't remember a single instant of my past when, under this roof, there was anything close to happiness. I'm not talking about old American movies, where everyone fawns on everyone else. I would have been happy with something more ordinary, more basic. If I think about something physical, I think of a lukewarm glue, a glue that holds pieces together. I'm here, and you're here next to me. The glue unites us, helps us understand what we're doing. But here there was nothing. There were two people in that house, and those two were as close as a wall and a shoe. Then a third came along, and it was something else again, a shovel for instance. The wall, the shoe, and the shovel lived together under the same roof. That's all.

Honor thy father and mother. This commandment, at a certain moment of my life, scared me more than any other. By then I'd learned all about how children were born and the tyrannical law that makes the world go around. At a given moment, all mammals go into heat: males look for females and mating takes place. Nature has a tremendous imagination. It has come up with endless tricks to make this happen. In their own way even trees mate. This strained music accompanies everything.

I gradually came to understand that the commandment does not mean, as everyone thinks, be kind to your parents, don't pocket any of the change from your grocery errands, and don't talk back. They want to make children believe that that's it, but it's not the truth at all; it's only a cover, a patch on your sweater to hide the hole. The truth is quite different, and it's embarrassing even if all you have is an intuition of it.

Honor thy father and mother means: never imagine the instant in which they conceived you. Keep thinking about storks and cabbages, flocks of storks and immense fields of cabbages. Do so until the end of your days because otherwise you'll have to realize that in that instant, in the majority of cases, there was no loving plan, just a mundane calling.

21

No one imagined the being that would come into the world, no one desired it, no one anticipated its otherness, its eyes, its hands, its new way of seeing things. In all simplicity, there was an itch somewhere that had to be scratched. There was a moment of distraction, and in that moment your mother and father became you.

There are of course exceptions. There are always some — few — lucky ones in the world, but I, at age fourteen, was well aware I wasn't one of them. I'd watch the big ogre eat. He would break bread into pieces, drop them into his soup, ruminating without raising his eyes. I'd watch him and know he had conceived me the same way. While I proceeded from morula to blastula, while my being grew, he snored obscenely, his breath heavy, his mouth open.

22   I was on the threshold of adolescence. I felt like an animal at the end of its hibernation. All during middle school, I had thought only of the void. Of the void and of what was or wasn't behind it. They were thoughts veiled with sadness. There was melancholy in every one of my movements. I sometimes spent entire afternoons in my room, looking out the window. As I stared at the void, I sometimes even broke into tears. I entered so completely into my own thoughts that I could no longer find a way out. I was sad and that was all there was to it. In a sense the tears were a kind of consolation.

People had noticed the change at school. They called my mother and told her, "It's not normal. The boy is behaving like an old man." My state had not escaped my father's notice either. Once during dinner he gestured toward me with his chin and asked my mother, "What's the matter? Is he sick?" I was always bewildered by how he never addressed me directly. Was he maybe afraid I didn't speak the same language? Every time he had to ask me something, he would turn to my mother. "Where is he going?" he'd ask, or, "Why does he come home so late?" I watched them talk, following the conversation like a deaf mute, watching the lips of one and then the other.

This state of apathy lasted until I was about fourteen.

Then a sort of inner thaw took place. It was as if my blood had changed its color, the intensity of its flow, its propulsion. There was a different vitality inside me. Each day I grew taller, stronger. With a bit of genetic luck, I would have become as tall and strong as my father. Then I would have finally been able to appear before him and say, "I hate you." Hatred was the feeling I'd felt for him since my earliest memories. I don't think he felt the same, at least not up to then. For most of my childhood I think he didn't feel one way or another about me. Sometimes I was a nuisance, yes, but nothing else.

Children were women's responsibility. Men came in later. I imagined a sort of bus stop. My mother would get off, leaving me there; a little later my father would arrive to take me with him on another part of the route. I was a mail-order package whose content had to correspond to the description in the catalogue. If it was different, it would need to be returned.

I was born too early. If I'd been born nowadays, my father would have used the most modern genetic methods. He would have filled out a form with so many checks, one

23

next to "male," another next to "healthy," a third by "communist," a fourth by "not queer."

My father considered himself so perfect that he couldn't even remotely imagine I could be something less than a copy of him. He was the top. I had to be equal to that top. Here is the big, scary contradiction. Human beings more than anything else fear difference, but nevertheless they continue to put children into the world. A child is necessarily always different. It's poison you lace your own food with.

In reality the right way to reproduce oneself would be the one chosen, or at least endured, by Frankenstein. A puppet with coils in its head. Electricity runs through the coils, and the deed is done. You have another form of life, identical to the model that was lying there beside you. The world would be more peaceful, boring perhaps, but with less suffering. Instead, one day your mother leaves you at the bus stop, where you're lost like Tom Thumb. Your father arrives, looks at you, and says, "What's this piece of garbage?" And you no longer know what to think of yourself.

One night, while talking about me with my mother — I was there with them, in the same room — instead of saying, as he always had, "the kid" or "the boy" — which was tantamount to saying "the dog" — he said "your son." He said it as if my mother were a snail or one of those creatures capable of doing everything by themselves. He said, "your son," and the words had a tone that was not at all neutral. That was how I came to understand one of the laws of nature — that isn't written down anywhere — which is that if children function, they belong to the father, but if they don't they remain for their entire lives an appendage of their mothers.

My mother was a silent, peaceful woman. I was quite surprised when she told me she'd met my father at a dance. It was the harvest festival and they'd danced together the whole night. At the time she was seventeen and in her last year of the teacher's training school. She liked children, and in any case, in those years, there were few choices for women who wanted to study. They could be teachers for elementary school or typists. There was a picture of her in her black school smock, surrounded by her classmates, taken just before she got her diploma. I used to look at it often. And the more I looked, the more convinced I became that the young woman was not my mother but someone else. There was a light in her eyes and a smile on her face that would have made even stones fall in love. I couldn't help asking myself which of the two was the actual her, the happy or the sad one. You change as you grow up, so I was always told. Why should the change always be for the worse? There'd been a dance and Ada had met Renzo. It hadn't been a simple encounter but a stroke of lightening. Then the war had come, an even bigger stroke. The war had separated them. For the entire period she had waited. The thought of him never left her, not even for an instant. Upon his return they got married. Then came me, many years later, the me that was or should have been the crown of that dream. A beautiful, touching story, if it had been a play. In the end, everyone would have clapped enthusiastically. Instead, there was nothing to be enthusiastic about.

25

When the three of us were at home, we were like three goldfish trapped in a bowl without anyone changing the water. The lack of oxygen intoxicated our gills. When we opened our mouths, all that came out was air bubbles.

My father used to always lose patience. He lost it over nothing—because he couldn't find a sock one morning, because the soup was over-salted, or because I scratched my head with a pencil while studying. Home was a continuous explosion. He'd utter the worst curses, throwing everything on the floor, kicking the walls and the cabinets. Then, when there was nothing left to break, he'd leave the house, slamming the door behind.

Once I read in a book that even seagulls do such things when they get mad at one another. Instead of attacking, they start furiously ripping out the grass. The tear it and throw it down, pulverizing everything they can get at with their beaks. They go until they exhaust themselves. Only then do they stop and resume their previous activity, as if nothing had happened. They do this out of convenience, not goodness. It's against the law of survival to destroy individuals of your own species.

My father's behavior was identical to that of the seagulls. He broke the dishes and chairs in order not to break the heads of his wife and son.

I grew up in terror. Growing up in terror, I learned that in the end even terror becomes boring. I used to dream that one day, suddenly, something different would happen. I don't know, that he'd yell, "There's no salt," and she'd answer, "Go get it yourself"; or he'd sit at the table and say, "I've never had anything so extraordinarily good." That never happened.

The road to hell is paved with good intentions. Once you choose the lines of a radio melodrama, they remain the same always. It's a little like donkeys turning a millstone: in the end, through the monotony of going round in circles, they become convinced there's no better life than that.

So up to a certain age I considered myself my mother's protector, her solace. On one occasion, when I'd learned to ride a bicycle, I even suggested we run away together. I'll deliver milk in the mornings, I told her. We'll be happy forever. He won't find us, and even if he does we won't open the door. I was at the naïve age when you expect clear answers. I wasn't yet aware of how radio melodramas work. I was convinced she was the victim, and, as victim, she could do nothing other than say, "Yes, let's run away together."

That my mother was complicit I understood much later, in late adolescence, when she began to attack instead of defend me. Only then did I realize that, no matter how incomprehensible, crazy, and unreasonable it was, the most important thing was their relationship. The melodrama of hatred. I had provided the background noise for many years. I was the opening and closing of doors, the creaking of a bed, a cough, a sneeze. I was — and should have remained — all that.

The very day on which I raised my head and my voice, asking for a role of my own, even my mother turned against me.

Perhaps that, of all things, was the heaviest, the hardest to bear. For many years each of our lives had validated the other's: we existed for each other. Then, suddenly, she took a black marker and blotted out her eyes, her smile.

What happened next? I regretted having been good. Just that. From one day to the next I wanted to erase my past. I was ashamed of all I'd been. Of my good, accommodating nature. Of the fact that, "thank God," I hadn't been "a problem child." It hadn't cost me any effort. Being silent and nice was part of me, a way of living, expending less energy. Even with terrible thoughts in my head, I kept saying, "Yes, teacher."

I wasn't first in my class, or second or third even. Excelling was a stupid waste of energy. But I was singled out. Mothers and teachers would say, "See how Walter never bothers anyone." So I thought, if I'm born again I'll piss on the desks, I'll nail kittens to doors. If I'm born again, I'll be a pest from the very start. There isn't a single reason to make life easy for those who will make it hard for you later.

For the first fifteen years I'd been losing the game. Understanding that was an important achievement. It was as if I'd stepped up on a chair. The landscape I saw was the same as always, but I saw it from a different perspective. I started provoking people. Not a day went by when I didn't say something nasty to my mother. With my father I didn't yet dare. Insulting her was a way to test the terrain. What happens when one departs from the script of the melodrama, I wondered?

So I taunted her. "You let him treat you like a slipper," I told her. "To him the whole world is toilet paper for wiping his ass. You're a piece of it, but I won't be." Then she'd start doing something with her hands. She'd clean a shelf with a sponge or something of that sort. It was still the trick of the seagulls. She would clean, her eyes fixed on what she was cleaning, and hiss, "Don't talk that way about your father. I won't allow it." "And why shouldn't I?" I'd say. "You're afraid of the truth, but I'm not. The truth is that he's an asshole." "Where did you learn to talk like that?" "Where? Where? You really want to know? Just you try and imagine, come on. From that same asshole."

We'd go on that way for hours, until we were exhausted. She'd keep cleaning, and I'd keep screaming, passing back and forth through the room. There were no victories or defeats. We both wanted the impossible. She, for me to go back to being background noise. I, for her to admit her hatred.

"Why did you marry him?!" I screamed one day.

"Because I loved him," she answered, looking me in the eyes. "Because I love him."

The war was always her great excuse, what she thought should put everything to rest. "You can't understand," she'd say when cornered. "Your father was in the war. He was a partisan."

The war was the resistance carried out in the mountains. He'd been away for a long time, and no one had heard anything from him. Not even he would say what he had done in those years. I knew Tex Willer, Pecos Bill, and a couple of other cartoon characters that had accomplished important things. The heroes of films and cartoons had nothing to do with my father. They were brave, strong. Before they fired, they always stared into the whites of their enemies' eyes. Someone who kicks chairs and walls, I thought, is nothing other than a frightened man. A vile coward with a fixed insult on his lips. There was nothing great in my father, nothing memorable. You wouldn't have

29

given him your hand to cross the street, let alone when you found yourself at the edge of a precipice.

The only noteworthy thing in him was contempt. It was something so strong that, already as I child, I could smell it. It was sour, sharp, a mix of hormones and adrenaline. It hovered about him, following him like a cloud.

On the days when he was talkative, he too would start up about the war. It happened when I complained about not being able to do or have something. Then he'd begin: "A war would straighten you out," he'd say. "I'd like to see you running with bombs hissing all around, or trying to escape a mop up team. You need to have a German chase you with a Lugar in his hand. To cry from cold and hunger."

He went on for hours with similar pleasantries. The moment I became distracted, he struck the table with his fist and screamed, "Pay attention!" The essence of it all was that I had to consider myself lucky. One war was over and no other had broken out yet.

Some years later I heard a story that my father would have liked. It was about an American boy, born of a couple who had survived the Nazi camps. He'd come into the world when the ashes were cold. Nevertheless, from the day he'd started to understand the meaning of words, his parents had done nothing but repeat, "You didn't live through what we lived through. You don't understand horror, deportation, hunger, humiliation. You don't deserve to exist." He never replied. He waited patiently to grow up. On the day he came of age, he enrolled in the Marines and shipped out to Vietnam. He came back at the end of the war, blind, without arms or legs. His father and mother took turns pushing the wheelchair. While they passed through the colorful streets, he'd say, "You don't know what it's like to live in darkness. You don't know what it means to not be able to walk, to not be able to pick a flower."

My father would have liked it a lot because it's what he always wished for my future: a son maimed by the fury of history. I've never been able to classify this feeling of his. Female cats defend their young by tooth and nail, just as all other living creatures. There's nothing more precious to defend than genetic patrimony. It's not me but science that says so. Perhaps, my father too was inspired by Darwin in a certain sense. He had in mind the triumph of the law of the fittest. Exposing newborns to frigid cold and the elements, exposing them to wounds, constantly undermining the physical weakness of their bodies: this was the best way of seeing if they functioned. If they didn't, too bad. It meant they didn't deserve to see the light of day. No one's indispensable in this world. Not even your own children.

31

The other feeling that kept him alive was hatred. Hatred and contempt were like Castor and Pollux, two twins walking hand in hand. The eyes of one were used to observe things, those of the other, to aim one's spittle at them. "Your father fought for a better world," my mother would repeat. I looked all around and wondered, where is that world? "He risked his life to fight the Nazis, the fascists, the Ustashe. Many others would not have had the courage to do that." This was the refrain I heard continually at home. Without him, without people like him, the world would have never changed.

This was true. There were no bad people anymore. Now those uniforms, those crosses, those legs up in the air, could only be witnessed in movies or in some old documentary.

At school we'd studied the Second World War. Children luckier than I even had model airplanes of the Wehrmacht. The teacher had told us no war like that could ever take place again.

The third one, the worst of all, would have fallen to us. Two or three bombs would have cleared the tables. Those bombs would have generated a hot wind, hotter than anything else in the world: its gust would have blown us all up like puppets. The plants and animals would have died with us, every life form would have disappeared, and any that survived would have fared even worse.

That same teacher had once taken us to visit the Museum of Science. There was a big stuffed whale hanging from the ceiling. It had a lot of teeth and seemed to be smiling. All around were glass display cases. They were full of jars with a yellowish liquid. Translucent looking things floated in the liquid. "They're fetuses," she had explained, pointing at them with a sweeping gesture. "You were like that too before you were born."

There was one fetus of a dog and one of a hedgehog with all its spines. I was examining the hedgehog when she clapped her hands. "Look over here, children!" she exclaimed. We turned and she indicated a larger jar. Inside was a ghostly pale baby. Instead of one head it had two. Two heads complete with everything: four eyes, two noses, two mouths, four ears.... "Hiroshima," said the teacher. "Hiroshima and Nagasaki, remember? Over there, after the bombs, children like this were born. This is what happens: suddenly nature can't remember the right way to make things. Two heads, six arms, three legs, there you have it...."

Naturally, these words had provoked immediate snickering on the part of my classmates. All of them were hinting at the multiplication of genitalia. But I was more interested in the doubling of heads. I considered: perhaps nature should have done that from the beginning; a single head is really not enough. There's too little space in there and too much confusion. Many people use it only to hold up their face or to make their hair grow, like having a garden with good soil for flowers. Even scooters have spare tires. Why shouldn't it be the same for heads? One for show and a second that does the actual work.

The fact that nature could lose its form had shocked me. I envisioned an elderly woman with disheveled hair, wandering about a messy house. Everything was turned upside down, the drawers, the wardrobes, as if thieves had ransacked the place. She wandered through the rooms with a lost expression, without even knowing what to look for.

33

In the end, I told myself, creating people hadn't been a good idea. Having them there, rummaging about the earth, was tantamount to nursing a viper in one's bosom. Ever since the world has been the world, animals have done same thing over and over: they were born, mated, took care of their young, preyed on other species in order to survive, then, one day, they died, and instead of feeding their young, they fed the hyenas, the crows, the saprophytes, the earth, and the flowers that grew upon it. There had never been a bear or a lion that had planned destruction. But man had, almost from the very start. He began at the very moment when, instead of there being two on the surface of the earth, there were four.

If Adam had murdered Eve, or vice versa, the story would have ended right off. Instead, Cain and Abel came along. And after a while Cain murdered Abel only because things were going better for Abel than for him. Abel had snow white lambs whose wool he groomed, and Cain couldn't stand that. So he picked up a club and did him in. "Where's your brother," asked God some time after. He didn't know what to say. Mouth shut, head down. While wandering through the barren lands, he felt like a poor wretch. He didn't know he was as important as a king or an emperor. After him, men almost all men behaved in the same way. He was the true prince. Since then, envy and prejudice have been the drive belt of the world.

I remember having a dream on the night after the museum visit. I was walking in a meadow, and suddenly a hot wind came toward me. It seemed like a giant hair dryer had begun to blow. I looked up and saw the sky was dark. Above everything there were fantastic fireworks. I had never seen such a light. It seemed to pass straight through you. In that very instant I felt a unique sensation: my cells and atoms, bones and tendons were melting away. I felt no pain, only heat. It wasn't an unpleasant sensation. Then the heat turned into something else. I had wings instead of arms. They were long and powerful like those of a pelican. I began to move them and slowly rose up higher and higher. Beneath me the trees and houses were mere dots. Mine looked no bigger than a crumb. Around it was the town, the city, the entire region, the frayed edges of the coast and the pointed outline of the mountains. The wings responded perfectly to my commands. It was beautiful to be up above, with a body no longer my own.

III

The region in which I was born is not a happy one. It sits on the borders of three countries. For that reason it has often been visited by war.

My father's father, that is, my grandfather, was born in central Italy. When he was little more than a boy he'd come up here to fight. He belonged to a unit of the Assault Troops. You can tell by their name they were among the bravest soldiers. With no more than a bayonet in hand, they crawled towards the enemy lines. They crawled in the dark and cut the throats of anyone who came within reach. I don't remember him well. He died when I was still a child. The little I have in my memory is only incredulity. I'd hear him boast about all the accomplishments of his youth, but all I could see before me was an old man with a meek expression. One of the two images had to be false. Maybe he talked like that to get attention, so someone would listen to him amid the room's silence.

He couldn't stand not being believed. Which was why at the beginning of each spring he'd insist we all take a trip together, always to the same place. We loaded up our little sedan with blankets, a radio, and plastic containers with picnic food.

The field where we were headed wasn't just any field. It was one in which my grandfather had fought. He'd been wounded there. For getting that wound he'd been awarded the bronze cross for military valor. During the trip he wore it on his lapel. He recounted the same episodes every time, as if they'd happened the day before, but no one listened anymore. My mother would once in a while say, "Yes, Papa." My father kept the radio glued to his ear to listen to soccer matches. But Grandpa was happy despite the lack of interest. Coming home, he'd say, "What a nice day that was...."

The last of such outings when I was old enough to understand a few things — I realized it was really funny to go and have a picnic on a field that had been fertilized by so many prematurely extinguished lives. Grandpa said it had been a real bloodbath. There'd been so many bodies lying one on top of another that you couldn't take a single step. You'd have needed a giant's legs to climb over all of them and move on. I looked at the grass and flowers as he spoke. Among the grass were gentianellas and anemones. The wind would gently stir their extraordinarily delicate petals below the open sky. The same sky as the day of the slaughter.

I'd look at everything and wonder what the sense of it was.

Cain had been ashamed of his action in a way. It doesn't say anywhere that he went around boasting afterward. He'd

37

done a bad thing and knew it. But my grandfather was happy. I never heard him say, "I think about the families of those I killed," or anything like that. He was simply happy he'd been quicker and luckier. He didn't care about anything else. Yet he wasn't a bad man. When he died, a lot of people came to his funeral, all of them weeping.

Once I asked my mother, "Is Grandpa a murderer?" She turned to me and said, "Where do you dig up this nonsense?"

Then I understood at least one thing: killing without a uniform makes you a murderer; killing with a uniform earns you medals. Even as a child I was of a rather speculative nature. I couldn't help but wonder whether the lives of those who die are valued differently. Before becoming adults and then cadavers, those men had been boys, newborns, and fetuses. Mothers had brought them into the world, had fed and raised them. Perhaps they hoped to have grandchildren. Instead their hopes had ended up scattered amidst the stones of a streambed or the mud of a field.

One day in school I even asked a teacher, one who'd inspired me with particular confidence. She listened in silence and then answered, "These are very big questions." Then she'd added something that I didn't quite understand about history going forward, taking misfortune along with it. History, I thought then, must be a kind of carriage that had lost its brake, a carriage without anyone on board, crashing down a slope and trampling everything in its path.

But in the smaller history — the one having to do with our home — there was something that remained quite unclear to me. My father had also been in the war, the second one chronologically, yet we'd never gone for a picnic in any of his places. And there was no picture of him in uniform on the kitchen credenza. By then, the only form of communication between him and me was silence. So I didn't have the courage to question him about his potentially heroic deeds. He didn't talk about it, and I didn't ask.

There were only two possible scenarios. Either he'd fought in the war without killing anyone, and therefore was ashamed of having failed in his duty. Or he'd killed but without wearing a uniform, so the shame he felt was that of the murderer.

In the end I didn't really care much which of the two was true. By then I'd understood there was an unexploded bomb in our house. It was buried under tons of rubble, the rubble of unspoken words. The powder was dry and fresh, the timer ticked with perfect precision. The bomb was the true heart of the house. It was what held us together and might blow us up on any given day.

In the school yard there was a color poster that filled an entire display case. Above it were a number of sketches like those in comic books. There were kids in short pants playing in a field. While playing, they found an oddly shaped object. They were curious, and to see what was inside they struck it with a stone. Just after, there was a huge explosion. The kids flew backwards as if pushed by an invisible hand. Next, the same kids were there, but they weren't the same as before. One was missing a leg, another an arm, a third had lost his sight. *Children, beware!* was written at the

39

end. *If you find something strange, don't touch it. Call your parents or the police immediately.* Below these words several objects were portrayed. One looked like a pine cone or a pineapple. Others resembled gigantic suppositories.

So some bombs were inside people, and others were hidden in the ground like lily bulbs. Maybe those bulbs too were the misfortunes sown by history, which killed grandparents, fathers, and then left little presents for their children and grandchildren. Its carriage had passed by long ago. There were no longer enemies on either side. Yet people died all the same.

IV

Mother wasn't a believer when she was young. She became one in the years when my father fought in the mountains. The war had separated them at the beginning of their love. She thought she'd landed on a safe, lush island where she would spend the rest of her life. Instead, from one day to the next, she found herself hanging onto the edge of a cliff. He disappeared, not for weeks but years. At first she still got a few letters or messages passed from person to person. Then a long silence fell on his destiny. It was then she decided to turn to the most powerful of all, God. Their pact was very simple. I'll follow you forever, she told Him, if you let him come back safe.

You could say many things about my mother but not that she wasn't steadfast in her vows. When she made a commitment, she was faithful and punctual in observing it. My father returned and she believed. They must have fought a lot about this at first. He couldn't stand the fact that his companion had turned into some kind of bigot. "You let yourself be duped like everyone else," he'd yell, even when I was grown up.

My mother died first, opening up a lead on him of nearly ten years. I was living in Rome then and didn't give a
damn about their lives. My father must have been filled
with rage. It had all started with a stomach ache. People
close to her said, "It's your grief. There's too much of it. It
doesn't know where else to go. So it settles there." That's
what she believed. When she finally went to the doctor, it
was too late. The grief had spread all through her body. Si-
lently, diligently, it had begun to devour her insides.

For many years I hadn't had any contact with them.

One day I was surprised to find her in front of my
door. It must have been ten or eleven in the morning. I'd
been drinking the night before. My head was heavy and
my mood foul. Opening the door and seeing her there
was an unpleasant shock. The box with the time bomb in
it was behind me, or so I believed. I hadn't asked to see
her. Nor did I have any desire to. Homesickness was a
feeling I never experienced. I didn't understand the reason for that surprise visit. I looked her over without hiding my irritation, while she stood before me, holding her
shiny purse tight.

"Has something happened?" I asked, even before letting
her in. She looked lost. She said softly, "Nothing has happened. I just felt like seeing you." The woman standing before me was different from the one I remembered. She had
clearly changed. But I thought the change must be due
solely to age. I was too young, too inexperienced, too furious to be able to read the signs of serious illness.

If she'd told me, "I'm dying," maybe everything would
have gone differently. I would have stretched that day into

an eternity. But instead I immediately covered it in a shroud of ill humor.

"I wanted to see Rome," she'd whispered, as if apologizing. So I took her for a ride on the Circle Line. We were silent during the entire ride. She looked at the ancient monuments with the expression of a girl on a school trip. Sitting behind her, I kept looking at my watch. Every traffic jam or slowdown made me lose my temper. At the Coliseum we got off and had a sandwich. It was twilight when we got back onto the Circle Line, the twilight of a cold, blustery, winter evening.

"The light looks like gold," she said, and then asked immediately, "Are you happy?"

"Do you still believe in that nonsense?" I asked in response. "Happiness doesn't exist."

Her train left that same evening. I was busy and didn't feel like wasting time by taking her to the station. So I took her to the main street where all the buses stop. I wrote on a piece of paper where she had to get off and what changes she had to make in order to get there. It was dinner time, and we were the only ones at the bus stop. When the bus appeared on the straight, she suddenly hugged me. I was surprised since she'd never been especially demonstrative. I instinctively hugged her back. Only then did I realize that under her black coat with the musk rat collar there was almost nothing left of her.

Meanwhile the bus had arrived and opened its doors. There were just a few people on board. As it moved away, I saw her waving her open palm at me from the rear window. She had the faint smile of a lost child. A thin sticky rain was falling, and the extraordinary whiteness of the palm of her hand stood out against the darkness.

Two months later I found a message from my father on my answering machine. His voice was more than sorrowful, it was lifeless. Behind the circumstantial tone, you could sense his retrained rage. "Your mother is dead," he said, "and I've buried her as well." These were his exact words. It sounded as though he had buried her with his own hands, like a Doberman and its bone. After the message there was only a click. No greeting, no invitation to call back. So I didn't. I didn't care to know what had killed her. She was no more, and that was the only noteworthy fact.

My mother wasn't yet sixty when she died, but to me she had seemed old. With the cynicism of youth I made her disappearance fit into the cycle of natural physiology. As far as I was concerned, I'd been an orphan from birth. I wasn't able to feel any regret.

She's dead, I told myself that evening as I closed my eyes. I wanted to see whether it would have any impact, whether a tear might well up or something. Nothing. I turned to the other side and fell asleep. In the middle of the night, I suddenly opened my eyes. There was a strange noise in the room. It was coming from my mouth. My teeth seemed to be filled with rage and force. I was clenching them together as if I wanted to break them.

I didn't know then that the things that happen to us are never neutral. We can believe in them, be convinced by them. A clover seed keeps its life force intact for eighty whole years. This is also true of facts. Even if we cover them over with a blanket of indifference or blow hard to send them far away, they remain there below, quiet. They're the germ of something that will sprout sooner or later.

Something strange happens to people who are too sensitive. When they grow up they become the cruelest of all. The body has its laws, among which is this one. If something undermines its firmness, its antibodies are immediately set in motion. Violence and cynicism are nothing but this. They reverse your vision of the world in order to provide strength. I was never surprised to read about the lives of great criminals. There have been people who exterminated entire populations and, in the evening, watering their flowers, were moved by a little bird that had fallen from its nest. Inside us somewhere is a switch, which turns the heart's power on and off according to need.

Father and mother were not uneducated people. She'd been an elementary school teacher and had applied herself with passion. He worked in the shipyards as a technical draughtsman. A couple of years before my birth he had fallen during an inspection of a ship's hull and become disabled, one of his legs ending up shorter than the other. Nevertheless he'd refused to use a cane. They both knew I was intelligent, and they had great hopes for my future. Naturally, they were always their hopes. My mother saw me as a professor of literature or philosophy, my father, as an engineer. I don't believe they wondered even for an instant what my true passion might have been. And, in truth, not even I knew that. As a child, I imagined myself becoming a pilot or a policeman, a pilot to fly above things, a policeman to bring more justice into the world. But by the fifth grade, the time of my classmate's death, these dreams had already evaporated. The only thing I was conscious of was the surrounding void that lay in wait. It was difficult to move or imagine anything with that sword pointed constantly at your throat.

I felt alone, and loneliness weighed on me.

At first I'd tried to communicate my thoughts to someone. The reactions, however, had not been the best. After listening to me, they all remained in an embarrassed silence or changed the subject, as one does with people who have lost their minds.

In the solitude of my room I'd ask myself why I saw things no one else did. It would have been simpler, I thought, to have a talent for mechanics or physics. Everyone would have been struck by my questions then. With a few precise calculations I could have shown why something worked or didn't. Instead, the questions I asked myself never concerned anything concrete.

There were contradictions in the real world, and these obsessed me. People talked in one way and behaved in another. My father had fought for a better world and there was nothing heroic or exemplary in him. He wore a halo of hatred and contempt. As my grade school teacher used to say, there's a whole ocean between words and deeds, and it was that ocean I wanted to sound.

Actually, by watching my parents, I had already come to understand that the world was divided into at least two large sectors. One comprised those who believed that beyond the universe lay something else; the other believed that, in the game of life, there was but one time period. But

I couldn't manage to take the field for one side or the other. They both had a virtually infinite series of ready made answers, while those I found for myself were made to measure. They fit me but no else.

For my entire childhood I hovered at the edge of that immense void. Then came adolescence, and I took the plunge. One day I wanted to study medicine in order to go to Africa and rescue starving children. The next day I wanted to be a mere murderer. In the afternoon, instead of studying I'd roam the fields or the city streets. I'd walk for hours, my fists in my pockets, my eyes on the ground. Walking did not lessen the pain at all. On the contrary, it made it grow. Each step was a line of argument, a question that found no answer. I spoke aloud, laughing on my own. I knew I seemed crazy to others but didn't care. If the norm was what I'd seen before me for some fifteen years, if it was insults and lifeless gazes, sadness dragged through one's days like a cape, I didn't want to be part of it even for a single second of my existence.

At a bookstand in the old part of town, I found a book of poems by Hölderlin. I'd never read any poetry but what we had studied in school, which was of course boring. When I opened that book, I immediately experienced an overwhelming emotion.

There inside were things that I too felt, melancholy, pain, autumn, the sense of transience. All of a sudden I was no longer alone. Between believing and not believing there was an in-between space, a sort of hollow in which restless gazes dwelt.

Here was the truth. I held it in my hand. Everyone else could have had it too if they'd only opened their eyes. Those phrases had been waiting for me since my birth. Now here they were, mine, part of my life. Poetry and madness, I told myself as I walked, are like the two sides of a leaf. One has stomata and faces upward, the other discharges carbon dioxide downward. Between one side and the other there is a constant passage of humors, a flowing of molecules and fluids.

I was enthralled by the lives of so many poets gone mad. I felt an affinity with them. I too one day would change my name and lock myself in a tower. Hölderlin had become Signor Scardanelli and spent the rest of his days locked up there, playing the piano. Every once in a while he'd looked down at the tranquil flow of the Neckar and been content. True, he had found a pious soul to take care of him. It had been an honor for the carpenter to be able to care for such a great spirit. I had a suspicion carpenters were different in our own day. Apartments were small, without towers or stables. There was hardly space for grandparents, let alone poets. An additional point against me was the fact that I wasn't a poet, at least not yet.

My life very quickly plunged into chaos. There was no movement behind me, no protest. I shook things up so that a crack of truth might become visible. I'd always done that, but now I sought words to express the truth.

My mother was called to school. The boy, they said, has problems. He's distracted, careless, and doesn't wash himself. "Have you noticed anything strange by any chance?" they asked, insinuating.

On TV at that time the first debates about drugs were being held. My mother watched them, and from that moment on she lived inside a cocoon of fear. On one occasion, while looking for money, I had come upon a newspaper clip that listed, from one to ten, like a set of commandments, the reasons why a parent should become suspicious. I remember some: tardiness, lack of hygiene, strange comments, a tendency to lie, abnormal dilation of the pupils.

I even remember her face when she came home from that parent-teacher conference. She'd had the eyes of a lynx and the nose of a bloodhound. She'd sat down on my bed and said, "It'd be better if you told me everything." Then, faced with my silence and with the air of a mother who had already lost her son, she'd added, "If you don't confess to me, I'll have to tell your father." I'd broken into laughter: "Tell the alcoholic father his son's a drug addict," I'd sung, dancing around her.

My father and alcohol. A subject not to be touched. As a little boy I'd see him drink one glass of wine after another. I wanted to imitate him. Wine is for grown-ups, my mother would say, putting a few drops into my water for color. Only some years later did I understand that wine wasn't for all grown-ups, only for a few. Those few were like cars. Instead of running on gasoline, they ran on alcohol.

In the morning, while I ate bread and drank some hot milk with coffee, he'd pour himself an equal amount of black coffee and grappa. At eight in the evening, he was almost never at home. My mother would send me to call him. Finding him was easy. There were no more than three or four taverns he went to. Deep down I always hoped he wouldn't be there, he'd have had an accident. But I found him every time. I'd see his massive back where he was sitting at a table with his friends, talking loudly, gesticulating. His friends were like him. They thought he was funny. In fact, with them my father was very different. He was talkative. At home he hardly said a word.

I'd stare at him and my feet would grow heavy. I had no desire to approach him and say, like in a movie, "Dinner is served." I'd stand quietly behind his back for a while. Then one of his friends would notice me and touch his shoulder, saying, "Renzo, your son." Then he'd turn, slow and heavy like a bear. His eyes were puffy. "What do you want?" he'd snarl, while, instead of speaking, I'd point at the wall clock, all the while maintaining a proper distance for safety's sake.

The effect of the alcohol would evaporate, or rather change direction, as soon as he set foot in the house. His loquaciousness would become stubborn silence. Once in a while my mother would try to keep a conversation going. She'd share what had happened during the day. When she'd been a teacher, she had talked about things that had happened at school. But she was like a tennis player without a partner, or even a wall. Her words floated in the air, and when her voice stopped driving them they dissolved into nothing. He'd eat with his eyes down, which is what I'd learned to do as well. If he felt my eyes on him, he'd immediately turn and roar, "What are you looking at me for?"

He behaved as if he had a guilty conscience, like someone with a straw tail, a long big fluffy one. It would take but the slightest error of movement for the tail to brush against the embers and catch fire. That's why he often looked behind him with the ferocious glance of someone preparing to attack.

After dinner he'd sit in his armchair. Most of the time he fell asleep in front of the TV. When he couldn't sleep, he'd start making comments about the programs in a loud voice, a sort of constant grumbling. To him they were all a bunch of dirty, stinking, exploitative capitalists, rotten queers. Seated beside him, my mother would embroider pillows for decoration. To her the rambling was like the sound of the sea. It had been thundering in her ears for so long she no longer noticed.

I was scared to death of alcohol. I saw it as something that got inside people and spoiled them.

When chaos entered my life, it did so as a pure element. It was mountain air, diamond, quartz, not something obtuse and dirty that resulted from vice. Lucidity was its strong point. It gave me infrared binoculars instead of eyes. I sounded the depths, searching. I was certain the apparent banality of things was nothing but a shield that had to be shattered. Poetry would rise from its fragments. Not other people's poetry, which I read in books, but my own. There was a great stirring deep inside me. From the stasis of childhood I had shifted into perpetual motion. Thoughts, ideas, feelings, moved about like clouds driven by the wind on the horizon. Instead of going to school, I would walk through the Karst hills. I'd recite Srečko Kosovel's poetry aloud as I walked:

> I am the broken arch of a circle,
> the force bitterness has torn asunder.

Those words were my gospel. I sensed a tremendous strength. I knew I was great. I was no longer Atlas but a Titan with unencumbered shoulders. I had always sensed the confusion and chaos of the world. Now for the first time I was no longer inside it. The chaos was mine only. I created and dismantled it every day. I was certain that out of that chaos order would be born, a crystalline order in which I would be the first to call things by their proper names.

In my walking life I had no friends. I wasn't at all interested in the things my peers liked. There was no one to confide in except the open sky above the fields, the wind, and, at night, the darkness and silence of my room.

I know now that one single person would have been enough to change my destiny. One gaze, one afternoon spent together, a glimmer of understanding would have been enough. Someone with a chisel in his hand: a chisel and the disposition to blast through the clay mould in which I was constrained.

For sixteen years solitude and despair had been at work inside me like twin bellows, which huffed and puffed without rest. By now every feeling, every perception was inflated beyond belief. I called the feelings greatness, poetry. But they were perhaps merely the desire to put an end to it all. I'd wake up in the middle of the night and, in a little notebook, scribble down words that were supposed to be poetry. In those moments I was like a drunk. My arm and wrist trembled, as did the pen against the paper. I felt finally the sluice inside my head had been raised. The veil of illusion had fallen. Truth shone resplendent. It was a spring landscape whose colors had been revivified by a rain. I saw the tender grass and the tree and flower buds open and bloom amid the green. When I went back to bed, a great sense of peace came over me. I fell asleep as happy as a child loved from the day of conception. It seemed to me I'd reached firm footing, a point from which to start out and re-establish everything in a different way.

But that happiness did not last long, just enough time to have breakfast and wash my face. As soon as I sat down again at my desk and re-read those pages, I felt the universe cave in on top of me. There was no light whatsoever in those phrases, which opened no greater realm. They were my usual thoughts, only more confused than during the daytime. The words were as banal as those of a love-sick girl writing to a help columnist.

Still I didn't give up. After the dejection came rage. I told myself: you dug down but not far enough. There isn't enough chaos. There are still too many pots boiling with their lids on.

Then I discovered Baudelaire. I became feverish reading him. To be honest I also felt somewhat cheated. Those were my words, the most profound words of my being. *Il faut être toujours ivre.* How could I deny the truth of such an affirmation? Chaos alone was no longer enough. To reach what I was looking for something else was needed. It was like being a child and having to reach for an object on an armoire. You climb onto a chair, and if that's not enough you put a stool on top. Drugs or alcohol were not the goal, only a ladder to reach what was hidden from me.

I found some hashish at school. I waited before smoking it until I was alone in the woods. I'd never rolled a cigarette before. My hands trembled with emotion. When I took the first draw, I felt like Ali Baba before the magic cave. That smoke was the open sesame, the magic key that would unlock the door to another dimension. I expected explosions of light and color, dragons, marvelous shapes. Nothing happened. The trees were barren, the grass, yellow. There was a jay above me. With a graceless caw, it hopped from one branch to another. Aside from nausea and dizziness, each thing was just the way I'd always seen it.

I spent a couple of hours in that field. Just before it got dark, I went home, and there the open sesame had its effect.

It happened during dinner. My father came into the kitchen and suddenly was no longer my father but a circus bear. A bear with a small hat on its head and a miniature bicycle beneath its paws. The transformation was so real I broke out laughing. Just then, my mother became a monkey. I saw their restless mugs fussing before me. They were so comical that my laughter turned into howling.

"Care to tell us what you're laughing about?" shouted my mother.

My father slammed his fist down on the table. "This has become a mad house."

I quit laughing, and answered, "It's always been that."

Then I did what he usually did. I kicked the cupboard and slammed the door shut behind me.

It was cold outside but I didn't care. The streets were deserted, the kitchens lit up. Peaking through the windows, I glimpsed score upon score of small domestic hells, served by people seated at dinner tables and in front of

54

televisions. I couldn't hear their words, but I knew them all nevertheless. I sensed the unhappiness seeping through the window panes.

I took the main street of town. At the tram station I stopped to buy cigarettes and then walked out onto the main road. I needed to breathe more freely. I wanted to get to the sea.

The tram passed right by me. Aside from the driver, there was only an old man with a long beard on board. I waived at him like children do. Then it and all its lights disappeared, and I remained alone in the night. I started to sing.

In the square with the obelisk a car was parked with a couple inside. I sat down on the low wall of the belvedere and lit a cigarette. To tell the truth, it was rather disgusting. But it burned after all, and I enjoyed seeing its small circle of fire against the dark sky.

55

Beneath me lay the great city, beyond it the dark space of the sea. Just outside the roadstead you could make out the enormous outline of an aircraft carrier. All around it flickered the smaller lights of the fishing boats. It was strange. In that moment I felt everything inside me. I understood everything. I was everything. I heard the words of the fishermen and saw their wives at home waiting for them in front of their TV sets. I saw fish swimming through the algae and the white nets that dropped before them. I saw taxis stopped in from the station and people on incoming trains looking out the windows. I perceived their thoughts, which were my own, as they were those of the child just then being beaten by his father, or the old woman dying all alone in a retirement home, and the pigeon watching her die from the windowsill. There had never been so many thoughts in my head, never such a precise consciousness of what was all around me.

I don't know when I got up from that spot. At a certain point I felt a shiver of cold. The excess of emotions had worn me out. The lovers were gone. I lit another cigarette and started for home.

Nearly all the windows were dark. Only the sleepless and the sick were awake. My house was dark as well. I didn't know what time it was and didn't care. I rang the bell and waited. Nothing happened. I waited a few more minutes then delivered a kick to the door and went away.

By then I was truly cold. I thought the station would be the only warm place. The road there passed through a large square where trucks from the East often spent the night. There were three just then, which had come from Bulgaria and been directed to the slaughter house, the destination of all the cattle trucks coming across the border.

One carried horses, another, cows. The contents of the third were unclear, so I went up and looked inside. Little lambs. They were so small and short they seemed like a soft, white, undulating rug. Some of them must have seen me. One raised itself on its legs and approached me. It bleated, making its way through the others. Perhaps, for some mysterious reason, it had taken me for its mother. It poked its muzzle through a slit. Its black, glistening eyes held a question. I extended my hand and touched its forehead. It was warm like a baby's. "What's the matter?" I asked softly and in that very instant, the spell of the open sesame ended. I broke into tears. It bleated and I cried, knocking my head against the side of the truck.

The world is pain, nothing more.

The next day my mother didn't say a single word to me. I didn't even see my father. Instead of going to school, I stayed at home and slept. I didn't care at all anymore about school. I attended the lyceum for classical studies and was supposed to be wracking my brain over the aorist. We studied things that were dead and buried, and I couldn't make sense of the reason for such studies. Even philosophy, which might have somehow interested me, was taught in a horrendous manner. There were many gentlemen who talked like statues in a desert: noumena and monads, the transcendent and the immanent. They seemed to be madmen describing a world known only to them. There was death, solitude, the void, the enigma of birth and destiny; there was suffering that ground out every hour of the day in its vice. What relation did all this have to those incomprehensible formulas we were supposed to commit to memory?

With the air of prophets the professors proclaimed, "Now you don't see the meaning, but when you're adults you'll understand the importance of Greek and Latin." Their attitude reminded me of my father's when he said, "A war would straighten you out." I perceived a subtle cruelty beneath such words, the desire to make others pay for the senseless years of their youth.

That was also the period when the first student unrest began. Out of curiosity I attended two or three meetings of the school's collective. They talked about the struggle against capitalism and the dictatorship of the proletariat,

57

the very same things for which my father had also fought.
There was nothing new under the sun. I told myself people
loved to come up with the same illusions over and over.
They were all scared so they invented dreams, something
to give them a sense of belonging and meaning: it's nice to
be part of a chorus, with everyone repeating the same
things. Chicks like to be kept warm under the light of the
incubator. People like the warmth of utopias, of impossible
promises. Not everyone can be on the outside; not everyone has the strength to contemplate the true essence, the
long, dark tunnel that, from birth to death, we're forced to
make our way through, on hands and knees.

When I was in my first year of the lyceum, one fall afternoon I went to a birthday party of a girl in my class. There
must have been around fifteen of us all together. We weren't
little anymore and not big either, so we didn't know quite
how to behave. There was a table with snacks, drinks, and
a portable record player. We all had pimples and difficulty
mingling. At one point, someone said, "Let's play musical
chairs!" and we started to play.

The game was very simple: the number of chairs was
smaller than the number of participants by one. A record
was placed in the player, and everyone began to walk
around the room. Then, by surprise, the music would stop
and one had to rush to sit down. There was a lot of running
and elbowing, and in the end, someone was left standing.
That one person was always me. Each time there was a penalty to pay. On the third time — the penalty was to take off
one shoe, hop on one leg for three minutes, and lap Coca

Cola from the dog's bowl, then walk on all fours carrying the fattest girl on my back. I said, "I quit" and left the game. Someone voiced a faint protest, someone else hissed, but I pretended I didn't care.

It was the beginning of December. Off the sitting room was a balcony. Ignoring the cold, I opened the door and went out. Despite the fact that it was afternoon, the sky was dark and filled with stars. A cold north wind blew, clearing the air. The antennas shook, as did the connecting wires. A symphony of cables and rattling metal. I watched my friends through the thin curtain. The marble floor of the living room shone polished and disinfected like the slabs of a morgue. They continued to run in a circle around the chairs. I could see their grimaces, winks, and awkward expressions. For me they were all skulls, jaws, and tibias already. The confusion enveloped them and would continue to envelope them forever. Their lives appeared to me like the blueprint of a house under construction. There were foundations and walls, plumbing, and a roof. I knew everything about their future; they'd do everything that they were supposed to. There they were, inside, in the light, amid the warmth, their mouths filled with empty words. I was outside the window.

Alone, in the dark, surrounded by the cold of night.

V

One day my mother had a surprise for me. I came home and found the priest there.

When I saw him, I asked, "What happened? Did somebody die?"

"Don't be irreverent," she whispered.

"I was passing by," said Father Tonino. "If I'm disturbing you, I'll get out of your way."

"Please...." said my mother, and he remained seated.

My father wasn't at home that day, so he stayed for lunch.

We ate in silence. Or rather, I kept quiet, and they talked about an upcoming pilgrimage to Lourdes.

"I'd like so much to join you," said my mother, "but you understand, with my husband...."

"What matters is the intent," the priest answered. "You'll have an opportunity sooner or later."

That topic exhausted, they turned for a while to church bells. There was a collection to buy new ones, but they were far from reaching their goal. From one pleasantry to another, we got to the end of the meal. At that point my mother stood up and, with a blush of falsehood painted on her face, said, "I hope you'll excuse me if go lie down a bit. I've got a terrible headache."

"You should learn to act your part a little better," I retorted without turning, upon which she closed the door.

The two of us were left alone, with breadcrumbs and orange peels in the middle of the table. There was a rather long silence. Then he began rubbing his hands together as if he was cold and said, "So how's it going?"

"Why are you such a hypocrite?" I asked.

"I'm not a hypocrite," he said. "I really want to know how you are. Your mother is worried about you."

I changed the position of my legs, and the chair creaked.

"She could have worried before bringing me into the world."

Father Tonino was playing with the remains of the bread, making little balls that he then squashed with his index finger. It was with him that I'd studied the catechism. When I was a child, he had seemed old. Only at that moment, watching him, did I realize that he must have been just over fifty. I had never disliked him, but at that moment he was the enemy.

We spent almost an hour together. He talked and talked. I didn't listen. Now and then a word reached me: "gifts... the prodigal son...." Outside it started raining. I found it much more interesting to watch the trajectory of the drops, the way they ran down the electric lines, the shining, barren branches of the tree in front of the house.

When he left, I didn't get up to walk him to the door.

61

Meanwhile things were getting worse. There wasn't a single instant of calm for me anymore. Instead of speaking, I shouted. I managed to be still only when I was in a state of exhaustion.

One night, lying in bed, I realized blood was no longer pulsing through my veins. In its place, glowing volcanic lava flowed; driven by my heart, it rushed from my feet to my head, flooding my brain. It reached my eyes and turned them into embers.

I hardly slept at night. My childhood insomnia had come back. At best, when I'd drunk or smoked, I would sink for a couple of hours into a dark pit without images or sounds. I'd always wake up suddenly, my eyes wide. I don't remember any particular dream except one. I raise my eyes and above me, on a rock, I see an enormous, immobile lion. Its very shadow is terrifying. I sense it's about to pounce. There's pure ferocity in its glance, which paralyzes any possible desire to escape. I want to scream but can't. At the moment it jumps, I realize it's no longer a lion but a goat, a bull, a python, a distant offspring of the devil. Its eyes have an other-worldly intensity. Its nostrils and tongue are firebrands. Above me the bloody claws dart like sparks escaping from a fire. Only then do I call out, and, with a scream, I wake up. From the street I hear the noise of trucks changing gears as they start the climb. In the kitchen a faucet drips. My father's snoring in the next room. I try to go back to sleep without success, and spend the rest of the night in a restless half-sleep, grinding my teeth, banging my head against the wall and tugging at the sheets as if they're a straightjacket.

The following morning I'd be dead tired. Getting up was hard, going to school impossible. I'd leave the house with my books, go into town, and duck into the first open bar.

Rage had brought thirst. My throat burned constantly, and so did my stomach. There was a fire, and I had to put it out. Beer was the best thing in the morning. I felt immediately better. Right after the first pitcher I calmed down. Thirst and anxiety were now one and the same thing.

So without even realizing it, I started drinking. I both knew and didn't know what I was doing. In any case, I kept telling myself: "It's different from my father. He drinks because he's a failure. I just need help in order to know myself better. One mustn't demonize anything in this world. Things are not valuable for themselves. They are valuable for what you can do with them."

At home we avoided each other. We were two mirrors that didn't reflect each other. At lunch time he was never at home, and I tried not to be there, too. My mother had got used to it. She didn't even ask where I'd been. She'd eat by herself in front of the television, then put her plate away and pick up her sewing.

During the last year her hair had turned gray. Fatigue must have also arrived with the gray. Somehow, perhaps, she was content with the apparent peace. But the peace was indeed apparent. We were all walking a tight rope with a balancing rod. Suddenly the rod slipped from our hands, and we fell.

It happened one Sunday. My mother had cooked a roast and was carving it. She placed a slice on my father's plate at the very instant I entered the kitchen. They turned to look at me as if I were a Martian. They were pale and motionless, like statues of salt. I moved my chair noisily and let myself drop onto it. My father's reflexes were slow. It took a few seconds before he slammed his fist on the table. The silverware and glasses jumped in the air.

"This house is not a hotel!" he shouted.

I took a new potato from the plate. It was tender, flavorful. "Strange," I said, biting into it, "I hadn't ever noticed that."

Then he got to his feet.

"You're a disgrace!" he howled, raising his arm to slap me.

I was quicker. I blocked with my right and struck with my left. My fist struck him square in the face. I could clearly feel the bone of his nose bend. He collapsed on his chair, covering his face with his hands.

64

I went to the door calmly.

"And you, what are you?" I said to him while my mother patted the wound with a handkerchief.

On Sunday afternoons the roads are terribly empty and sad. I felt like having some fun. The posters on the walls announced the arrival of a big fair. I took the bus to get there. I spent the afternoon riding the bumper cars. As soon as I saw anyone looking happy, I would turn my car and ram them.

I left with the fair people. At closing time, I asked if they needed a hand. "A hand is always helpful," they answered. No one asked how old I was or why I wanted to leave town; there wasn't any pay, only some tips, a roof, something to eat, and the possibility of having fun every day.

The next day we took down the structures and left. I could have called home to ask how my father was, but the thought didn't enter my head even for a moment. A kind of dark vortex had formed in my mind and, spinning in on itself, had swallowed up my past.

I spent the day from morning to evening with others. It was cold and rainy. They all helped themselves to alcohol in order to get by. It was the first time I was drinking with others. I didn't mind the effect at all. I was witty, likeable. When I spoke, people around me had fun. We changed locations every day or nearly. We never went far. We went to fairs, markets, and neighborhood festivals.

Of that period—it must not have lasted more than two or three weeks—I have no clear recollection. It was as if I held a kaleidoscope in my hand. What stood out most were the colors: the gray of an abandoned shed, the wall paper of a tavern in the hills, the sky blue of a bus emerging from the fog, the sharp orange of persimmons in a barren garden.

65

I had erased the past and, in doing so, the future as well. In place of thoughts and self awareness there was only a kind of fever. In those days I called it entertainment. My throat burned with the endless talk and laughter. I drank and drank, and no drink could put out the fire any more.

Then one afternoon, in the men's room of a bar, I saw my face reflected in a mirror. Who was that person staring at me? Those were not my eyes. I'd never had such dull eyes. They looked like the eyes of a chicken or turkey—glossy, polished, empty. And below the eyes were two swollen bags and a complexion that ranged from gray to yellow. What the hell! I told myself it must be because of the lousy light in this shit hole. I was about to leave when I suddenly had the sensation I wasn't alone in there. There was someone else with me, and that someone else was sad. I couldn't see him, but I sensed his presence.

Suddenly, for no reason, the thought of the guardian angel crossed my mind. The men's room was cold, damp, foul. It had a folding door made of plastic. The floor was soaked with urine; the light was dim. What could a guardian angel possibly be doing there? Rather than live in latrines, I thought, guardian angels followed children on the edges of cliffs or on suspension bridges hanging over the abyss.

It was afternoon. Within the hour we would have to open the bumper car rink. The tavern was rather far from the town where our fair was. There were four of us that day. They'd told us the wine was good "up there," which was why we'd gone up the hill. We passed the time drinking and playing cards. When we got going again, we were very late. The fog was lifting from the plain. The road was curvy and full of potholes. The suspension on our tiny old car was shot. I was in back, and it occurred to me we were going too fast. At that instant, right in front of us, the dark silhouette of a truck materialized.

VI

In that last year — before I became a legal adult — only two important things happened. After a month in the hospital, I went straight into a rehabilitation center for alcoholic minors. That was the first. The second was that there I finally found a friend. His name was Andrea. We shared a room. When I saw him for the first time, he was lying on his bed with his hands clasped behind the nape of his neck. His open eyes stared at the ceiling. I said, "Hi," but he didn't turn. I introduced myself, extending my hand, and he remained motionless.

He ignored me for two whole days. The only contact we had was through our eyes. He followed me everywhere with his gaze. He watched me, but I couldn't do the same. His irises were of a strange color halfway between blue and light green. They made you think of a watery surface closed in by ice. They were water but also fire, burning at the slightest contact. His face was handsome, with regular features and a fair complexion. Beside him I felt awkward, misshapen. He was always alone, aloof.

In the evening, after dinner, all the center's guests gathered in a room to watch television and play cards. Staying in your room wasn't allowed. There was lots of noise, so he would move his chair to face the wall, turning his back on the rest of the room. For two evenings I joined in the company and took part in their game of briscola, making comments about the TV shows. But I actually felt more alone than ever. So on the third night I followed his example and joined him in watching the wall.

"Are you copying me," he asked, without turning.

"No," I answered. "It's just that I can't stand all the rest."

In our room that night we talked for a long time, the darkness concealing his gaze. We shared the same interests. We used the same words to describe them.

From that moment on, we never left each other.

The center was a small building in the midst of the psychiatric hospital's grounds.

The more important wings had a rather old feel to them and must have dated back to the beginning of the century. Nearly all the windows were protected by thick grates, and the window pains behind them were opaque. Inhuman screams sometimes filtered through from the other side. The only time I'd heard anything similar was in movies set in the jungles of the Amazon. They resembled the screams of tree monkeys.

Once, when we were passing by the ward with chronically ill patients, Andrea told me he'd heard of a girl our age locked in there who could not be left without a straight jacket even for a moment. The moment her hands were free in fact, she started destroying herself. She pulled out her hair, slashed her face with her nails, mauled her forearms as a dog does with a bone. There was nothing, absolutely nothing one could do. She'd behaved like that since she was little — a lesion at the moment of her birth or something. She would go on acting that way until the end of her days.

"Keeping people of that sort alive," said Andrea, one morning when we walked near the ward, "is one of the many instances of hypocrisy. All it would take to make them happy is an injection." Then he paused. "In a way, we're linked to them by the same destiny."

I looked at him without understanding. Then he explained that the structure of human kind was a pyramid. Those poor wretches stood on the bottom step, where the animate world met inert matter. We, on the contrary, occupy the highest level, at the summit. It was the level of our awareness that raised us to that point. Just as they were in contact with the naked earth, we were in contact with the infinite air of the sky. We were locked up in that hospital through the law of opposites. For different reasons, both the lowest and the highest levels irritated those vegetating in the middle. Or rather, one was an irritant, the other was a threat.

69

"We live under the dictatorship of the norm, haven't you realized?" he said, brushing my shoulder. "No one can stand the superman."

"Who's the superman?" I asked.

"Me," he said without hesitating, "you. Those of us who see what the others don't."

Then he spoke about nature. There too, things proceeded in the same way. There were the herbivores, the carnivores, and, above them, the super-predators, which were none other than certain carnivores who happened to be meaner than all the others. Aside from the elements and hunters, no one could do them harm.

"For animals," said Andrea, "it's just a matter of survival. Some eat and some get eaten. For humans, the question is much more subtle. There are primitive beings whose only aim is to fill their bellies and mate. Those are the wide base of the pyramid. Their minds are primitive. They live mainly on drives. Give them a stimulus and you can be sure of the response. Their reflexes are not that different from those of an amoeba. Above them are people slightly superior, people who have something of a consciousness, but it's a diluted consciousness, like salt in pasta water. To survive, sometimes they invent an ideal or something of the sort, a weak, infantile invention. They're lame. They need a cane to walk with. If you take it away, they fall to the ground and crawl like worms.

"Above this slime," he continued, "are the elect. The elect have enjoyed each of their talents in higher doses than the norm. They're eagles, not worms. Their natural condition is flight. They understand beauty and truth, and they don't mix with the filth that lies beneath them. But once in a while they retract their wings and plunge down headlong, with their majestic power, and destroy the enemy."

I listened, fascinated, to these speeches of his. I had never heard anyone talk like that. At the very moment his words reached my ears, I experienced an instant of wonder. The

70

instant passed, and I immediately recognized the justness of those words. They were the truth. There was no equality on earth. Even if we all had two legs, two arms, and one head, we belonged to different species. I thought of the livid faces of my father's tavern friends or about friends from school who only ever had girls and engines on their minds. With them I'd always felt uncomfortable. Then I was still ignorant of the fact that between them and me lay an abyss. I belonged to the eagles, they to the protozoans. From morning to eve they merely reacted to the law of stimulus-response.

Andrea's words provoked the same exaltation I'd experienced with my first readings of poetry. But to this was added a sense of profound release. The world proceeded apace in this manner. How was it I hadn't understood before?

After eating we'd go smoke a cigarette near the park fence. Spring was coming. The mimosas and precocious shrubs were already in bloom, the sun tepid. We'd stand there chatting until it was time for our therapy.

"Why don't they say it right away?" I asked one day. "It would all be simpler."

Andrea answered with another question: "In your opinion, who is it that governs the world?"

I felt ashamed of my superficiality. It was clear the accepted reality was that spread by the protozoans, the stimulus-response beings. They were the ones holding the reins. And I'd met dozens, hundreds of them since I was in kindergarten. Their strength was in quantity, not quality. They were the hard mud of the pyramids, without light or thrill.

It was impossible they might ever reveal how things actually stood. Not through meanness or calculation but through pure ignorance of the world's essence.

He always said the Indians had found the best solution with the invention of castes. There everything was clear from the very start. There was no floundering or useless waste of energy.

"Only in our country do people waste their time pursuing things they can never attain. Then of course there's the question of race. Depending on the continent on which one is born, one has a greater or lesser possibility of rising to the top. Think about blacks, for instance," he added, pacing. "Have you ever seen a black man conducting an orchestra? And yet they are foremost in athletic contests. No one runs and jumps like they do. What does that indicate? That they're closer to lions than they are to philosophers. It's a natural, logical reflection. It leaps onto your tongue spontaneously, but you could never say it aloud. We live in an age of undisputed hypocrisy. We're all equal—that's what they want to make us repeat like automatons."

If it hadn't been for my friendship with Andrea, that period of my life would have been truly sad. Life inside was ordered by rigid timetables. You could neither leave nor receive visitors. They fed you poorly, and you were forced to undergo therapy. There must have been some fifteen patients, all of them rather young. But I hardly had any rapport at all with them. Andrea and I had fashioned our own cocoon. He talked and I listened. I was a thirsty stag drinking clear water.

Therapy was conducted all together or individually. They were kind young misses who pretended you were very important to them. I understood very well that the only really important thing was their pay check at the end of the month and the fact that it was they, and not someone else, who were warming those seats there. Which was why they could afford to allow themselves a little affability, because, at least for the moment, in the jungle of competition, they'd made it.

Most often I stayed silent with them. The only sound in the room was the ticking of the clock. I knew silence bothered them a lot, even if they pretended it was nothing. They smiled at me. Then they started toying with their pen or their earrings, pulling them forward and back, as if they wanted to take the whole lobe away.

Andrea had told me about the strategy of silence. "If you like saying stupid things," he'd said, "go ahead and talk. They'll be happy. They gulp it down like a drink. But if it doesn't suit you, then stay silent and you'll see them go crazy."

In the quiet time many things would come to my mind. Things that had to do not with me but with young miss sitting opposite. I'd see her life as a string of slides: graduation from school, first kiss, decision to study psychology, satisfaction after taking final exams, college graduation party in pitiful pizzeria, with parents all dressed up and friends, then exhausting search for work, permissible and less permissible strategies for obtaining it, fiancé's desertion—"I can't stand the fact that you take so much care of other people"—tears, tranquilizers, a decision to focus completely on work, meetings, conferences, special training courses,

73

tripping up colleagues to get ahead, miniscule gains in one's career, changes in clothing and facial features. By then it was an old maid's course, an esteemed, intelligent old maid following an unbending road. At the end of it, as at all ends, a zinc box lined with the most precious wood awaited her.

Several minutes before the hour was up, the miss would lean a little forward and ask, "Has anything in particular occurred to you?"

I'd look in her eyes and say, "No, nothing."

Andrea said one of the powers shared by eagles was their ability to see the lives of others without any screen. "Before us everyone is naked, defenseless. They offer us their insides like fruit on the market tables." When I'd leave the room with the therapist, I knew it was the truth.

Andrea was the son of Istrian refugees. He hated nothing more than the reds. "They're the cancer eating away at our society," he'd say. "They get the mediocre drunk on their nonsense. You need to crush them under your heel to keep them from doing harm, like worms, and just leave mush on the ground." He thought there hadn't ever been so much tragedy in the world as since the communist delirium was born. "Human society has existed," he said, "for thousands of years, and it's always kept going like this: whoever's better is in charge; the others just have to follow. But these people have created a paranoid power structure, knocking things upside down, so the less capable have the power to make decisions, and everything goes to the dogs. If you're a worker, you can do whatever you want. If you're a professor, you're a piece of shit. They make you clean toilets or break rocks to make asphalt for roads. Every morning you have to kiss the boots of your bosses for the simple fact that, so far, they haven't decided to liquidate you.

"For them," he said, "people don't exist. Only trades do, and Party roles, among which preference goes to that of the spy. Brother denounces brother, sons denounce fathers. Betrayal and denunciation are the backbone of the system. A system that works like a concrete mixer, grinding up human beings instead of rocks."

I listened to him in silence. He had much more experience than I did and knew about more things. Plus there was a tone in his voice that didn't seem to allow any sort of objection. From half phrases and hints I'd gathered that his father must have gone through something terrible. The fury that often came over Andrea in the midst of his speeches was perhaps nothing other than that, the echo of a blow inflicted on his father. The echo of my father had been much different: with his heroic struggle to change the world he'd vaccinated me against all possible revolutions. For that reason I'd always been exclusively concerned with what was inside me. What was outside was rather indifferent to me. And my father, in such matters, was my guilty conscience. Losing Andrea's respect was the last thing in the world I wanted. If he'd found out that my father was a communist, he'd have probably thought I was one too. So I kept silent.

75

But one afternoon I took my courage in hand. We were smoking a cigarette on the park bench. All in one breath I said, "You know, you're right. My father's a communist and he's a real shit."

He wanted to know everything, whether he was a radical activist or less, whether he'd been in the war and where. I disappointed him a little with my answer. "He never talks about it. I know he was one of the partisans and that's all."

Andrea snuffed the end of his cigarette with his heel. "Probably has something dirty on his conscience."

In school he'd had run-ins with reds. "You wouldn't believe how sorry I felt for them," he'd say. "Some I knew since middle school. They were good kids, sensible. But it's common sense and sensitivity that those worms play on. They toss out their nets at the age when people are most sensitive, when they're dreaming of a better world. They're dragnets, and a heap of fish end up inside. Liberty, justice, equality. It's nice to fill your mouth with those words. They're just little lark mirrors, and the larks fall down on them. That's why I felt sorry for them: they didn't see the hand behind the mirror. It's a twisted, dirty hand. With the slightest movement it sheds blood. Then, sure, once in a while somebody figures it out. That invasion of Hungary would have been enough to prove the whole thing's a mistake. But it's sad to get off the train. You've been traveling in the convoy for such a long time with people singing the same songs as you. You didn't see anything beside the tracks during the trip. You were looking ahead with everyone else, to that unspecified place that was the future, a future radiant like the dawn. That's where you were going, trustful. How can you get off? If you get off, you'll be alone in the desert, you'll become aware of the hunger, the cold. The train with its lights pulls away, night falls, wolves circle. Why should you risk so much? It's much better to stay on board. You stay on even though you know the future isn't radiant, but it makes no difference. They eat and sing on board. The words you sing make you feel different; the noble phrases are your commitment. You have a meaning in the world because of it. If you quit you're a defeatist. Sing, keep singing, bray like a jackass with the others. Like a jackass put blinders on so as not to see outside. This colossal lie is the beast, get it? The 666 in its final form. It'll destroy the world before the millennium is up."

I didn't know what 666 was. It actually sounded like it could have been a hotel room number. So I asked, "What does that number mean? I've never heard it before."

"The apocalypse of St. John. 666. The beast. Satan, the master of the world, get it?"

"Communism is Satan?"

"Of course."

All of a sudden I began to think of a cat biting its tail. When I'd asked my father if there was a devil, he'd answered it was the fascists. But for Andrea it was the communists. So what then? If one blamed the other and vice versa, where did the real blame lie? That ancient problem began to torment me. Inside there wasn't even a priest. If there had been, I would have asked him two or three questions about what there was or what there wasn't on high. The only interlocutor I had, besides Andrea, was the therapist.

So one day, at the beginning of our session, I asked her point-blank: "Who is the the devil?"

She smiled, clearly satisfied. "What association of thoughts brought this up?"

I didn't feel like explaining the question of contrasting forces, the reds and the blacks dividing up the chess board, so I said, "In here I've had a lot of time to think. I've thought about all that's happened to me. I would have so liked to be good, but I'm not capable of it. So I ask myself whether it's my fault or whether someone else had a hand in it."

"There is nothing outside yourself," she answered reassuringly. "What you call the devil are your own insecurities, the fears you've carried inside since you were a child." She paused, then, her voice lower, added, "You think you want to talk about it?"

Now I was at the dance and had to keep dancing. So, as if I were drawing out the words from some deep recess, I started from when I was a child, from the fact of coming into the world and not feeling wanted by anyone. Every time my father had come into my room, I'd had the impression he was a killer sent by a neighboring realm. I was heir to the throne and he, through some problem of territorial supremacy, had the task of killing me. Her eyes showed agreement as she listened. I could already imagine the paper she would give at her next conference. It was nice to have an attentive listener—the bard singers of old must have experienced more or less the same. All I had to do was keep adding ever more astounding details. It wasn't hard. I had no idea where I was going. Every phrase that came out of my mouth surprised me first of all.

When the hour was up, the psychologist opened my chart and made marks with the pen as if she were checking off blanks on a form. Then she stood up and walked with

me to the door, saying, "I have the impression we're coming to the main point."

I responded with a meek smile.

I didn't feel like going back to the room. Andrea's talks
had brought me to a kind of saturation point. I wasn't fed
up or irritated. I just needed a silent rest. Too many
thoughts in too short a time. I wished we had a beach there,
an open place where I could walk and see the horizon. As
there wasn't one, I took a little walk around the wards.

I once saw a metal ball as part of an exhibition of torture
instruments. In its time burning coals would have been
placed inside. Thank heaven I don't remember its exact
use, but I felt as though I had something like it inside me.
There was still a fire in my body—I could feel its heat. But
it was a domestic fire now. Its flames didn't lick at everything as they had under the influence of alcohol. The only
difference was frailty. Being sober was like having a turned
off switch. I walked through the park, wondering whether
I'd ever need to turn it on again. Could one live like that,
with one's engines on low?

79

VII

The close tie linking me to Andrea did not remain unnoticed for long. While the others were deadly bored, we were always talking. It must have caused a certain jealousy because one morning written outside our room we found the words "fags."

I thought Andrea would be furious, but he just shrugged. "Slime," he said. "Slime doesn't think of anything but that. Its horizon is too low to allow it to contemplate the height of our friendship."

We were separated the next night: nothing should impede the process of our recovery. I shared the room with three strangers, one of whom stunk so bad the air was unbreathable. During the day we were obliged to keep away from each other. Despite this, after lunch one afternoon Andrea joined me on the little bench and whispered, "We're out of here tomorrow."

Without changing my facial expression, I whispered, "What? Are you crazy?"

"You afraid?" he asked.

"No, but it seems silly when in less than a month you'll be able to go home."

He stood up suddenly. "Stay in the slime then," he said before going away.

I was extremely agitated the whole afternoon. I'd made myself look like a worm. After all the pretty phrases I hadn't been able to take up the tiniest gesture of rebellion. Between friendship with Andrea and the norm I'd chosen the norm. I'd been afraid of imagining what would happen to me if I went out. I was a chick, not an eagle, a chick that growing up would become a chicken. I saw him eating alone at dinner, sitting at a table near the window. He didn't eat, he nibbled. There was something melancholic about him I'd never seen before.

As we were going to the recreation room, I passed nonchalantly and said under my breath, "Okay."

"One o'clock in front of the kitchen," he answered.

It was May, and the warm night air was filled with the cloying scent of flowers. We reached the back of the hospital's psychiatric wards in silence. Behind the garbage depot Andrea had found a hole in the wire fencing. My heart beat fast. I was torn between euphoria and fear over what we were doing.

We started running as soon as we reached the outside. There were dug up fields and, after them, a narrow asphalt road where no one passed. I didn't know which way we'd set out, believing like a child that Andrea had everything thought out. We'd take off like cabin-boys for a boat pulling out, or something like that.

"Where are we going?" I asked after some time.

"I don't have the foggiest idea," he answered, unconcerned.
I nearly screamed, "So why did you get me to come out?"

"Nobody forced you. You came out on your own, with
your own two feet. As for me, I felt like taking a little trip in
the middle of the night."

"And if they find us?"

"They'll hang us."

A suffocating resentment came over me. The idea of a
grand adventure evaporated. I was running a useless risk.
For an instant I even thought of going back. In less than
half an hour I could have been back in my bed. Andrea
meanwhile was walking ahead, his hands in his pockets.
He seemed engrossed, as indifferent as a stone to my presence. It was I who was incapable of not following him. I almost had the sensation of needing to protect him.

In the end we came to a parking lot with lots of cars in
it. Andrea pulled a small canned meat opener from his
pocket and opened one of them.

"Is this your?" I asked.

"Are you coming?" he said.

We took the bypass out of the city. Andrea struck me as
sullen, and I was afraid. I didn't dare ask any more questions, but a part of me was convinced this was a race to the
death. At a certain point he was going to turn the wheel and
we'd go flying into the rock wall alongside or into the
guardrail and then straight down to the sea. It wouldn't be
an accident or because he was distracted but because he'd
wanted to do it from the very start. How had I got stuck in
this? My legs were straight out in front of me as if there
were pedals under my feet.

82

But after several kilometers, he flipped on his signal light and turned onto a white road. It climbed upward in tight curves. Two or three hairpin bends later he stopped in a large square, turned off the engine, got out, and took a deep breath. Below us was the sea, all around small fields, steep vineyards, orchards.

"What now?" I asked.

"Now we're here."

The moon was high. It lit up his face, which seemed less tense than before, almost even cheerful. We sat down on the grass near a low stone wall, where grape vines had given way to two great cherry trees.

"There," Andrea exclaimed, "this is what I wanted. At least for a night. To see the horizon and open space. I was thirsty for this."

I felt the same. I said: "Psychology and closed rooms constrain the head." Then I told him about the first time I'd smoked a joint, about the effect that burst on me later, this very need to see the horizon, the line of the sea, the line of the sky, and of how that horizon and all it contained had suddenly poured into me. Everything lived inside me, and all that everything was, first and foremost, pain.

We talked for a long time that night, and though we'd had nothing to drink, our words had that confidential laxity of those who've tossed back a few. The satellites mingled with the stars above our heads. From the grass came the rustle of the first crickets. The insistent song of a nightingale filled the silences.

"Who knows," said Andrea at one point, "if there isn't up there a great big hat with all our names inside, like in the lottery or a bingo game. At a certain point Walter or Andrea comes out, and you have to go there, see your house, your parents, and you know already you'll be unhappy with them. You know it but you can't protest."

"If they've got a hatter," I put in, "then he's mad. Anyway it's either a madman or a blind man who sends everyone to the wrong place. My father, who would ever want him? But it turned out to be my turn. Of course I had to go. It's not nice, is it?"

"Not nice at all," Andrea answered. "Me too, if I could have chosen, I would have chosen something different."

A little later there was no longer any rhyme or reason to our discussion. We talked for a long time about what we'd have liked to become if we hadn't become us. Andrea would have wanted to be a knight living in the Middle Ages, with splendid armor and a shining horse, and with the possibility of upholding justice all by himself, with his sword and mace. I hesitated, indecisive and confused. In reality the life I yearned for was one of extreme quiet. In the end I said, "I'd have liked to be an accountant."

"An accountant?!" Andrea shouted and then burst into laughter. It was the first time since I'd known him. He slapped me hard on the shoulder. "An accountant! Come on, no joking!"

"I'm not. Try to imagine someone who, from the time he was little has thought only about accounts. He adds things together, and when he draws a line underneath everything is exact, everything adds up." I paused. "It'd be very nice," I added.

Soon we were overcome by sleep. We fell asleep next

84

to each other, feeling each other's warmth. We breathed as one. He was a knight, I tallied everything up. The heavenly vault was no longer menacing, it was reassuring. We slept there like two tired kids who no longer had any need to ask questions.

During our brief slumber a light breeze sprung up, shaking the cherry trees and making petals fall. I opened my eyes and found myself covered with a strange snow, a fragrant, tepid snow. Andrea was still sleeping, his fingers interlocked across his stomach. His expression was truly that of a knight. He had petals on his eyes, his cheeks, his hair. I looked at him for some time. Without the rage of his eyes or the sarcasm of his words, his face almost became something else. On his strong, regular features there was a veil of sadness. He was a knight on whom a spell had been cast right in the middle of a battle. He lay on the ground, and from his body emanated the cold wind of tragedy.

85

It was still dark when we got back into the car. We needed to return quickly in order not to be found out. Andrea's mood had changed. Against the dark sky the white leaves of the cherry trees stood out against the dark sky. Before leaving he turned to look at them.

"That's what we forget about too often," he said.

"What?"

"Beauty."

Then he added, "That's how I'd like to die, in a meadow, covered by something white. Snow or rose petals."

Discharge day was approaching. And with it the big question of what I would do with my future. Just a few months separated me from legal adulthood. Those months I'd be spending with my parents.

A social worker had in the meantime been trying to patch up our relationship. She had even convinced my mother to have a few sessions with the same therapist because—she must have said—if I was like this, in some manner the fault must also be theirs.

I could already hear my mother's words. "This child is my despair. When he was little, he was a treasure. Even though we weren't well off, he never lacked for anything." Just the thought of it bored and irritated me.

Still, in that place I'd come to understand I wasn't disposed to a life like everyone else's. Now that I was no longer dependent on alcohol, by paying proper attention to what was commonsensical I could have made up the year of study I'd lost, then entered the university and got a degree. Military service I would almost certainly avoid because my father was disabled. So after graduating I'd have started the dance of temporary positions. One fine day I would meet a nice, sensible girl. We'd marry and she decorate a smallish apartment with mass-produced furniture, though in good taste. Our first son would be born, and I'd try to be different from my father, kindly and soft spoken. If he liked soccer, I'd take him to the stadium. And then one day, eating dinner, I'd catch the look of contempt in his eyes, the same contempt I felt for my father.

I walked along the little paths of the park, thinking about it all and trying to imagine some different life. Between despair and normality there must be a cross-roads. It's like being in a forest. There's the path you're following,

86

well beaten and marked with a red line on maps. But you're sick of it. You've covered it too many times. You go a little to the right, a little to the left. In the end you find another one, a new one, whose entrance is hidden in the bushes. You don't know where it leads. But it makes no difference. Your new-found happiness makes you walk differently.

Why not say it, at heart I envied those who had a precise idea of life, those who'd been born holding an umbrella. Rain, snow, hail, they're always protected. They don't let it go even when the sun's out. But envy was not a strong enough incentive to make me take the leap. I could have closed my eyes and plunged into any kind of existence at all. But I knew only too well it would be a short-lived leap. Initial satisfaction would be followed by a slight sense of unease. In a short time it would devour every other emotion, and I would be unhappy. Unhappiness would be accompanied by malice. Despising oneself and doing harm to others are two sides of the same sentiment. I wasn't cut out to be a murderer. My malice would becommon, petty: nastiness, humiliation, backbiting, rotten little tricks. That was how my father had always acted. Then that escape valve would be insufficient, just keeping me alive. Something else would be needed. Rather than exploding, I would implode. One morning I'd get up and again set out to destroy myself.

A great part of unhappiness — by now this much was clear — depends on the wrong road taken. Walking in shoes too tight or too loose, you start cursing the world after a few kilometers. What I couldn't figure out was why one couldn't choose the right size shoes from the very start.

I walked about, bewildered by such thoughts, and, without knowing how, ended up at the crazies ward. I knew one was not supposed to call them that. In that place no word was considered more obscene. In all the posted signs they were noted as "customers" or "carriers of a psychological handicap."

Andrea had pointed it out to me. "Look," he'd said, "now even words are enough to make people afraid. So as not to dirty their mouths, they use cleansed words. By themselves words aren't offensive. What's offensive is the hypocrisy behind them. Craziness has its own greatness. Turning it into the normality of a postal form means negating the power of its mystery. There's a point in fact where the human pyramid loses its dimension of depth and changes into a triangle. The triangle is a flat form, so it can be rolled up. When it's rolled, the top can actually touch the base. Craziness nullifies distances. It strikes very high or very low. Who's to say that one day our destiny won't turn into theirs?"

"I don't get it."

He started to talk about Icarus, about how one can burn one's wings by flying too high.

"If you no longer have wings, you fall. Gravity pulls you down like a rock. You run a risk by going too high. A strong light burns your sight, not just your wings. You go blind. You spend the rest of your life walking in a circle, muttering things without sense. You become a customer like all the others." Then he'd enumerated a series of poets and philosophers who'd gone mad. I lit up: "It's true. Even Hölderlin became Scardanelli." "And Nietzsche?" he said. "Nietzsche started weeping and embraced a horse."

Now the crazies were before me. There couldn't have been more than twenty. It was hard to figure their age: sickness alters the features, rendering them timeless. Some were very fat, others extremely thin. To look at them all together like that, the first thing that occurred to you was their absolute solitude. Some were standing as motionless as stones. Others rocked back and forth. Their rhythm and expression were the same as great carnivores locked up behind bars. Still others crossed the courtyard with excited steps, like generals haranguing their troops before the final battle. This was solitude. None of them perceived any other. Their situation resembled that of an astronaut who leaves his module to take a walk in space. Around their body they have a hyper-equipped suit, with oxygen, appropriately regulated temperature and air pressure. A microcosm of sorts lives between the fabric and the body. Outside is the darkness and silence that brush against eternity. The people before me seemed to have done just that. Between them and what was around them was an interspace: from it, probably, they drew breath and nourishment. And it was always thanks to that interspace that they defended themselves against the surrounding world.

At heart, I told myself as I looked at them, they're the most sincere. They don't pretend not to be alone. Perhaps that's why they cause so much worry. Nobody likes to have the terrible and absolute solitude of human life thrown in his face. To hide it, you worry yourself from birth to death. You play castanets and tambourines so as not to see the cadaver that floats to the surface, so the cadaver won't shout out the fact that we're alone, all desperately alone. Dust in motion, nothing more.

I too had always been afraid of crazy people. When, as a child, I ran into the one from our part of town, I'd cross to the other side of the street. But soon after, witnessing the cruelty of the passersby had left me between a feeling of terror and a desire to weep. I was afraid of the unpredictability of what he might say or do and moved by his helplessness before the malice and stupidity of other people. As a young child, I experienced an overbearing desire to protect the weak, but the feeling vanished when it occurred to me that I myself fell into that category.

Excessive sensitivity isn't a safe-conduct, it's a trap. You don't figure it out right away. Early on you get praised. It's later that it becomes a problem. Slowly, whoever's around you realizes that sensitivity, rather than being a gift, is dead weight. The world is made of foxes, hyenas, and elbow jabbing. You're a soft-pelted rabbit with no possibility of moving ahead. That's why, from one day to the next, everything changes. Around you there's only irritation and annoyance at the fact that you're not like everybody else. From the great rabbit massacre, only those who know how to do something exceptional are spared.

In my class, for instance, there was a boy who could play the piano without ever having studied music. He only had to hear a song once to be able immediately to repeat it with perfection. For this, adults treated him respectfully. They were even in awe of him. They called him little Mozart and moved around him with the greatest delicacy, as if he were a glass ball.

All the others had to face the great sickle of normality. Either you gave in to her or she cut you down. Why normality had to be that of the foxes and hyenas, and not that of the rabbits, was a mystery I've never understood. Watching those unfortunates behind the wire fence, I felt very close to them. Andrea was right that maybe at some point the extremes came together. I managed to perceive clearly what might have happened in their lives. They'd been worn down, that was the whole of it. Rather than continuing to pretend, they'd slipped on their space suits. Concerning the others, however, the ones who'd been born that way, I had no answer whatsoever.

"Who does?" I said aloud, and, naturally, no one answered. "Nature's mistakes," Andrea had said. "Inexact duplicates of the genetic code."

Just when his words came back to my mind, a man turned to look at me. More than a man, he was a youth. His face was swollen, his tongue kept coming out of his mouth. I don't know why, but I had the impression he was happy to see me. He started slapping his open palms against the fence. The male nurse looked up from his sports page and immediately lowered his gaze once more. The youth kept jumping and striking the fence. He wants me, I thought. Instead of coming closer, I backed away.

Within two weeks of each other, Andrea and I were both released from the center. That week Andrea became a legal adult. I still had several months to go.

I'd been home for just a few days when he called for the first and last time. He wanted to go for a walk.

He rang the bell at two. I went down instead of having him come up. We quickly got to the field road. It was the first days of June.

As we walked in silence with our hands in our pockets, I thought one of the things I'd missed most was having a brother. It was something I came to realize during those two weeks of solitude. For me, Andrea had become like a brother. I wanted to tell him but refrained. I was too afraid of his sarcasm.

When we'd left the town behind, he started to talk.

"We're free," he said with a profound sigh. Then he laughed and added, "We've been redeemed. See, now they're satisfied because they're convinced they saved me. They don't ever realize that I've just learned to play my part well. You too, you've become a passable actor in my school. Drinking was my conscious choice. I've never been a victim of anything. This is where the game changes, see? Between submitting to things and choosing them. I wanted to explore a different state of consciousness, to make others believe I was lost. I was interested in the limit, that's all. And then, in a way, I performed a good deed. I gave the people watching me during those months the illusion of rehabilitating a human being."

I told him about how something analogous had happened to me. At a certain point I'd discovered poetry. I felt it in my blood, in my bones, but couldn't manage to reach it. I thought wine might give me a hand, that it might be as good a way as any of breaking the monotony of my sensations.

The road started to climb. He listened in silence, then said, "The person who wants to cross over a boundary keeps something great inside. That doesn't ever happen with normal people. The boundary they place on themselves is always material, something concrete they want to obtain. A nicer house, a job with more money, a love interest different from everyone else's. From birth to death they wallow in these minuscule things without ever lifting their heads."

"Are you saying I could be something great?" I asked timidly.

"Sure," he said. "Otherwise you'd have been satisfied like all the others."

"Still, I don't know what to do. I only know what I don't want. I don't see any road opening up for me."

"Now the path is going up, and we're working harder than before. Greatness is like that. It never contemplates ease. Otherwise what kind of greatness would it be? Instead of a path it would be a highway during summer holidays. For the moment you only know you're different. That's already a very important point. Keep not giving in, living outside the rut, and you'll see sooner or later your calling will come to you."

"But you don't have even the slightest idea what I could become?"

Andrea stopped and looked me in the eye for a long time. It was always hard for me to sustain his gaze.

"I don't know," he said. "Maybe you could be a philosopher, or an artist."

"Why a philosopher or an artist?"

"Because I know you by now. I'm sure that as a kid you used to sob over every leaf that fell from a tree. Death is part of your breathing. It envelopes you, dominates you. All your emotions come from contemplating it."

I sometimes felt terribly annoyed by Andrea. It was as if before him I was being subjected to an X-ray, and I didn't always feel like putting myself through it.

"What about you?" I asked, slightly raising my voice. "Haven't you ever cried?"

Andrea laughed. "The moment I was born, sure I cried, but I stopped right after. It didn't take me long to figure out you always need to see things from above. Altitude is a fine antidote to emotion."

"So you're not an artist?"

"I might have been. But I renounced that the day I decided not to cry."

"So?"

"So there are two ways of escaping mediocrity. One is art, the other is action. There are connections between the two, but action is superior to art because it doesn't entail any sort of involvement. There's only been one artist who understood this—Rimbaud. First he wrote poetry. Then he went to Africa to sell weapons."

We'd reached the top of the hill. There were no trees at the summit, only grass. A light breeze stirred the blades and the petals of flowers growing in their midst. We lay down next to each other, our hands clasped behind our heads. For some time we were silent, looking at the sky. Once in a while a swift darted quickly by just above us. Andrea was the first to speak. Without looking at me he said, "I'm leaving tomorrow."

"Where to?"

He didn't answer. Two sparrow hawks glided above us, one higher than the other. They seemed to be playing, full of grace and power, with short sharp calls, chasing each other in the air.

On my return home, my mother had asked what my plans were, whether I wanted to take up my studies again or work at something else. "I don't know," I'd said. "I need to think." In the meantime I wanted to work during the summer.

94

She set out immediately to find me a position. It wasn't hard. The husband of an ex-coworker of hers had a trattoria in a small town nearby.

And so, the week after I was already working.

I left by bike in the morning and came home in the evening towards nine-thirty, after the kitchen had closed. Not being around at meal times, I never saw my father. At other times he and I avoided each other with the same caution wild animals show in avoiding man. They smell or hear something suspicious and off they go into the most inaccessible parts of the forest. My mother and I talked about the weather. If it was nice out, we were silent.

Once in a while in her eyes I'd read something resembling a faint hope. Even if she didn't yet dare to show it openly, she must in a certain sense have been convinced everything was resolved. The darkness was behind us. Thanks to those fine doctors, things had been patched up. Before her was materializing, once again, her son the college graduate. And after graduation, a long line of grand children for whom she'd sew baby outfits and sweaters until the end of her days.

I tried to send that look far away so as not to see it. Or to see it from above, as Andrea had taught me. I didn't always manage it. The times I was unsuccessful, right in the middle of my chest I'd feel an acute pain like the prick of an insect.

My own plans were obviously much different. Some time before I had decided to leave. I wanted to get far away from this suffocating town. I'd understood by now that greatness was like a plant: to grow it needed full light and fertile soil. By staying there I would surely have started drinking again, or would have become one of those pathetically

95

eccentric beings that populate the provinces. I wanted to unfold my wings like Baudelaire's albatross. Even without having flown before, I felt their power and weight. If I hadn't opened them up to that moment, it was because my course had not taken me to a large enough sky. It's strange, but at that time I slept soundly at night, and the few dreams I had were all innocuous. I was suspended, in anticipation. In me was the calm of the man who knows he's going to meet real life.

September came and with it a precocious autumn. At daybreak fog would shroud the landscape. On the morning I became an adult, it was so thick that the linden in the courtyard was barely visible.

I'd quit working at the trattoria the week before.

I got up very early and dressed in silence like a cat. The train would leave a little before seven. My father was still snoring loudly. The table was set for breakfast. Next to my plate was an oblong package with a red paper and a gold bow. Under my cup was a card.

I picked it up and opened it. Inside was written, "You're all grown up!" And below, in her clear elementary teacher's handwriting, "Your Mama."

I weighed the package. It couldn't have contained anything other than a watch. I didn't take it. On the other side of the envelope, with the butt of a pencil I wrote in block letters: "I don't want your time anymore. I want my own. Don't worry."

I left with a light bag. In order not to make any noise I left the door half open. Once on the street outside, I felt a stab in my sternum.

96

EARTH

I

Temperature is the critical point in a body. If it's too high, the cells are no longer able to communicate among themselves. Faced with an excess of heat, therefore, the body must have recourse to some means of lowering it. It needs to evaporate; otherwise, everything explodes. Explodes or implodes. Either way the matter passes from one state to another.

In my first days living in Rome, I had the impression this was just what was happening. I'd walk and walk and, walking, give off steam. The more days that passed, the lighter I felt. It wasn't sweat that went away but the poisonous stench assimilated during growth. Sometimes I even had the impression I was becoming transparent. The beauty of the street and the monuments was reflected in me. It could be reflected because there wasn't anything left inside. My glance was no longer a ray beam but a sponge. It imbibed things and let them pass by. I'd sometimes find myself laughing without any reason. In the same way I'd cry. Behind both these states lay the very same feeling. I laughed out of a sense of liberation and cried for the same reason.

Rather than make judgments, I just let things reach all the way to my heart. I sobbed before the Imperial Forum illuminated by the rosy light of a sunset. I laughed before the sparrows that twittered bathing in the fountains.

Andrea's words were always in my ear. In those days spent doing nothing I understood my path wasn't the love of learning but art. I didn't consider, I felt. This was the sign.

Of course there were also practical problems. After a couple of weeks in a *pensione* near Piazza Vittorio, I went looking for work and a regular place to live. I found both on the same day. The work was that of a dishwasher in a restaurant at Campo dei Fiori, the room, a bed in a widow's house behind via dei Giubbonari.

Unfortunately, there was another boy in the room. His name was Federico. He came from a little town in the Marches. He must have been four or five years older than me. He was a literature major but quite behind in his course of studies. He had an elusive chin and black, excessively mobile eyes.

Fortunately our schedules differed. Our beds were next to each other. At night, to avoid the intimacies of sleep, we'd lie down on our sides with our backs to each other.

Federico annoyed me just as the loud, smelly work in the restaurant did. But these were rather superficial inconveniences. I was a great big hound, and these nuisances were fleas. I went calmly forward toward my goal with strong paws, without paying attention to them. The evaporation of excessive heat had cleansed me. The cleansing was called distance. Distance from home, my parents, ugly memories, furious walks. And Andrea.

The sky had cleared. I watched the limpid horizon and waited for something to happen. Inside I already glimpsed a flash, not of a fire anymore but of creation. Energy that licks and excites, that doesn't melt but creates. That emptiness was the kind diviners or mediums obtain within. It was an emptiness with an echo, a cavity prepared to resonate. What I was looking for didn't have a precise name or form. I approached, receded, approached again. It was a continuous pursuit. I knew of no lure or attraction. All I felt at times was a fearful acceleration of the heart. A word appearing from the void like a wild animal amid the vegetation.

I soon started spending all my free time in the library. Being in the midst of books was like being in a magnetic field. I'd found one close to home, in the interior of a cloister. In the middle there was a moss-covered fountain and, all around it, orange trees. When it opened I was already there, and I'd stay until it was time to go to the restaurant. I had no plan or program. There too the only law that applied was that of resonance.

I chose volumes randomly, taking four or five to my table at a time. I would enter the first page as if it were another world. I was no longer myself but some kind of wild animal, a seeker of precious stones. I was hungry. I wanted diamonds or gold. I often made my way forward through the pages as through a desert. There was sand all around and blinding sunlight. I walked and walked and found nothing. The words were dead weight, lifeless bodies, rocks. They hindered your passage and led nowhere. Often, through exhaustion and boredom I would curse the fact that I'd set out on the journey. But then, suddenly, when I'd nearly lost all hope, a miracle would happen: the page and I were one chord vibrating on the same instrument. Then time and space would disappear. The library could have gone up in flames and I wouldn't have noticed.

Sometimes I'd be late for work. I'd get there in a daze. They'd always have to repeat their orders twice. I'd wash the encrusted pans, flaying my nails, and I was no longer alone. With me were Prince Myshkin and Don Quixote, Captain Ahab and Prince Andrei, Marlowe, Raskolnikov, and David Copperfield. They were all there. When the pan was bright and shiny, they were reflected with me inside.

Several months passed in this way.

At that time my mood shifted between euphoria and the blackest despair. It was a little like being on a see-saw. I passed from one state to another, searching for something. One moment I felt as if I was close to it; the next I was sure I'd never get anywhere. I wanted to write but didn't know how. I lacked the magic word that would open the way toward work. A fire was inside me again. But it was different from the one I'd known before. Closing my eyes now and again I'd catch a glimpse of its tongue-like flames, low flames that follow the burning of the stubble. The purification had come. Now the rest was supposed to.

One particularly hard day I thought of Andrea and his resolute manner of confronting things. I thought, maybe an artist needs to be something of a warrior, decide to act, to fight.

That afternoon on my way to work I bought a large white notebook and a pen. The apartment was empty when I got home. I was agitated, not sleepy. I opened the notebook at the little table next to the window. From the moment the pen was perched above the paper it started rushing forward. It rushed on like a little sailboat impelled by the wind. I made no effort and felt no suffering. I felt more like a medium than a writer. Someone was dictating, and I went ahead. It was as if the book had already been written in some mysterious place and I was merely the humble servant, the scribe charged with writing it down.

Federico came home about three. "What are you doing?" he asked, seeing me at the table. Without turning I said, "Writing to my girl."

At six I went to bed. From the square nearby the sounds of the market could be heard. I was tired and wide awake at the same time. I wanted to sleep but couldn't. The words flowed and flowed. They were no rivulet; they were the swollen torrential flood of a monsoon.

I filled up sheet after sheet for a whole month. During the day it was all I thought about. I scraped pans and repeated phrases as if I were singing a song. Walking on the street or in the restaurant kitchen, I'd sometimes be struck by a feeling of great alienation. The dimension in which I was moving was mine and nobody else's. There was reality and there were thoughts. Between these two states was the interspace of poetry. That was where I lived, distant and very close, neither above nor below, but to the side of things. I was the demiurge of that space. On the waves of memory I created and destroyed destinies. I gave palpable voice to a universe in which the only rule was suffering.

I traced the words "The End" at dawn on Christmas morning. I was alone in the apartment, and the holiday church bells were ringing. I wanted to tell someone the

104

news. At eight I went into the kitchen. Signora Elda had put the coffee on the stove, whose neon light made the clear skin of her head beneath its few remaining hairs shine.

"I've written a book!" I announced in the doorway.

She turned with a pot holder in her hand, looked at me in confusion for a moment, and said, "Congratulations."

I tried to rest by wasn't able to. I didn't yet understand that this kind of work emptied you like no other in the world. You write "The End" and feel you're a lion. Some hours later you're a rag, the embalmed mummy of a pharaoh. It's taken everything from inside you. What's left of you is just your skin. As soon as you move, it crackles like that of a chicken on a spit.

My legs were sort of on edge, so I went out. The streets were more deserted than I'd ever seen them. Everyone was still at their tables doing justice to the Pantagruelian Christmas meal.

I walked and walked until I'd climbed to the top of the Giancolo Hill. The afternoon was clear. At my feet was the entire city and then, farther off, the exhausted volcanoes of the Alban hills. No sound reached me, neither car horn nor ambulance. It seemed as though a spell had been cast over the city. My thoughts wandered a bit as I considered that a large part of my imagination was made of what I was seeing there down below. It was as if the only kind of history we had studied was Roman since that was all that had remained in my mind. To call it "history" was maybe too much because I didn't remember a single date. It was personalities rather than history: Anco Marzio and Tullius Ostilius, Romulus and

Remus and the rape of the Sabines, Cornelia, mother of the Gracchi, and Cincinnatus, the Horatii and Curiatii, and Nero, plucking his zither as he sang out his insanity before Rome in flames. Such personalities had spoken a phrase or used a gesture and for that single phrase or gesture had impressed themselves on my memory. I sat on the low wall of the Gianicolo looking down and wondered where exactly Caeser had been killed, which was the bridge of the Horatii and Curiatii.

I spent a half-hour in such fantasy before I started to feel cold and got up. It was as good a way as any of filling the pneumatic void that had sprung up inside me.

Then, coming down from the Gianicolo toward Trastevere, I began to feel something strange between my diaphragm and stomach. It felt like someone was shoving his finger in. Maybe more than a finger. It was more like an expansion screw, for the discomfort radiated outward.

By now the people were swarming out of their houses. There were small knots of them everywhere, hugging and kissing. They all had the excited, befuddled air of those who've just come from a long family gathering. At such moments the tension, hatred, and petty envy were annulled in the frenetic engagement of food and alcohol. It's the brutishness of the libations, not the birth of the Savior, that creates the simulacrum of love.

At our house nativity scenes were strictly forbidden. If you wanted to see one, you had to go to a church in secret. Once, on my way back from the dairy, I had slipped inside. I was maybe seven or eight at the time. It was afternoon. The nativity was beneath the altar, and there was no one else in the church. The baby was already in the manger even though it was still many days before Christmas. Joseph and Mary were looking at him with an affectionate expression, the same as that of the oxen and the ass. Everything was peace, tranquility. I observed him and wondered if he knew what was coming. All that intimate sweetness, one day, would be destroyed, and upon that same child all the meanness and stupidity of men would bear down. A terrible sadness came over me. "You're the kind of guy who sobs over every leaf that falls," Andrea had said. It made me furious, but he was right.

I was thinking all this as I forced my way through the well-fed crowd, and the sadness, rather than going away, grew out of all proportion. The pain between my diaphragm and my sternum was so strong I almost wasn't able to breathe.

Who knew if my mother and father had had a Christmas meal. I saw them around the Formica table covered with the cross-stitched table cloth my mother had made, eating in silence, looking into space in opposite directions. After the Christmas cake, my father would drop like a dead weight into his recliner in front of the TV. He barely had the time to say, "A bunch of bullshit," before falling asleep. My mother, behind him, would wash the dishes and go to the bedroom to do crossword puzzles.

Did she miss me? I was in no position to say. Probably I was a weight she'd shrugged off. Or maybe no, maybe at that precise moment she had locked herself in the bathroom to look at my pictures. She was sitting on the toilet lid, caressing the pages of an album the same way she'd caressed my newborn skin.

I realized then that the emptiness inside me wasn't pneumatic. It was neither impermeable nor pneumatic. It was a magnetic void, fragile and wretched. A void that attracted all the thoughts I'd never wanted to have. Before such thoughts I felt tremendously alone, tremendously exposed.

By now the street lamps were lit, and a north wind had begun to blow. The human herds had gone back to their respective homes, and the streets were again deserted. Tin cans and scraps of paper whirled up to the level of cars' tires. The sadness went from a mere feeling to nearly a physical state. I felt it emanating from me just as spite towards my father had once emanated.

I reached Ponte Sisto at a slow walk and looked down.

The rains of the preceding days had turned the river into an impetuous rush. It was so yellow that it sometimes looked more like a river of mud than a stream of water. I had abandoned my mother and felt guilty. In my enraged flight I hadn't even taken a picture of her. She hadn't done anything to make my life easier, but I felt guilty all the same.

On the bridge I remembered an old tenant of Signora Elda's who used to go fishing in the Tiber every morning. I couldn't believe that fish lived in all that scum, so one day I asked him, "What do you catch?" and he showed me his prey. They were called *ciriole* those fish; he kept them in the bath tub filled with running water. It wasn't an improvised aquarium but the place they went to be cleaned out before being eaten. There were four or five of them, floating on the water's surface, their grayish gills all swollen.

Even someone who grows up in mud, I told myself then, can step back at a certain moment in his life and become pure, return to his original innocence. But what was original purity? Maybe just this—the state in which one hasn't yet been touched by pain.

Watching the turbid eddies that formed and disintegrated before my eyes, I cast back in my memory. Months and years retreated, and I was already corrupted. To what point had I lived in innocence I asked myself, but could not find an answer. All my days had passed in the naked obscenity of evil. My friend's death had merely been the instant when that state became visible, but for some time before that, corruption had lived inside me, a sordid vein in the marble's white purity.

My mother's face rose before me on my way home. She was young, seated on the bed, sobbing. I was a little over a year old, sitting in front of her, touching one of her legs. I was calling mamma, and she, instead of smiling or answering me, kept crying. So there was something that made grownups cry too. At that precise moment my certainty in the world crumbled. I was a little plant that had sprouted on an outcropping of rock that, shoved by an unknown force, was slipping down.

At the apartment, Signora Elda had gone to sleep. I quickly got into bed. I felt exhausted, hot and cold at the same time, as if I'd come down with a fever. I fell asleep almost immediately. And with sleep came a dream. I was walking in a snow-covered plain. I didn't know how I'd got there or where I was going. I thought: it must be the Padana plain or the lower Polesine, and at that instant a ball of fire appeared before me. For a moment I thought it was a tire, but there was no smoke or stench. I came closer and saw it was a bramble of blackberry bushes. It burned but created no heat. I had a cane in my hand, which I extended in that direction. Just as I grazed it, something strange happened. The bushes started to unravel. They unraveled by themselves. As they came apart, I understood they weren't bushes but barbed wire. At each of the barbs the flames were higher. They rolled out and ran ahead as if indicating a path. So I followed, and after several steps something still stranger happened. The flames went out, and pearls appeared in their place. Polished, bright shining pearls. A string that seemed it would never end. But, suddenly, it was over. I was no longer in the plain but on the brink of a precipice. One after another the pearls were being swallowed up. I leaned out. At that instant someone called out to me. The voice came from below and echoed. Once it reached the top, it went silent. I recognized that voice immediately. I knelt at the edge and shouted: "Andrea –ea –ea –ea."

I woke up in the middle of the night with a high fever. I took an aspirin and got back into bed. Half-asleep I thought the splendor of pearls is born from a wound. That was what I was, a pearl diver. From the time of my birth I'd done nothing but plunge into the most profound depths in order to draw treasure up to the surface.

II

My fever lasted through to the beginning of the new year.
Federico came back just then. He was a little fatter than
when he'd left.

"You didn't go home?" he asked, seeing me wandering
through the room in my pajamas.

I said, "I don't have a home."

His appearance didn't irritate that much. Observing him
was actually as good a way as any of entertaining myself.

During my convalescence I discovered that university
study was just a façade for him. His real work was the telephone. He had an address book as fat as a preacher's Bible.
Little pieces of paper with additional notes were attached
to every sheet. He'd get up relatively late in the morning
and, after his coffee, attach himself to the receiver. We had
a party line, and that drove him crazy. He would often go
onto the landing to pound on the neighbors' wall to get
them off the line. It was over the phone that Federico would
round up invitations to lunch, dinner, and after. Over the
phone he'd get himself still other phone numbers. What he

wanted most to do was work in the world of movies and TV. He confirmed this for me one day when he as particularly talkative.

"College is for my father. Otherwise he'd close off the finances. I'm actually an artist."

"An artist?" I asked. "What kind?"

He spread his arms wide: "A Renaissance artist—all kinds."

I went back to work after Epiphany, once my fever had passed.

One evening I came home and, strangely, found Federico. He was almost never at the apartment at that time.

"Why didn't you tell me?" he asked, without even saying hello.

I blushed all of a sudden and asked in a low voice, "Tell you what?"

"That you write, that you're a fantastic writer."

"You read it?"

"I didn't want to be indiscrete, but the first page caught my eye, and after that I couldn't stop myself."

"You pulling my leg?

"No. Seriously. It's a masterpiece."

I suddenly felt all hot. It seemed as if something was set free inside me. My blood ran extraordinarily fast. Its sweet warmth invaded every part of my body. I should have got angry at such an invasion of privacy, but I was honest enough to know that in a way I'd been complicit in it. I was the one who'd left the manuscript there, in plain sight, on top of the desk.

Federico seemed truly enthusiastic, and talking about it roused him further. He actually quoted several passages from memory. In the end, when we were dressed for bed, he said, "It would be a crime to leave a work like that in a drawer. We have to find a publisher and get it published right away."

Sure, but how? I didn't know anyone at all.

"Don't you worry about that. Next week We'll go see Neno. He'll help you out."

In the days that followed I discovered Neno was a famous screen writer who'd even been nominated for an Oscar. He had also published four or five novels and a couple of collections of poetry, all well reviewed. "Neno," said Federico, "is an extraordinary man. He has everything he wants: money, success, talent. He can afford not to give a damn, but still he'll give you a hand if he can. Every Monday he opens his door to anyone who wants to go see him, no matter whether they're friends or complete strangers."

113

The feeling I had wrapped myself up in on my arrival in Rome was starting to return. My life was taking its proper course and without any undue effort on my part. Neno received visitors on Mondays, and Monday was my day off. Such coincidences couldn't be anything but a sign of destiny.

The only worry was my wardrobe.

In my closet I had two pairs of bell-bottom pants, three shirts, and three sweaters, plus a jacket with synthetic fur inside that, when it was warm, could be removed. How could I appear before my patron dressed like that?

So Sunday I got up early and went to Porta Portese.

There, on a bench, I found a nice white shirt that looked like a nineteenth-century poet's. I bought it and went home feeling triumphant.

The next evening when I put everything on, I understood the whole tragedy. The shirt was not a man's, it was a woman's: on the front rose up two starched pyramids that were supposed to hold boobs. I tried to flatten them out by rubbing them with my hands, but the material was synthetic and too resistant. After a second the protuberances were back out front. By then it was too late for any alternative, so I put on a sweater with brown and purple diamonds on it, the only one that was clean, and resolved at all costs not to take it off.

At nine we set out from home. Neno lived close by, in a large *palazzo* between Piazza Navona and the Pantheon.

"How am I supposed to act?" I asked as we went down the street.

"However you think is best," Federico said. "You'll see. At Neno's it's all informal."

He listed a long series of names, people who had come by Neno's one day and, thanks to him, been successful.

On the intercom there were no names, only numbers. Federico pressed the eight, and the thick, heavy door opened.

It was on the fourth floor. To get there you took an enormous stone staircase. The walls were painted in frescoes, and every niche had an ancient Roman bust in it.

We entered in the general indifference. Here and there were small groups of people. Coats were piled up on a big armchair. Federico tossed his onto the top, and I did the same with my jacket with synthetic fur. Then somebody called him from one of the groups, and he ran off to them, while I was left standing in the middle of the room, not knowing what to do.

He'd been really right about just one thing. It was all informal there. Nobody looked at you or asked who you were or what you wanted. The people present gave the impression they all knew each other pretty well already. There were a bunch of little groups in spirited discussion. The thickest assemblage was around Neno. I spotted him right away because he was the only one there with long, gray hair. He was seated in a huge armchair with the supple laxity of the Sun King.

After standing halfway between the entry and the main room for ten minutes, I thought, "Maybe the best thing to do is go toward the bookshelves and look interested in the books." I spent a good half an hour in that position without any other result than making myself hungry. It was ten o'clock already. So I decided to make my way over to the food table on the opposite side of the room. If the food accorded with the furnishings, there would be nothing but salmon, caviar, and expensive champagne.

The buffet was terribly disappointing. The things laid out on the plastic plates were much less impressive than what we used to have on grandpa's picnics. There were little squares of mortadella and some thin slices of bruschette, a Tupperware bowl filled with industrial French fries that had gone completely soft from being out for too long, and the remnants of some cold pasta. The drinks, in small plastic cups, consisted of two big, crown-cap bottles of Frascati.

I looked cautiously around. Almost nobody was eating. They were all gathered around Neno, not discussing anything, just squawking like barnyard geese. Neno's legs were crossed, and the soles of his shoes had holes so deep you could see his socks. After some time he opened his hands to calm the waters, and his voice dominated all the rest.

"In my opinion," he said, "you have to consider the dialect of the whole. We have to ask ourselves if, in a society that's changing as quickly as the present one, what we're doing still has any sense? I mean," he went on, after a pregnant pause, "the artist still exists, can exist, or is the artist the collective?"

The little square of mortadella that I'd put into my mouth almost stuck in my throat. What was he talking about?

"Art is the expression of the bourgeoisie. The end of the bourgeoisie is the end of art," proclaimed someone heatedly.

"Or the birth of a different form of art," someone else added from his feet.

"Exactly," said Neno. "The era of art as an expression of the individual is finished. The singular artist, suffering and privileged, no longer has any reason to exist. It's the collective that now has to express a sentiment..."

"And the director?" asked someone at the back.

"Bravo," answered Neno. "The director doesn't make sense anymore either, for the simple fact that film is the most collective form of art that exists. If you think about it carefully, it's a little like the cathedrals of once upon a time. Imagine how many artisans, how many manual laborers contributed to constructing them..."

"Slaves of the capitalist Church!"

"Slaves certainly, but slaves without which the building of those masterpieces would never have been possible ... , and the cinema, the cinema is the same thing. The epic of the bourgeoisie is finished. Its decline is evident down to the smallest, most nauseating details, and another is being born: the despotic director, the keeper of some vision of the world, is no more. Collectives are springing up everywhere, school collectives, factory collectives . ... The screen writer as a social figure must modulate to this key. What you have to become is, in my opinion ... Look, you have to become seismographs. You have to go around like the most sensitive needles, registering the vibrations of the revolution ... ."

I hadn't drunk any of the crown-cap Frascati, but my head was spinning. How was this possible? Neno wrote books and said it was impossible to write books anymore. He talked about the revolution. He'd probably become infatuated with it through books. He'd already twice cited Chairman Mao, and his cat was even called that. He must have simply forgotten, or maybe he didn't understand, that revolutions aren't made by words but by the rage of people who've eaten poorly or not at all for their whole lives and who've worked to get the little they have had.

Whether the revolution came or not didn't really interest me much. What smarted was the thought that the artist might not exist anymore. I had worked so hard to become one and knew I was one but wasn't able to be one anymore. Films would no longer be made, nor books written, so what was it I'd come into the world to do?

It wasn't true that artists were just bourgeois. Artists, I said to myself, were like mushrooms that sprout up here and there in the forest, spread by spores. Some are born rich and others are born poor and have to work, but that was just bad luck; it didn't have anything to do with art. Jack London was the son of a traveling astrologer. At first he didn't have a dime and only later became really rich. He never hurt anybody. On the contrary, he made a lot of people happy with his stories. And if he came back to life now, who would tell him he couldn't write books anymore and he had to yield up his pen and paper to a shoe factory workers collective?

I was immersed in these thoughts when I saw some commotion amid the crowd. Neno was gesturing to me, calling me over with his arm.

"Hey you!" he shouted. "What are you being an individualist over there for? Come sit with us!"

I had barely come up when he reached out his hand toward my manuscript. "Give it here," he said. "Federico has told me everything." Then, before I'd even sat down, he asked, "What do you think of Godard?"

III

I didn't sleep a wink that night after coming back from the party.

"It went great," said Federico over and over, but I felt like I'd looked like an idiot. On Godard, in fact, I'd been too vague. I knew he was a director but had never seen any of his films, so while everyone was looking at me intently, I had said simply, "Well, some like him and some don't."

After this my debut, the conversation went back to them, and they started quarreling about Godard, having forgotten all about my presence.

"The only advice I can give you," said Federico, "is to be more active. At Neno's you can say whatever you like. People go to argue, dispute. What's the point in going if you're going to play mute?"

"But do you think he'll read it?"

"Sure, but you shouldn't be impatient. Impatient or pushy. He's always got a thousand things being shoved at him. You keep going every Monday, and you'll see one day, even when you least expect it, he'll say something."

I didn't understand why Federico was so forthcoming in trying to help me. It was really pure chance that we'd come to share the same room. So one day I said, "I'm really pleased that you're helping me, but I don't understand why you're doing it."

"What do you mean, you don't understand?" he asked, dumbfounded. "It's more than obvious: you know how to write, and I know people. We're a perfect partnership for success. If you think about it, some of the most famous people always work in pairs. There are even people who write books with a partner. I could become a famous director, and you, my screen writer, get it? It's a perfect opportunity because what one of us might miss the other won't. You always get farther with four legs than with two."

Federico's arguments reassured me. After all he knew that world much better than I did, and he was probably right—the best thing to do was to trust his experience.

It just so happened that the week right after Neno's party, at the opening for an exhibit, Federico had met an important TV executive, one of those people who got four stars in his address book, like the ones used for big hotels. He had seen this man's bewildered gaze directed toward the crowd surging around the buffet, and he'd sacrificed himself, elbowing right and left, managing to bring him a glass of sparkling wine. The executive was so grateful that they'd spoken like old friend for nearly two minutes.

When I came back from the restaurant, I found him completely revved up. He kept standing up and sitting back down on the bed, saying, "It's done! You understand? Done!"

We started working that same night. I'd be sitting at the desk while he walked around the room. The story we were writing was supposed to be used for a TV movie. In my opinion, it was rather woolly, but as far as Federico was concerned, the ingredients were blended so skillfully that success would be guaranteed.

Of course it was set in the Marches. "Not in Fermo," Federico had said. "Too autobiographical. Let's say in Osimo." It was the story of an authoritarian father with an only son who was supposed to inherit the family business. The business consisted of a chain of bakeries scattered here and there throughout the region. The father had started as a humble dough maker, who, in a few years, thanks to his skill, had become the king of sandwich rolls. He was a rather narrow character, tied more to material things than to ideals. "So," Federico had said, "a typical representative of the older generation." From the first scenes it was clear that the son could not have cared less about baked goods. Unlike his father, he had ideals. As a child he had even considered entering the seminary in order to become a missionary. As he got older, luckily, he'd come to understand that religion was the opiate of the masses and, thus, had decided to abandon the bakeries and become a sociologist, a profession his father did not at all appreciate. Obviously, there was a girl involved too, Patrizia, daughter of a fisherman from San Benedetto del Tronto—"a little bit of Visconti's *The Earth Trembles* always goes over well," said Federico, making the floor tremble with his feet. The boy, Corrado, loves the girl and is loved back by her. Her family adores him. Every time he goes over for dinner, they serve him

121

grilled jumbo prawns. The perfect son-in-law. Until the terrible day when he shows up to ask for Patrizia's hand, announcing with pride that he has broken with his father over the sociology issue. Storm, tempest, and fireworks! Her father starts cursing in straight local dialect and kicking everything around. The mother cries, the two kids escape, hand in hand, because love is much stronger than petty self-interest. They run off to Rome, and while he's studying, she waits tables. Meanwhile back in Osimo, a ghost appears in his father's house (there had been a TV movie on the paranormal a few years before that had been quite successful). It's the ghost of a distant ancestor who was something of a witch. Strange things begin to happen. The sandwich rolls no longer rise properly. A few loaves explode, others remain as flat as pizzas. No one understands what the hell is happening until the ancestress writes in flour on the marble floor of the formal sitting room: THIS IS REVENGE.

It took us a couple of weeks to draft the script, amid doubts and second thoughts. We worked every night, after my job and his parties. Federico dictated the plot, and I enriched it with poetic details. Finding a title wasn't easy. In the end, after two days of attempts, we agreed on *The Leavening of Revolution*.

The next morning, Federico went to a printer and made three copies, one for the executive, one for Neno, and one for us.

"It's no use calling the executive," he said then. "He probably won't recognize my voice, and he might not remember my name."

There was only one thing to do, he thought: go there, to the station, and bring it to him in person.

So the following Monday, early in the morning, we went down to the riverfront to catch the bus. Federico was wearing a velvet suit with a turtle neck and beige raincoat. I wore my usual jacket with synthetic fur.

We hadn't even left when he said, "It's clear that you're coming along for the ride. He's never seen you. If I took you inside right away on the first day, it wouldn't make a good impression at all. It would seem like I wanted to force you on him or was being arrogant, you know, something like that... ."

His proposal didn't offend me at all. On the contrary, I felt relieved. I had already suffered enough at Neno's house.

It was a sticky, hazy day. Along the Tiber there were rows and rows of cars stopped in traffic. The light on the bridge was broken, and there was a traffic cop directing. We waited for the bus for forty minutes. Off and on a light drizzle fell, greasy like dish water. When the 280 finally pulled up, the doors opened onto a scene from hell, the likes of which I've seen only in certain modern paintings, where a head is in one place and a leg somewhere far away.

"It's too crowded," I said.

He didn't listen to me, and with the skill of an eel he slipped inside. There wasn't any room for me, so I stood on the step, and the folding doors closed on my body like a pair of pliers.

It took us more than an hour to get to the TV station. The bus hiccupped along, a long halt for every step forward. Walking would have surely meant less time and fewer unpleasant smells.

When we finally got off, Federico explained the strategy he was going to use. Getting into the TV station wasn't easy.

There was a check-point you had to pass, and to do so you had to show your credentials, that is, the proper documents and an appointment verified by someone upstairs.

It was obvious that the executive, on hearing our names, would never have let us go up, not out of meanness but for the simple fact that he didn't know us. It was an obstacle that tripped up everyone who wanted to get inside, which was why Federico, who wasn't born yesterday, had put a lot of thought into it.

It had happened during the summer, in a ballroom dance hall on the outskirts of town. Federico loved that kind of dancing. In that very hall he had met a rather unattractive girl, or really, the way he put it, it wasn't that he'd met her, it was that she'd literally jumped on him. The thing would have ended then and there if, after they had danced and were sipping a drink, she hadn't told him she worked as a secretary at the TV station. He didn't let the opportunity slip, and he wrote down her number straight off. She was flattered. "Get it," said Federico, "a scag like that doesn't get asked for her number by somebody like me every day." The girl became his personal wild card. Every time he needed to get into the building, she let him in. "Unfortunately," he added, "she works for someone in administration so she can't be of much use to us. But you have to make do with what lady luck deals you. If you ask too much, she gets fed up. You know how it is, eh? Too much is too much."

Meanwhile we got to the front of the building, which was all of glass without even an antenna on it. Behind the iron gates there was a poor horse in the throws of death. It

124

looked like it had been shot because its hindquarters were resting on the ground and, its head raised upward, it was neighing in agony.

Looking at it, I thought, "What the hell kind of people could possibly be inside when they put up a dying horse as the symbol of their work?"

Federico said, "You wait here. I'll be right back."

In front of the building there was a barren little park full of scraps of garbage. The drizzle had stopped. I sat there and lit a cigarette. Then I smoked three more. With the fourth I decided to go back home.

I didn't really care much about the fate of our script. As they said in school, it wasn't my own work. I had chipped in, that was all. The only thing I cared about in the deal were the economic possibilities. I was fed up with dishwashing and making just enough to get by. Now I wanted a room of my own, a scooter to get around with, and a good coat. I was also a little puzzled by Federico's methods. I would have never had the courage to act that way. But he was more experienced. He'd been sailing those waters for four years already. I had to trust him.

Federico came home at five, his face so pale it looked as if he'd had his air cut off. But there was a hint of satisfaction just visible in that pallor.

"So?" I asked.

"Great! I did it."

"Did you give them our script?"

"Well, not too fast. I got in to see him."

"Which means?"

"From eleven to three I never left my post. At two fifty-

125

five he came out of his den. I approached him. 'Hello,' I said. 'How are you?' He looked at me, surprised, and I reminded him of the episode at the opening. 'Oh, right,' he mumbled, and then I had the presence of mind to offer my hand. 'My name is Federico Ferrari,' I said."

"And him?"

"He shook it and said, 'A pleasure.'"

I was astounded. "You were there all those hours just for that?"

Federico gave a condescending sigh as he slipped off his shoes. "It's clear you're from a small town and don't know how the world works."

That afternoon, sitting on the edge of the bed, I learned how the world works, at least that world. The most important thing was getting in. Once you were in, it became something between a treasure hunt and a stake out. You needed to have an important name written in your address book and, if possible, a direct connection to go with that name, I don't know, an evening together at the house of some friends, having sat together at a reading, that kind of thing, skin-deep, because the main thing was to imprint your face clearly on the executive's memory. "Naturally, if you had something else between your legs," he added, snickering, "the road in would be very different. It wouldn't be a road, it would be an interstate. They even say that somebody on one of the top floors has a special desk—if you tap a button, bang, it turns into a bed. Banging is all they do up there."

The more Federico went on, the more I realized it wasn't a question of hunting so much as a war of attrition. Once

126

you found the right door, you had to keep going there day after day for weeks and months, standing guard without being distracted, in the hope that sooner or later the object of your desire would gesture your way and say, "Come in."

"It's obvious there are short cuts for us too," concluded Federico. "Otherwise what kind of fucking equality would that be? But it's a tricky field, like quick sand. You have to sniff your way, sift through. When you make your move, you can't be wrong. You have to understand what side the person you're interested in is on, and then, once you've figured that out, what direction the political current is flowing. But that's not enough. You have to have spies informing you if he's about to fall out of favor or not. Everything inside there is in a state of delicate balance, which from one day to the next can be upset. The best thing would be to have two tickets, two sets of connections, so that, no matter which way the wind might blow, it's always behind you. Got it? If you want to make it, you have to work your butt off, so you should even be thanking me for today, considering that I stood there all those hours for you, too."

That night it occurred to me that what Federico had told me was a lot like the customs of Ancient Rome. Life at the Forum and life in TV were pretty much the same. There were the powerful and the needy. To understand who might be powerful or not, all you had to do was look outside the door. Wherever there was a line, there was power.

Neno was in Paris for a conference. Although several weeks had gone by, he hadn't told me anything about the book yet. I couldn't fall asleep nights. What worried me most was that he might not have liked it.

IV

Months passed. By March it already felt like spring. In the few green areas, there were trees covered with yellow flowers, their smell so strong it went straight to your head.

The situation had remained the same. I worked in the kitchen, and on Monday evenings I went to Neno's parties. There hadn't been a single word or sign from him. I was beginning to suspect the book had gone straight from the shelf to the garbage can. My suspicion become almost a certainty when, one particular Monday Neno didn't give me a single glance during the entire evening. Federico continued to be an errand boy. He ran himself ragged, standing guard at different doors all day long.

Every once in a while, early in the morning, his dad would call and they'd spend a good half hour fighting. His father was fed up with sending him money and wanted him to go back home to work in the family business—which wasn't a bakery but a little shoe making establishment—and Federico would insult him, saying he didn't understand a thing and it would be stupid for him to leave everything just before his big break.

When he'd come back into the room, he'd be in a nasty mood.

"Lucky you're an orphan!" he'd say every time, getting back under the covers.

That month I tried writing to my mother. It happened one night when I was very sad. My life was at a standstill, and I could no longer see which way I was going. It felt deadlocked. Waiting for an answer had worn me out, even stifling any desire I might have had to write other things.

The smell of spring agitated me, made me want to be somewhere else. I was nostalgic for my long walks in the Karst. I was sure that all I really needed to clear my mind and understand everything was a whole day of walking up there alone amid the first crocuses and the meadows bitten by winter frost.

129

In the city I was never able to find places that had the same effect on me. Anywhere I went, there were too many things coming at me, things too beautiful or too ugly, and this excess stood in the way of any depth of thought on my part.

I didn't walk on the street with the self confidence of my first months there. I was no longer a young dog exploring his territory. I trudged along with the indolent and doubtful step of the old hound. It was the anxieties of spring, sure, but also something else. Walking and walking, sniffing and sniffing, in the end I lost all trace of my way.

I didn't yet know, in that confused wandering, that shortly thereafter destiny had a sudden turn in store for me.

As if by design, everything happened on April 1. The mild temperature lured people outdoors in droves. Those days the restaurant was packed. I hardly ever had enough time to finish one pile of plates before another came my way. The swinging doors between the kitchen and the dining room would open and close like those in a comedy film. Once in a while a customer would come in by mistake in search of the bathroom. I was always the one who said, "Just outside on the left." So as not to waste any time, I'd say it without looking up.

So that day too, when a man's voice asked for the bathroom, I said without looking, "Just outside on the left, the light is right behind the door." But instead of wheeling around and following my directions, the guy planted himself in front of me.

"Look who's here!"

I looked up. Before me stood Neno, wearing an old velvet sport coat, his eyes shiny as if he'd been drinking. I didn't know what to say besides good evening.

"What are you doing here?"

It seemed to me an idle question, if not a stupid one. What I was doing was more than obvious. Washing dishes for next to nothing. But I was still polite. "This is my occupation," I said.

He lingered there in the doorway a little longer, then muttered, "Well, see you later," and left in the direction of the restroom.

I said nothing to Federico. Partly I was ashamed of having been discovered, partly a sixth sense told me it was better to keep quiet.

The following Monday I didn't want to hear about going to Neno's. I felt like everyone would catch the whiff of bleach and detergent about me, so, as soon as Federico started getting ready, I said, "Go ahead by yourself. I'm tired tonight."

"It's out of the question. You're coming and if you won't, I'll kick you there myself. Neno called this morning and was really insistent. He wants you to come, too."

I went like a donkey circling a grindstone, my head lowered, my tread heavy. Federico, by contrast, was euphoric. Actually I'd never really seen him any other way. He had convinced himself that Neno had finally read our story idea and that, not only had he read it, he'd loved it: he was summoning us both that evening to congratulate us and tell us to forget about television because he already had a contract lined up with a movie producer. At every step his megalomaniacal projects got more and more gigantic while in me all that grew was my ill humor.

The moment he saw me Neno came over and greeted me warmly, wrapping his arm around my shoulder, and he didn't let go for an instant the rest of the evening. He wanted to know everything about me. There didn't seem to be anything more interesting in the world to him than my life and what I thought about things. At first, to tell the truth, I was rather embarrassed. I wasn't used to so much attention. Then, after a few glasses of Frascati, things started to go a little better.

A couple of hours more and I was doing great. It was nice to talk and be listened to. I'd never had so many adults around so enraptured by whatever came out of my mouth.

131

I talked and talked and talked. There was no stopping me. I felt as if my cheeks were purple, my ears too, but could not care less. For those people I was important, and that erased everything else.

I was among the last to leave the apartment. Federico had disappeared from my sight just after our arrival. When it came time to take my leave, the church bells were striking two. Neno was at my side.

"You've written a masterpiece," he said. "If you allow me, I'll help you publish it."

V

Neno seemed truly enthusiastic about my manuscript. It had been years, he told me that night, since he'd read anything so strong and fresh, so innovative, so anti-academic.

"It's clear you didn't come out of some university," he'd said. "You can feel the pure despair in it, without any kind of filter. There isn't any intellectual mediation, self-indulgence. It's just the scream and rebellion of a life at the margins, a life without prospects and without consolation."

I was speechless. I mumbled a thank you.

"Why don't we say *tu* to each other," he said, giving my arm a firm squeeze.

Within a week we'd become close friends. He took me with him everywhere, introducing me with the words, "You'll soon be hearing about this guy." Whatever was being discussed, he would ask me, "And what do you think, Walter?"

I kept blushing, more so the first few times, then, as time passed, less and less. At the start I thought he was overdoing it. After all, I had written only a first and very autobiographical novel. But hearing it repeated so often, I came to believe it. At last everyone had realized that there was something superior about me, and I was happy such superiority was finally recognized and respected.

At the end of the month he informed me that my book would come out with a publisher in Rome.

Seized by euphoria, I wrote my mother at the beginning of May. It seemed a nice gesture to resume contact with good news. I filled three entire pages explaining to her that I'd come to Rome because I had something great to accomplish. Everything had happened very fast, and probably before August she'd be hearing about me in the papers, not because of drug use or alcohol, as she assumed, but because I'd become a writer. I ended the letter by saying that I wasn't sending my address because soon I'd be leaving my room for a new apartment all to myself.

Yes, because among the daydreams I indulged in during those days was the one about money, and it wasn't a little one.

Money was something I'd never had. Until that moment, my focus had always been internal, in good times and bad. I hadn't even noticed that I didn't have a car or a stereo. Money and all you could get with it was very distant from me. I didn't judge people by that measure, and didn't want to be judged by it. So not having ever thought about money, I didn't know its dangers. Only then did I discover its subtle and omnipotent power. In the exterior world there was an invisible fabric, and that fabric was made of money. Everything was for sale, and every person could be corrupted. With a few extra bills I too would be able to purchase my worldly security. With some nice clothes my debut would be completely different.

When I'd started going to Neno's place in the evenings, my first thought had been about clothing. I knew I was inadequate and had no taste at all. That was how I'd acquired that unfortunate nineteenth-century poet's shirt, which turned out to be not the poet's but his fiancée's. Afterward, trying to improve things a little, I'd made two or three other purchases. Federico was horrified when he saw them.

"Where did you find that garbage? You look like even more of a hick than before."

I was terribly disheartened. Maybe it's stupid to say, but I was more ashamed of my shoes than of any potential lack of culture. I had no doubt whatsoever about my intelligence, but plenty about my appearance. I felt like a snail dragging its house behind him: the house was the apartment where I'd grown up, with its constant kitchen odors and cat piss in the stairwell, my father's alcohol breath, my mother's quaint needlepoint on the walls. I was convinced that anyone could read all that squalor in my face.

Just to confuse me more, at the beginning there were Neno's clothes too. I'd noticed the holes in his shoes the first evening, then the ones in his sweaters, to say nothing of his sport coats without any elbows or his corduroy trousers so worn they had no ridges on the seat anymore. Everyone imitated him, some with more holes some with less.

I didn't understand. If they're so badly dressed, I told myself, why should I be ashamed of my synthetic fur jacket? I tried to make sense of it all, telling myself, "Neno and

135

his friends are richer than I am, and they go around in rags; I'm not as rich as them, there aren't any holes in my clothes, but I'm ashamed of myself all the same." One Sunday morning, strolling on Piazza Navona, I finally understood it all. The great difference wasn't in the holes but in the material that surrounded them.

The revelation came while I was watching the people sitting in the sun as they took their aperitifs. You needed a lot of money to be able to sit around in those bars. Farther on, before the doors of the church there was a beggar with terrible, eggplant-colored fake leather shoes. Tracing the gulf was a simple matter. With poor quality, wear and tear quickly becomes rupture; with good, it makes the leather nobler. In short, one could easily divide the world in two on the basis of shoes. This law also held for sweaters: an abyss separated the uses of cashmere and acrylic. Those holes worn with indifference meant just one thing: "I've been living in comfort for such a long time that I don't lend it any weight anymore, I've got much more important things to think about."

I signed the book contract at the beginning of June. The editor was nice. He had a beard, wore a scarf, and never stopped talking. His company was a just few years old and specialized in "wild" authors, which meant those who had done other things in life and then up and wrote a book.

A Life in Flames—that was the title. It was set to come out in September.

I was a little disappointed that no one ever talked about compensation, but then I told myself, "That's really

peripheral. The main thing is that the book should be printed. From then on surely doors will start opening for me."

I had a summer of leisure before me. All that remained
to do was take pleasure in it as in an unanticipated gift. And
in effect that's what I did.

Every Monday I went out for dinner. The coming of the
first warm days had thrown open the terraces. It was
beautiful to be out, under the stars, with a light breeze
caressing your hair and making everything easy. It was
nice to eat and drink well, and talk to people who knew
who you were.

Then at two or three in the morning when I came back
out onto the street, I'd go walking until morning. The light
and air were soft, the city welcomed me with its extraordinary beauty. I walked near the Forum and then alongside
the Coliseum. A few blackbirds would be searching for
food amid the fresh morning grass, the cats coming out to
stretch among the ruins. All that excessive quantity of harmony and history were there for me, I was part of it.

The hours I wasn't in the kitchen I spent sleeping.

Federico had gone home on vacation. I was happy in
the solitude of my room. I kept the shutters half closed.
The sounds that came from outside were my alarm clock.
When I heard the screeching of the martins, I knew it
was time to get up. Washing dishes didn't even feel
heavy anymore. I had all the detachment of a person
there by mistake.

On July 31 I went with Neno and his friends for lunch
in Fiumicino. The next day they all left, him for his home in
the country, the others for destinations elsewhere.

Even the restaurant closed at the beginning of August, the city suddenly emptying, and the sudden absence of people and cars was stunning in its shabby grandeur. I strolled down the deserted streets with the same ease as the year before. For the first time in my life I felt truly on vacation. Which meant observing everything from outside. Handing out the benevolent compassion of one who knows he is already out of danger.

From dusk on I would be on the move, on foot or by bus. Sometimes, during the day, I'd take the old metropolitan all the way to Ostia, where the sand was black and the sea was the same yellowish color as the Tiber.

Once in a while I'd go to the movies or, after walking in the sun, take refuge in the coolness of the empty churches.

138

The nineteen years of my existence up to that point had been completely erased. I was no longer interested in knowing what was meant by emptiness or death or whether there was a principle of evil acting in men. All the questions I'd once asked myself had disappeared. There was no order or disorder anymore, or the chasm of nothingness that opened up between one thing and another. I looked at the horizon above the sea, and the horizon said nothing to me. I was thinking about what I'd wear on the night of the launch or about the jealousy my old school mates would feel when they found out.

The auger that had always been drilling inside me had pulled up. Layer by layer, earth and rubble had covered up the fire that burned below.

From the era of incandescent magma, without realizing

it and without any act of will, I'd passed on to the era of skin. The skin of apples, pears, nut kernels, banana peels. Only the outside interested me.

I'd forgotten that skin can be slippery. You put your foot down and go flying head over heels.

The book came out at the end of September.

At the launch, which was held at Neno's place, there were a bunch of important people. I'd learned at last how to dress right. Behind the Campo dei Fiori I'd discovered a used clothing store that sold only cashmere and tweed. For not much money I'd managed to put on a whole outfit that was perfect, with holes everywhere that I didn't dream of hiding.

Everyone was hanging around me, making compliments.

"It's been such a long time since we read anything so extraordinary," they said. "This book marks the beginning of the rebirth of literature." Then they wanted to know everything, if I was still washing dishes, or if the protagonist was some kind of alter ego, or if I too drank from morning till night. I said yes, it was true, the story was autobiographical.

At a certain point a lively discussion erupted by the fireplace. One person was saying he thought there were echoes of Julius Evola in the story while another was in absolute disagreement. The disruptive force of the text, its absoluteness, came only from the fact that I was a "wild" narrator. Even London had been one, though he'd always been a socialist. He knew Spencer as well as Protestant pastors know the Bible.

I was confused but not unhappy. All this was new but also felt right. I had a few interviews in those days as well. Reading them left me disappointed. I'd spoken passionately for hours, but the image that came across was just of some drunk provincial.

In the mornings I'd go around to the bookstores nearby home to make sure the book was displayed. "How's it going?" I'd ask the sales people, pointing to it, to which they'd answer "Well, it hasn't taken off yet."

I was beginning to get a little worried when, through Neno, a movie producer turned up.

"This story would make a fantastic film," he'd said, and, a little later, I'd signed a contract for an option on the rights.

Reality was approaching my dreams. I had a piece of paper in my hand that would guarantee me more money than I'd had in my whole life.

At last I could allow myself to stop washing dishes. The restaurant owner didn't seem especially saddened. He paid me for the month, forgetting about my severance pay. After all, I'd been working off the books.

At the end of October I moved to a new apartment. It wasn't in an attic, as I'd hoped, but a basement. It was at Tuscolano, on a street named after a Roman consul. This was just a temporary settlement. I couldn't complain. The place had one bedroom, a little bath without any windows, and a tiny kitchen, also windowless. Light came in from something like arrow slots that ran along the sidewalk.

Luckily the phone was already hooked up, so I could

call the producer and get calls without having to run around to phone booths. The shooting for the film was supposed to start in the first months of the new year, but first the script had to be written. From one day to the next I waited for the call.

Federico called first. He knew about my good fortune and was afraid of being forgotten.

"Don't forget you owe me a favor," he said before hanging up.

"Don't worry," I said, "I know how to be grateful."

I was telling the absolute truth. The moment the producer called me, I would have invited Federico to join in on the script.

But the producer was silent.

After ten days of no word, I decided to call myself. The secretary answered that the doctor was out. The next morning he was at a meeting, and the one after that he was out of town.

In the meantime, a man from the radio had called me. He'd read my book and wanted to do an interview. I went to the recording studio and had a pleasant meeting. The journalist was a good listener, calm and well prepared. He had intelligent questions that I was able to answer naturally, as if I'd been behind a microphone my whole life.

"Why don't you come work for us?" he asked at the end.

I would have liked that. It was nice there in that reclusive, padded world, but I couldn't. I turned down his invitation, saying I was very busy with my film.

This was true and false. It was true in that I had a contract for an option. It was false in that I wasn't doing anything. I was convinced it was a question of days or at most weeks.

By the beginning of December the producer still hadn't called.

So one morning I took the scooter I'd purchased in the meantime and went to his offices. Two hours of antechambers later he saw me. He was affable and smiling as before.

"There were some obstacles," he said. "Those slowed us down, but now they're getting resolved. You think about the names of some actors. That way we can sign them up so as not to risk losing them when it comes time for the shooting."

VI

A year went by.

Shooting for the film never started. There wasn't even any contract for the script. During the first months my tenacity in tracking down the producer was pretty strong, then it weakened and, weakening, turned to depression. I couldn't understand why anyone would behave like that. After all, if there were problems, wouldn't it be better to talk to me about them?

While I waited I'd even bought myself an answering machine. It was a kind of oracle. I'd get home and immediately look to see if the light was blinking.

It never did. Not even Federico was contacting me anymore. He'd found himself the right connections and now had a regular position at a TV station. I had sought him out a couple of times and he'd been very evasive, as if he was afraid I was going to ask him for something.

The money from the option and what I'd saved from the restaurant was almost gone. I didn't know how I was going to make more.

I went to see the publisher. I hadn't seen a lire from him yet so I asked him to settle up. He burst into laughter and gave me an affectionate slap on the back.

"Come now, don't you know that you can't live off of books?"

Then he showed me some invoices that I couldn't make heads or tails of.

"Look," he said, pointing with a pencil at a few lines, "you haven't sold even three hundred copies. Next week the rest is going to be pulped. It was a nice book you know. Too bad no one realized it. I lost a hefty sum on it but I'm not sorry."

I was in up to my neck. At the beginning of December I decided to ask Neno's help. According to him, it had been a terrible mistake to leave my work at the restaurant. If I wanted to be a writer, I could very well wash dishes. "Experience of life, that's what counts." But in the end he gave me the number of a script writer.

"He's always got work. Rather than writing he scripts comedian contracts." I didn't understand, so he explained. "That's what they call people who write those stupid demented scripts cooked up for comedians with big box office sales. Producers are always hard on their heels so they need people to help. Tell him I told you to call," he said. "He'll find you something, you'll see."

The scripter for comedians was named Orio, and he lived in the hills outside Rome. He'd agreed to meet me almost immediately. I was afraid of being late, so I took a bus that left four hours before our appointment.

The country village turned out to be an overgrown little town, something mid-way between an industrial park, a

Neapolitan nativity scene, and a barracks camp. Everything was unkempt, shapeless, shabby. The roads were precariously illuminated by sad Christmas decorations. The more I walked the more uncomfortable I became. Nothing bad was happening really, I told myself. I was just on my way to see a script writer who would give me work. But all the same I felt like a prisoner in some nightmare I wanted to wake up from as fast as possible.

The villa, Orio had explained to me on the phone, was ten minutes from the center. You had to turn right after the community soccer field, left in front of a dump for construction materials, and you'll be there. His house was the only one there, you couldn't miss it. Along the road, I wondered, "What the hell would make someone want to live in a place like this?"

At exactly four o'clock I was in front of "La dolce vita," which was written on a ceramic tile above the bell. Below was another charming watercolor of a man sleeping blissfully on a hammock.

There wasn't an actual garden but an expanse of gravel from which a cypress sprung up here and there. In back you could make out a house of tuff colored bricks, the windows of its two stories adorned with curled iron bars. I made my appearance. Orio was waiting for me at the door with his hand extended so that I had to cover the last few meters at a run.

"Come in, make yourself comfortable," he said, taking my hand.

He was smiling, but it was a smile I didn't like at all. The lips and eyes didn't match. He wasn't tall. His face was

145

puffy and of an unhealthy pallor, his eyes watery, his cheeks flabby. He had on a threadbare house sweater, saggy velvet pants, and a pair of worn out slippers.

He had me sit down on a stiff chair. The white marble floor hadn't the comfort of a throw rug. Between us there was a little table with an arrangement of dry flowers that were dark and covered with dust. They looked like they'd survived a fire.

"So," he said softly, fixing me with his glance, "you would be Walter .... Good. So Walter, what can you tell me?"

I had brought a copy of *A Life in Flames* along like a business card. I pulled it out of my coarse leather bag and gave it to him. "Here, I brought you this."

He took the book as if he were accepting the carcass of a dead rat. He opened to the first page, read over a few lines, then he turned it over and read the blurb on the dust jacket, shook his head, sighed, and handed it back.

"Thank you for the thought, but I don't want it."

I was paralyzed. I'd never imagined a response like that. I sat stock still while my thoughts raced. He had acted rudely, I told myself, so I could too. I'm going to stand up now and give him a slap and then a kick in that saggy ass of his, the old filthy stinking shit. My blood started to boil as I thought this, but I continued to sit stock still meanwhile. I couldn't do it. I had no money whatsoever, and this man was the only one in a position to get me some. And so, faking a smile, I spoke like one of those wretches who sell encyclopedias door to door.

"Why not? It's a very nice book."

146

He burst into laughter. He had a mocking laugh, his teeth thrust forward, his body jerking, like a hyena.

"Listen, Walter," he said at last, "I want to be honest with you because I like you: can you imagine how many youngsters have sat here before you in that chair? If you can't guess, I'll tell you. A hundred, two hundred, I've lost count. They were, no, they are all the same. You come from the provinces, you want to make movies, you're convinced that you're artists, geniuses even. To show me what you're worth you all come with a book or a script in hand. You're going to think I'm mean, but you're wrong. Look around you. What do you see in this room? Shelves filled with books from the floor to the attic with not a space to be had. And do you know what's on these shelves? Only classics. That's why I don't want your book, just as I didn't want any of the others. You write to show that you're noble souls, but to me your noble souls are utterly unimportant. If in thirty years somebody says that this little book of yours is a masterpiece, maybe I'll read it and make a space for it, but for now I'm not interested. You need work? I can get you work. But forget poetry, young Werther and all that...."

That afternoon I learned at least two things about Orio: that he wasn't a bulldog but a hyena, and that once he started talking he never stopped. He talked and talked and seemed in love with his own bark.

Meanwhile I'd begun to think about saprophytes. In thirty years he wouldn't be reading my book since by then he'd have become a picnic for them. The poor beasts would have had to devour that repellent man. I could hear his words in the background. One that came up often was

147

dough. He must have liked it a lot. He kept repeating, "When someone's got to earn dough, he can't be overly concerned with subtleties...." Dough this, dough that. It must have been a little like the war for my father. Their tone of voice shared the same contempt, the same desire for mortification.

When the great pendulum on the hall clock struck six, I got up and said, "I'm sorry, but I really have to go or else I'll miss the last bus." He scribbled me a phone number on a sheet of paper.

"His name's Massimo," he said. "He's one of my most reliable collaborators. A month from now a comedian's film is supposed to be out. Give him a call as soon as you're back in Rome."

He shook my hand at the door. "I hope I haven't given you the wrong idea about me. In any case I prefer to work this way and put an end to any illusions right away. If there turns out to be real talent inside, it comes out sooner or later. One day you'll thank me for this."

I gave him a warm handshake.

"I'm certain of it," I answered, and, as I moved away down the little street, I shouted, "Thanks for everything!"

The heater in the bus was broken. On the ring road we were held up for a long time by an accident. I had carried the discomfort from inside that house out with me. It was a kind of unease I hadn't ever felt before. I wasn't able to give it a name. By the time I got home it had taken on a strange form. I was there by myself, but I had the impression someone else was there with me. I was me and not me. I wasn't at all pleased being two.

Massimo must have been around thirty, maybe a little

older, and was on the friendly side. We met in a bar on Piazza Venezia. The busses and cars were deafening. I had trouble making out what he was saying. Unpleasantness seemed like the background noise for the whole experience as we said good-bye.

The next time our meeting was at his place, and there were four of us. He introduced me to the others, and I shook their hands in as friendly a manner as I could. The film of the famous comedian was supposed to come out exactly one month from now. We didn't have much time. Except for Stan and Oli and Charlie Chaplin, I didn't know any actors capable of making people laugh. I didn't know how to get laughter out of spectators.

But first we had to discuss the plot.

"There's him," began Massimo, "and then two actresses just starting out, a couple of nice pieces of pussy...."

I sat there for more than an hour listening in silence. It seemed like a meeting of truck drivers after too many hours at the wheel. Pussies, cunts, tits and asses followed one another with the regularity of milestones. Every once in a while great guffaws of laughter would erupt. Faking a smile took all my strength.

I felt like when I was at middle school and my classmates were telling dirty jokes around me. Most of the time I had trouble even understanding the meaning, and the whole little story would just hang around in my head like the questions without apparent answers that eastern sages toss out to their disciples. I remembered one that I must have heard in fourth or fifth grade. A man is shaving on his terrace with a razor. It's a sunny day, and on the balcony

149

below him there's a beautiful woman. The razor slips from the man's hand and the next instant a pear drops into the hand of the woman. For years I was tormented by that pear in transit. I couldn't grasp its meaning.

The jokes of my workmates had the same effect. I'd listen and pretend to laugh. But without understanding what there was to laugh about, I never managed to open my mouth to tell one of my own. After a while Massimo noticed and said, "Why don't you say anything, Walter? Here if you don't talk, you're not working."

I mumbled something about being new and needing to understand how the whole thing worked and, that time at least, managed to get through it.

What happened in the film was pretty simple. The heroine, Jessica, was a well-endowed, cheerful girl who worked as a nurse in a tourist village in the tropics. Naturally almost all the villagers were men, and the few women present had a subtle lesbian trace and were insanely jealous of their husbands. Following a short panorama of the village, the opening scene went like this. The hero, which meant the comedian, goes to the clinic with a small cut on the inside part of his upper thigh. The nurse, who's a handy seamstress, immediately takes up a needle and thread to tack him up. When she doesn't find any scissors, she leans down to cut the thread with her mouth ... .

When we'd finished sketching out the first act, it was dinner time.

"Shall we make some spaghetti?" asked Massimo.

During dinner I understood that underneath all the camaraderie and good will was a sharpening of blades. Orio

150

was the shark while they were a school of remora fish circling him, remoras that wanted to grow into sharks. You didn't have to understand much biology to see that it was a fantasy. Even just slightly changing the form of a snout took hundreds of generations. Imagine changing a sucking mouth into a jaw with six rows of teeth in a single life . . . .

Fortunately, I thought, as I rolled the bucatini all'amatriciana on my fork during dinner, I'm not like them. I don't want to become a screenwriter or a director. I'm just a writer making a little money to be able to continue my work in peace. I needed air. There inside, distance was the only breathing space.

I lived at Tuscolano, Massimo at Torrevecchia. It was December and bitingly cold. It took me forty-five minutes to get home on my scooter. That night I dreamt I was traveling through arctic waters in a canoe protected only by swim trunks and a T-shirt.

151

The next afternoon we had another meeting, and the evening after that one more. On my scooter I would try hard to imagine jokes I could tell. On the last night they divided up the scenes. Each of us had a piece to develop at home. Massimo decided who got what. He gave me the part with the bungalows. Which meant I was supposed to describe everything that happened in the bedroom. When we were leaving, he said, "If you have any doubts, any questions, just give me a call. I'm in town every day now."

One problem I had already was not having a typewriter. Up to then I'd always written everything by hand. It took me two days to find someone who would rent me one at a reasonable price. Then I closed myself up in my tomb and for an entire week lived with Jessica and the others in the tropics.

I went back to Massimo's to drop off the scene two days before Christmas. He called me a few hours later.

"I've read your work," he said without even a hello. His tone was somewhere between paternal and irritated. "That's not it at all. You should have told me right away, just come right out, there's nothing to be ashamed of. I would have given you a part you're more suited for."

"Well," I said, "you knew it was my first piece."

"It's not that. It's that in the sex scene there's no realism. Before going to bed the characters waste hours looking at the stars, and then when they do go you can't tell what happens. They could be having a picnic, and the result would be the same, understand? That isn't what the public wants. They're paying money and they want to see what they've paid for … . See, Walter, I don't like playing around with words. You should have told me right away you were queer, I mean, you don't have the proper sensibility to write these scenes. We could have given you the fairy part and everything would have gone smoother."

"Fairy? Queer?" I said, practically hoarse, "What gave you that idea? Maybe I did it wrong, but that's just because I lack experience. It can happen that way at first. What do asses have to do with it?"

"Okay, okay, don't get angry. In any case, I have to give the stuff to Orio today. He'll decide what to do."

On December twenty-fifth at seven fifteen in the morning, the telephone rang. Half asleep, at first I thought it was my mother calling me for Christmas. The room was damp and freezing, and I left my covers unwillingly to get to the receiver. On the other end was the arrogant voice of Orio. He didn't say hello or Merry Christmas or sorry to bother you or it's Orio. Enunciating carefully, he merely said:

"Young man, I thought I was clear. You're to take Werther and all the rest and throw it in the toilet. What you've written is garbage. What, you think when people have some nice cunt in front of them they're going to start looking at the stars? Where are you living? You believe you're a writer but you're not. If you really were, you'd live off your books, not come to me for dough. And if you need dough it means you're a failure. I'll give it to you because I'm generous, but you have to earn it, you have to do what I tell you, what people want. Do you know what people want? They want fucking, screwing, and more fucking from beginning to end. And when there's no fucking, there has to at least be ass groping and tit squeezing, got it? And don't start in with the old cliché story. The public lives on clichés and masks, and since they're the ones paying, we give it to them, is that clear? Remember that fine sentiments have never made anyone any dough. I should let you go, but since it's Christmas and I stick up for young people, I'll give you another chance. Five days from now I want the whole thing rewritten the way I said."

The call ended there. I hadn't been able to say a word. My feet were freezing cold. Outside the bells began ringing to announce the Savior's birth. I dressed and was on the street by eight. It took me an hour to find a newsstand. I had to get some porn magazines at all cost. I needed inspiration rather fast.

153

I turned in the work on the last day of the year. I had stuffed it full of all possible and imaginable vulgarities copied from magazines. Orio didn't call, so I thought he was satisfied.

No one had yet said anything to me about money. We didn't have even a shred of a contract. My situation was desperate now. For a month I ate only pasta flavored with margarine.

I let Epiphany go by and then called Massimo.

"So how are we working things with money?" I asked, without beating around the bush.

"Oh, that's rushing it!" he blurted out. "It's not like manna from heaven." Then he explained to me that the producer hadn't yet read the script. Only once he'd read and approved it would Orio get paid, after which Orio would pay him, and he would pay us.

"How much?" I asked anxiously.

Massimo was vague. "I don't know, it depends," he'd said. "Give me a call in a week or two and I'll be able to tell you more."

After two months of continual reminders, I received a million lire. I was as happy as a dog whose master's just tossed him a bone. That day I filled the fridge, paid the outstanding bills, and had the breaks on my scooter fixed. The feeling wasn't that different from when someone wins the lottery. I was sure I'd made a positive step forward in my life. Another job would be coming soon, and another after that. They weren't that hard after all. You just had to plug your nose and forget you had a brain. With the way I lived, that money would last an eternity. Before summer for sure I'd have the time and freedom to write another book.

The state of satisfaction in which I immersed myself

didn't last long. A month had passed and no one had contacted me. The nest egg was shrinking. So one morning I gathered up my courage and called Massimo. I didn't yet know that in this business nothing is certain, no one comes looking for you, no one ever thanks you. Only humbling yourself in the most abject servility can you hope for a certain regularity of work. To get a new job I had to subject myself to three months of strenuous shuttling between the hills outside Rome and Torrevecchia.

In the end I did it. This movie was the same genre as the first. Instead of a nurse there was a woman police officer. Two of the guys from the group had disappeared. Silence was the rule about the disappearances, but from half sentences and allusions I understand they were trying to make it on their own.

One day when we were alone, Massimo said, "See, working with Orio is like being in a life boat. You're not that comfortable, but there's food and water. And there above the water, you know that sooner or later a cruise ship will come along and take you on board. And if it turns stormy, you won't sink. Orio is the only one who always survives sea changes. Even if there were a revolution he'd find a way to stay in place. He's got a different ticket in every pocket, connections everywhere, in every circle. Sometimes I admire him for that. I don't know how he does it. He's like some kind of conjurer. If you try things on your own, what'll happen? You plunge in, manage two or three strokes, and in those few meters delude yourself into thinking you're free. Then the sharks come and you're done for. Is it worth it? I don't know ... ."

155

For some mysterious reason Massimo had taken a liking to me. Maybe I was suitably defenseless and stupid. My specialty was connection scenes, the ones no one else wanted to do.

I worked for several years, always for the same amount or sometimes less, with a certain regularity. A series of short TV movies, the Article Twenty-Eight of an incapable, arrogant beginner, a couple of other comedian movies. Months passed, and I continued to pay my rent and bills on time. By now I wasn't asking much more from life.

By the sixth summer I had put aside enough to be able to think about a vacation. After *A Life in Flames* I hadn't written anything more. I felt the time had come to do so. A little earlier a book of Dino Campana's had come my way. It had been years since poetry had struck me as strongly as this.

156   I got to the town of Marradi by train. I was convinced that this place, the place where the poet had lived, would favor my inspiration. Finding a room was simple. There was just one old hotel, and it was completely empty.

As soon as I arrived I went for a walk. The air was fresh. In the morning there'd been a summer storm. Surrounding the town there were little fields, hedges, patches of oaks and chestnuts. Having come from Rome, I was almost bothered by all the fresh air. I stopped in front of an imposing beech tree. The north side of its trunk was covered with soft moss. How long had it been since I'd looked at a tree, I wondered? I looked at it, and it said nothing to me.

The next morning, in my room, I sat down in front of the typewriter. I had neither a story nor a character in mind. I wrote my name to start and lit a cigarette. After working for so many years, the blank pages didn't frighten me anymore.

The first day I wrote twenty pages, then another forty in the next few. One word followed another with extreme ease. At the end of the week, I took up my work and read it through. I was convinced it was beautiful and yet it wasn't. There wasn't a single sentence I recognized as being truly mine. I tried to go on but felt uncertain. I smoked nonstop. Every noise was a disturbance. I didn't know who was telling the story, or why in the world he needed to tell it. I spoiled sheet after sheet simply in order to beguile the time away. The air of the hills wasn't good to me. Every day I grew paler and more nervous. I still had in my head the happiness with which I'd written *A Life in Flames* and couldn't believe that such magic couldn't be repeated. Anxiousness grew inside me, and I could give it neither face nor name.

Then one night, in the joyless bed of the *pensione*, I dreamt of Andrea for the first time in who knows how long. We were on a beach in winter, a joyless beach like Ostia or Fiumicino. The sea and sky were practically the same color, a monotonous gray in which it was next to impossible to make out the horizon. Andrea's back was to the sea, and he was sitting on a beached boat. I was sitting on a log in front of him. He wasn't the Andrea of my memory. He had the hanging arms and slouched back of someone who'd gone through a lot. He kept his eyes fixed on me without lowering them. There was a shade to his expression that I couldn't decipher. His eyes were a steely blue, more like a mirror than eyes, reflecting the joyless light of the surrounding landscape. I called him by name and extended a hand, but before I managed to come near he turned toward the horizon and disappeared. I was alone on the beach with just the roar of the sea all around.

I woke up overcome by a sense of profound solitude as in death. From outside came the calls of the swifts announcing the day. I looked in the mirror and asked who I was. I no longer knew. Andrea had come to find Walter, but Walter meanwhile had disappeared. He hadn't become an artist, or an eagle of any kind. He crept along at the lowest point of the pyramid. Walter was a worm, a jellyfish, ectoplasm. That's what he'd become the day he'd said, "Thank you for everything" to Orio instead of spitting in his face.

That same morning I packed and headed back to Rome.

158

More than once that summer I had the impression I'd caught sight of Andrea. It happened on the street or amid a crowd gathered for a movie. They were sudden visions that made my heart beat faster from emotion, and from fear. How could I have summarized those years? What words could have recounted the drifting of my illusions? I couldn't have found them, nor did I want to. I was where I was and had to go on.

At the beginning of September I started calling Massimo again. I got his answering machine and for a little while thought maybe he hadn't come back from vacation yet. There wasn't any reason he shouldn't get back to me since we'd said goodbye on good terms. After a few weeks I called Orio. He answered right off—he never left his little tuff villa.

"Can I stop by?" I asked.

"I'm here whenever you like," he answered.

Before heading for the hills I stopped at a deli to get him something. The people in the group had explained to me he didn't like it when you came empty handed. He did much for us and liked to have the much appreciated by little gifts. I took a jar with three black truffles. When I gave it to him, he merely observed, "These here don't have much flavor. Compared to the white ones they're like cardboard."

Then we talked a little about this and that, and between this and that I mentioned that I needed work. I'd been looking for Massimo for a month and couldn't find him.

"Work, work," he repeated after me, "do you have any idea how many people need that? There's only so much dough, and all around is an army of rats, all hungry, all needing a bite of it. Things change and nobody notices. They're all there with their mouths open, waiting for the mush to drop in. Keep looking for him," he said before sending me on my way. "A couple of things should be coming toward Christmas. Be persistent. Life doesn't come around for those who surrender, those who give in."

So that's what I did. After a few days I found Massimo. His tone was distant. "It's not so certain those things are going to come out. Call me back in a while."

"In a while when?"

"Whenever you like."

While I waited for something to happen, I started wandering around town. I'd leave in the morning and come back in the evening. I ground out dozens of kilometers trying to

159

discharge the fear and rage. Rome seemed completely different to me now from when I'd arrived. No longer was it a great stage on which dreams were played out. Now it was a city with feelers, destructive like all others, a Moloch like all others. The air stunk, and you were in danger of being run over at every step. The sidewalks were filled with people walking sullenly. The dark sedans of politicians darted from one place to another followed by the wails of their escorts. The palaces were falling to pieces. The streets were strewn with potholes. In contrast to all this, everywhere new posh restaurants were opening, and stores with utterly frivolous goods. At the stop lights foreigners would wash your windows even if you didn't want them to, and in front of the luxury the beggars grew, young, old, women, Italians, foreigners, gypsies. They asked you for money even if your own face was haggard from hunger.

160

That was when I first noticed it, but it was clear the change had had a long incubation period. I wasn't in the habit of reading the papers, and I only had a radio at home.

While my attention had been all taken up with developments concerning my immediate future, governments had changed hands. In that period of waiting, looking around me, I realized the landscape was no longer the same. There had been no revolution. Something more treacherous and slippery had taken place. It was a kind of toxic gas, invisible and odorless. Mixing with the oxygen in ever larger doses, it had infiltrated the lungs, and from the lungs the blood, and from the blood the brain. Slowly, without anyone noticing, day after day, month after month, it had intoxicated the whole country. It's true, at the beginning some had felt a little burning in their eyes, but that could have been caused by a thousand other things, so the poison had continued to spread in complete indifference.

Sixty-eight was a good fifteen years behind us. It was gone, but its tail was still around, the long, multihued tale of a peacock. The animal was already far off, but the tail was still sweeping the dust from the threshing floor. That tail had brought with it years of fog, the fog of cloudless days. In the fog all sorts of things had happened — bombs had exploded, trains had blown up. In the fog there'd been rumblings and traffic shuffles, with some fleeing and others chasing after amid the volleys and muffled blows of crossbows and cudgels. The fog concealed everything. The only thing it couldn't cover up was the blood, which flowed in dark, dense rivulets on the asphalt, soaking canopies, sidewalks, the entrances to buildings, parking garages. It flowed everywhere without impediment, like a river that had burst its banks.

Almost no one meanwhile had noticed that behind the fog there was a stairway. Those who'd seen it kept the news to themselves. It led to the heights, from which one could see what was invisible. There below was a tired country, a country too often cheated, dominated by gray and continual election rallies that led nowhere. The promises were always big. The results amounted to little more than a package of pasta. After each vote the work just begun got interrupted. Roads and highways were suspended in the void, schools without windows, unmatched shoes in the closet. The ancient country was governed by a band of bureaucrats, small, dull, Bourbonist. They held the reigns,

161

and everything was under an oppressive yoke. The bombs and explosions had barely scratched them. It was a country old before its time. Something needed to be done to change it, make it agile, brisk, European, sparkling. It needed to be made modern.

The Eighties were here, arrogant and determined like an icebreaker, as fatuous and deceptive as Pinocchio's Toy Land carriage. As it passed, the ship blasted its horn, its great flag flowing. It seemed as carefree and inviting as a cruise liner, and trailing was the scent of money.

The men at the top of the ladder looked like good people, not like ogres. They made nice speeches and exuded hope, ever smiling and tan even in winter. They had the perfect word for every thing, for every problem the right solution. What they took to heart most, more than their own lives even, was people's happiness. And happiness consisted in one thing only: possession.

It's easy to fight against an ogre. But why fight against those who want only good for you?

They weren't ogres but barkers at a fair. We would have needed a little quiet to see their goods were cheap. Perhaps that was why quiet disappeared from the country.

In just a short time a lot of new TV networks came to life. Now it was possible to watch programs at any hour. Even the newspapers talked almost exclusively about television. There seemed a land of plenty inside the cathode tube. Morning to night the same doubtful message was hammered out: it was wrong to live as you had up to that moment; money was the goal of existence, and the stupidest thing of all was actually working for it. All you needed

162

to do was turn on the screen and guess how many beans were in the jar. If the host was yelling, it meant you'd become millionaires.

A great howl went up across the whole peninsula. Breathing was enough to win. Manna fell everywhere in great wads. There weren't any distinctions of class or culture anymore. You didn't have to know anything. It was enough to be patient and wait in line. Sooner or later you'd get rich. And while they let the loose change fall from the sky like rain in a marionette theater, in the wings, the men of the ladder were emptying the real coffers. The handfuls of millions that sparkled on screen were merely the pocket watch for hypnotizing a sucker.

Every so often fruit trees are attacked by rot. Up to a certain point everything is fine. There were plenty of healthy blossoms, and mild weather promises abundant growth. Fruit follows the flowers and starts to grow. There's so much the branches bend under the weight. But suddenly one morning you notice something is changing. Some of the fruit has darkened. The consistency isn't what it was. The moment you touch it, it falls to the ground. At first you think of a natural cause—the tree's letting some of its weight fall so as not to be overburdened. But when you climb up the ladder with a basket you see there's nothing to pick. In a single night the ripe fruit has turned into dark, festering sacks. The tree's grown sick without our noticing. The rot crept up slowly, day by day, until it captured every edible part of the tree.

But rot and mildew and the infinite variety of parasites that infest plants only do so when the plants are off bal-

163

ance, when the earth is too acidic or too alkaline, when there's too much water or not enough, or if they're too exposed to frigid gusts of wind.

It was thinking about plants that had convinced me the horror of those years had been lying in ambush, preparing in silence during the long preceding period. There had been an imbalance in the land, which no one except the men on the elevator had noticed; they'd had an advantage because of it. They had puffed from above with a bellows to help disperse the spores.

At the decade's start everything was still unfolding in quiet. Distracted people like me might not have even noticed anything. Only the slightest of signals were visible on the surface, signs as difficult to grasp as the changes in an electrical field before an earthquake.

So in the course of that summer, while I was at Marradi trying to write a book and then back in Rome, wrapped in a cloud of discontent, a game of musical chairs had taken place, that game I had been losing since I was a teenager. Someone had sat in my chair, my miniscule footstool. Maybe he wasn't as good as me, or as skilled, but what made him superior was the ticket he carried in his pocket.

A dictatorship had installed itself, smiling and tan. There had been no physical altercations, no assassinations, no interventions of armed troops. The network of its power was determined by favors. As in any parlor game, the first rule of participation was having your marker of a certain color.

All this wasn't just a matter intuition on my part. Massimo told me to my face when, after a month, I finally succeeded in tracking him down.

"Have you really gone to sleep so completely," he said. "Everyone's gotten busy, but you're just sitting there like a post. You look at me with the eyes of a beaten down dog, as if getting yourself some mush just depended on me. Wake up, Walter! Find yourself some connections."

I thought of Federico. He was the only one who could help. Back home I found his number in my agenda book from two year before. After a few rings a young woman answered.

"Ferrari doesn't live here anymore," she said.

"Do you know where I can find him?"

She didn't have his new number. "If you're an old friend, try at the TV station," she said.

"He still works there?"

"What, you haven't seen him? He hosts a variety show."

Finding Federico took a couple of weeks. It was a matter of secretaries, lines, departures, sudden meetings, impolite receptionists. In the end I managed it. When he heard my name, Federico cried, "Walter, what a surprise! What's the good word?"

I wanted to answer there isn't any but instead just said, "I need to see you."

He invited me to come by the Palace of the Dying Horse, which is where he spent most of his time.

"When should I come?" I asked.

He answered like Massimo: "Whenever you like."

After a few days in ambush outside his building I managed to intercept him. He was on his way back from a top level meeting. He seemed happy to see me.

"Come on in so we can talk," he said. "I have a few minutes."

I sat on one side of the desk, he on the other. Mine was for petitioners. I looked around and felt a vague sense of unreality. Federico was barely a few years my senior. I didn't think he'd reached thirty yet. He was the one who first thought my book was so good and introduced me to Neno to help with getting it published. Together we'd written *The Leavening of Revolution*. I still remembered the fights he used to have on the phone with his father. Our roads had been parallel up to a point but then had split. Then he'd got on a highway; I'd taken a mule track.

I was before him now as he had years earlier been before his TV executive. What had he said then? I couldn't imagine it. My tack wasn't too subtle since I only had a few minutes. I just said, "I need work."

He rubbed his hands together. "Fine. Send me your resume and I'll see what I can do."

A month later I had a small post as a dubbing assistant for a series of American TV movies.

Just as on other occasions, I had the feeling of touching the sky with my finger tips. I was actually happy he hadn't offered me a referral. He knew me too well. In the midst of making a move, with masochistic precision, I would have done it wrong. So he preferred to give me my alms without any bigger scheme. There was the split in our lives, the highway and the mule track. What I didn't yet know was that my mule track didn't lead to an open field but to the edge of a ravine.

In the decade that followed, the earth wore still thinner, the rain and wind eroded the path. Every time I was on the point of slipping over the precipice, some little bit of work would arrive. Thanks to the small change, I covered a few more meters. My journey wasn't a walk; it was more like a kind of Russian roulette. I could hear the click in the chamber but didn't know when it would fire. There wasn't any point in front of me, where I might stop and rest. What pushed me forward was the inertia of hopelessness.

Money that isn't there provokes a kind of a spell, eliminating any thought whatsoever that isn't linked to its existence. You wake up at night making calculations in your head. You hope this or that doesn't happen because, you think, this or that would be a catastrophe. This or that turns out to be a broken pipe or a sudden toothache. You don't have the strength to even imagine real catastrophes.

If there really are rich people who think about money, they are truly sick, perverse people who immerse themselves in the claustrophobia of arithmetic needlessly.

167

In those years I thought only about money. The battle was constant — the phone disconnected, electricity cut off, unpaid bills, an empty fridge, getting service again. I lived walking against the wind, and the wind was those economic necessities, my powerlessness to fill them. The storm's hiss sucked all fantasy out of me, all joy, all capacity to look about or raise my spirits.

In the Orio days, I was a waiter who comes at the end of the banquet to scrape up the remaining crumbs from the table cloth with his hands. Then I changed from a waiter to a dog, a bony stray that shows up at the end of the feast and plunges beneath the table in the hope of finding a mouthful that fell to the ground. I begged for left overs. They were never small enough that I might die of hunger and never large enough to allow me to live with the dignity of a human being. This was the cruelty of those who tossed them to me.

After five or six years of shilly-shallying, even Orio let me go. "I don't want to see you anymore. You're too poor, too sad. I get depressed as soon as you come in."

My mother had died several months before. I hadn't even managed to say goodbye. Almost without being aware of it, I had started drinking again, not every day but by fits and starts. When I couldn't manage anymore, I'd buy cheap liquor and drink it in front of the TV. I had no girl, no friends, no relatives. I'd never cared to look for Andrea, and he'd never contacted me. I was alone in the world. If I'd died in my basement room, it would have taken days for anyone to find me, by the smell. I loved no one and no one loved me. I couldn't figure out in what moment my life had changed. Where was the eagle's flight Andrea had heralded? My career had begun with Federico. Now he grew more powerful all the time, while I grew closer and closer to being a bum.

I told myself it was destiny that had clipped my wings. If I hadn't given it such a name, I would have had to admit that at a determined moment I'd stepped on a peel, one I couldn't have avoided. Of course I could have looked for another kind of work. Actually I'd made a round of the restaurants, but no one wanted Italian dishwashers any more. There were foreigners who were much more convenient, cost less, and could be locked in the cellar when the authorities came for inspections. I didn't have a degree, or a father with a store, or a family business. In the dreams of adolescence I'd never imagined the merciless concreteness in which life works. You can play if your back's covered. If not, the game can turn tragic.

I started thinking about suicide. Committing suicide and becoming a bum were two sides of the same coin. Waking from a night of alcohol, I decided to end my life. But first I wanted to say goodbye to my mother. I wasn't convinced I'd be seeing her on the other side.

At dawn I took my scooter to the freeway onramp. At that hour the traffic was mostly trucks. I was lucky and made it Mestre with only four lifts. From Mestre to Trieste it was more difficult. Cars and semis raced by without stopping. After two hours, one finally did.

I reached the plateau near eleven at night. The truck driver was continuing on toward Hungary, and I asked him to drop me off a little before the houses started. I didn't want to be seen. I was dazed and confused. The seven or eight hundred kilometers that separated me from Rome had given me the impression of a movement in time rather than space.

The town looked different. There were many new buildings. There was a hi-fi store in place of the bicycle mechanic's shop. Where a movie theater had once stood now was a discount supermarket.

The cemetery was closed. I looked around. The stone wall was rather low, it was easy to climb. Once inside, I experienced a moment of dismay. I didn't know which direction to take. I walked bent over, reading the names on the

169

tomb stones by the glimmer of the votive candles. When there was no light, I used my lighter.

Making my way like that, I was surprised many times. Quite a few people had passed away in those years. There below was my first teacher and the band director, the baker and his six-year-old grand daughter. When at last I found my mother's tomb, I knelt beside it and caressed the plaque as if it were her cheek. The last fumes of the alcohol were gone. I felt empty and weak. Terribly empty and terribly weak. The woman who had brought me into the world lay down there. She'd gone away and I hadn't given her a final kiss goodbye.

I wept and felt furious for my crocodile tears, loud, useless, showy. I wept for myself, for the remorse that would take my breath away from then on. I wept and repeated her name. Then I was no longer caressing the stone plaque, I was beating it with my head.

170

The air smelled of methane. From far off the continual noise of the trucks reached me. Close by an owl that must have been hidden in a cypress hooted and fell silent. The hoot remained suspended in air with its sadness. Nothing ever comes back. My life had been just a tiny firework. It had gun powder inside and had taken off when they lit me. At the end of its trajectory it had filled the air with a little color. The light was very short and not very high. After the sparks, only the deep dark of the night had remained.

As the eastern sky began to brighten, I moved away from the cemetery, like a wild animal, making my way down the slopes of Mount Radio, and reached the train station.

That evening I was back in my Roman basement. The answering machine light was blinking. Someone had called in my absence. It was a tiny job offer. I called the next morning to accept. Death could wait. I didn't want to die like a rat down there. In that at least I would be great, reaching a mountain summit as if on a hike. From there, in flight, I would throw myself.

The decision gave me a strange kind of lightness. I started to see things with the distance of someone who knows he'll be leaving soon. To give myself the face of a winner, that night I didn't drink and went to bed early.

At the entrance barrier to the TV station there were bunches of people. In their midst I met the glance of Neno. It had been a good many years since I'd seen him. His hair had gone completely white, nor was he wearing it as long as before. He had on a blue cashmere overcoat and the shiniest black English dress shoes. He seemed happy to see me.

171

"How are you doing?" he asked, then answered his own question. "Good, it seems, you look good."

As the line went in, he asked me if I'd written anything else. I lied and said I was just finishing something up. Meanwhile we reached the service window. Neno took out his pass, I took out mine. We were awaited on very different floors. The palace was, like the inferno, divided into numerous circles. The lower you were, the more nobody you were.

I walked with him to the elevator. Before saying goodbye, he said, "I'm having a dinner party tonight. Why don't you come?"

"Why not." I said.

I could accept just about anything just then without the dreaded weight.

The house was the same and so was the furniture. But as soon as I entered I realized the atmosphere was different from what I remembered. There was no longer the variegated crowd of young people around the couches, nor the overlay of their voices in discussion. Along with them the long buffet table with its plastic plates had disappeared, and the Mortadella squares and the screw-top bottles of Frascati.

In their places were rather mature couples. They appeared to be developers, politicians, well-known journalists. Neno introduced me to each in turn, saying, "Walter is a very talented young man."

172

The Frascati had been replaced by Brunello di Montalcino, which rose up on a snow white table cloth ringed with porcelain plates, candlesticks, and crystal glasses. There was now a waiter from distant parts, who wore livery with gold buttons of a sort that I thought were only worn in movies. He walked among the guests offering aperitifs.

Even Mao the cat seemed to have changed the origins of his name: I overheard Neno explaining to a guest that the reason was purely linguistic. He was called Mao because whenever he saw his biscuit box instead of meow he would say mao.

I was even more a fish out of water. I got in with that crowd less than with the one from before. I knew Neno had invited me just to even out the dinner places and add a little folklore to his party. Every once in a while, to draw me out of my gloomy silence he would ask in front of everyone, "So haven't you written anything new?"

At which I would stammer, "I'm still working on things" and turn red because I've never been able to lie.

Neno's new friends talked about just three things—politics, food, and wine. I was completely indifferent to all three and didn't know a thing about them. I knew which margarine was the cheapest, not what vintage of Brunello di Montalcino was best. But Neno was passionate in such discussions, just as he'd once been about art works created by factory workers' committees.

Evidently he too at some point had climbed on the power bandwagon, sloughing off all that he'd once proclaimed in years past.

I wasn't indignant, nor did I feel contempt for him. I'd given up trying to understand many things a long time before. The fact of managing to survive absorbed the greater part of my energy. The consistency or lack of consistency of others didn't much matter to me. There was soft light in this house and beautiful table linen, and they were eating things I wouldn't have had occasion to eat in any other place. After dinner, there would be sipping of fine whiskey, more conversation, and me staring at the tips of my shoes in silence. That was all.

At dinner Neno had seated me next to a woman who was probably ten years my senior. She was thin and elegant. She had long hair of an auburn shade that fell loose around her shoulders. I had noticed her earlier when, her voice low, she'd asked Neno to excuse her husband's absence as he'd been held up by a sudden meeting at work.

173

Even before the antipasto the conversation had turned to politics. Above the white tablecloth before me I could see the woman's hands, which she moved with weary grace. She fingered her fork, the stem of her wine glass, and, with her index finger, crushed some bread crumbs. It was she who spoke to me first, gently bending her head in my direction:

"None of this is important to you either?"

I said, "Well, I don't follow these things much."

She took a sip of wine, then looked at me directly and whispered, "I read *A Life in Flames*. It was quite striking."

At that point my cheeks caught fire, my back turned to ice, and I started to sweat. I had utterly forgotten about that book. It was a sort of skeleton in my closet. Without warning or allowing me any presentiment, she had opened the door and shoved it with all its exposed vertebrae right in front of me.

"Really?" I said, then, hesitating, "but it came out such a long time ago."

"Time has no importance. If that weren't the case, we wouldn't read *Don Quixote* anymore or *The Odyssey*."

Then, looking me straight in the eyes, she added, "Don't you think so?"

Meanwhile the conversation had turned to an argument. There were divergent opinions about the current government, and every party claimed to be right.

"How boring," whispered the woman in my ear. She took a breath and asked, "Who are your favorite authors?"

Suddenly it was like when I was sitting at a desk in school. My mind blank, absolutely blank. She looked at me, smiling and waiting, and I groped for a name. I took a sip of wine to help in the search. I wanted a name, any name. At last one came.

"Kafka is great," I said in the same tone that one might have spoken about a soccer team.

"That's what I thought," was her comment, and she immediately launched into the minute particulars of his correspondence with Felice Bauer, citing one passage and another, speaking of love and the richness of impossibility, while I nodded in silence.

The whole evening we talked in low voices while the others were screaming at the top of their lungs. After Kafka other names came into my head. I cited Rilke, and Melville, and Conrad, and others. She looked at me and didn't stop smiling.

"I see we have exactly the same taste," she said as we stood up to make our way to the sitting area.

175

Neno came over. "You haven't even deigned to look at us. What are you talking about?"

"Literature," she said. "We've found many passionate interests in common."

A rather corpulent gent passed by and declared with a sarcastic smile, "Perhaps you haven't yet noticed but literature is dead. After Musil no one's been able to write a real book."

"Well you're wrong. This young man has written a wonderful one," she said.

The fatso gave me a condescending look up and down and said, "And it was all about yourself and about your unhappiness. Am I correct?"

"Well, in a sense yes," I answered softly.

"There, that's what literature's become today. A breeding ground for doltish autobiographies. Young people don't read anymore but plague us with their banalities, and claim to be producing art!"

The red haired woman came to my defense. "Why? Explain it to me. Was your last novel art?"

Her lips were spread in a nervous smile.

"I wasn't really talking about me. And anyway my book was a metaphor."

"A metaphor?" she said. "I didn't notice that. It seemed to me the story of a fifty-year-old in crisis who chases after a young girl with the eyes of a fawn."

"You're the same old provocateur," said the man and gave her a fillip on the cheek. "But I won't fall in with your games, even if you do have nice eyes."

That said, he joined the others and sank into a couch.

I took advantage of the moment to disappear. "I have to go. Goodbye, everyone," I said amid the general indifference. And I left.

The wind was stronger now than in the afternoon. The bus was nearly empty. There was a rather plump black woman and a drunk talking loudly to himself. I looked out the window, gripped by a strange sense. My heart was constrained, almost panicked, but at the same time I was lighter than I'd ever been.

Little plastic sacks fluttered past, and I thought there was really no reason for me to feel that way. What had happened after all? I'd had a little conversation. You've been living like a bear for too long, I told myself. A little attention from one person is enough to throw you into a funk.

The feeling stayed with me even at home. I turned onto one side and was wrapped in a warmth I'd never known before. I turned onto the other and plunged into icy cold. My teeth chattered, and I curled up trying in vain to get warm.

I fell asleep very late. When the phone rang I thought maybe it was dawn. I reached for the receiver angrily.

"Who is it?" I shouted.

Just then I caught sight of the clock. It was a quarter to noon. It was her on the other end.

"Hi," she said. "Were you sleeping?"

From that call a lunch invitation was born. I was going to her house the next day and didn't even know her name. I could have called Neno, but what kind of a schmuck would I have looked like then? He'd told me her name the night before after all.

I dressed and went to buy some fruit. The wind had died down, and a large cold sun burned in the sky. As I covered the hundred or so meters that separated me from the market, I realized the discomfort of the night before was becoming sheer restlessness.

I was walking fast, talking with myself. What was there to get worked up about? It was going to be a social lunch like any other. We'd eat well and then I'd go back home. There was nothing bad about it. I said as much but knew I was lying.

I spent the afternoon looking for suitable attire. Fashions had changed and holes were no longer in. I went up and down via Appia three times. Luckily the after Christmas sales had started. In the end I found a turtleneck sweater that seemed appropriate for the occasion. I didn't want to come off as a beggar, or as a provincial flaunting his nice clothes.

That night I went to bed early and didn't sleep a wink. Around three a.m. I decided I wouldn't go. It was cold. I could have quite easily pretended to have come down with a sudden flu. At around four I realized that not only did I not know her name I didn't know her number either. All I had was an address scribbled on a scrap of paper.

At five I got up, made some coffee, turned on the TV, and lit a cigarette. On screen was a full-figured woman dressed as a Gypsy. "The stars are talking to you" was written under her belly band, and she was discussing horoscopes. She had a Roman accent and pronounced everything very slowly. Why would she talk like that, I wondered? Maybe the long silences allowed her to listen to the stars. Maybe she was sleepy. After a bit, caressing her ball, she said, "Virgo," my sign, and then, "with the winter solstice Venus entered your sign ... ." Then she went on with Libra, Scorpio, Sagittarius ... ," and with that lullaby in the background, I fell asleep at last.

When I opened my eyes again, the Gypsy was still there, and now she was reading Tarot cards. It was eight in the morning, and she had a woman on the line. She turned over a card and said, "The Tower, my dear, misfortune comes."

Five hours later I was standing in front of the house phone.

I experienced a moment of panic because instead of last names there were just numbers. I found an eight written on the piece of paper I had, thought it must be the top floor,

178

and rang. I climbed the stairs two at a time. At the top I was out of breath. The door was half open. I gave a light knock. "Come on in," came a voice from inside.

"It's me," I said as I made my way in.

She was wearing a loose-fitting house dress. The room was carpeted wall to wall so she walked without making any sound. She gave me two kisses on the cheeks as if we were old friends.

"Make yourself comfortable," she said, then, "Is it cold out?"

The apartment had a window that faced the Forum and was very small. It seemed more like a den or nest than a place to live. Everything was warm, comfortable, and called for relaxation.

I sat down on a flowered easy chair, and she offered me an aperitif. I looked around discretely. I'd seen a fat wedding ring on her left hand, but there was no sign of a husband.

179

We were alone. I was starting to get a slight headache from the stress. It was like a web of metal strings wrapped around my temples. They must have been guitar or violin strings because every time I breathed in, someone seemed to tighten them a little more.

We made small talk, traffic, the weather. Then we moved on to Neno and how we'd met. I told her about the room rented from Mrs. Elda and about Federico.

"He took a different route than me," I said. "Now he's the host of all kinds of frilly shows."

"Federico Ferrari?"

"Yes."

"I really hope you don't envy him," she said.

I hastened to deny it. "Oh, no, not at all. We were very different from the start."

We'd started talking about German cinema, which directors we liked and which we didn't, when a timer went off in the kitchen.

"Excuse me, the oven," and she disappeared behind the door.

She came back carrying a glass dish. On our way to the table, I looked around, said, "It's cute here, but it's not much larger than my place. It must be difficult for two."

She broke out laughing. She laughed with her head tilted slightly back, like storks when they make their calls.

"This is just my study. My husband and I live in Parioli."

There were some cannelloni in the dish. It seemed unlikely to me she'd made them herself. The first bite confirmed it had come straight from a delicatessen. As far as the food went, I thought, things hadn't gone well. Just then she put down her fork.

"Tell me about your city," she whispered, looking me straight in the eyes.

My headache suddenly grew. Who did she take me for, a tourist guide? I swallowed, wiped my mouth with a napkin, then, noncommittally, asked, "In what sense?"

She smiled. Now she looked more like a cat than a stork.

"It must be a very interesting city. Let me see it with your eyes."

So I set off like a promotional pamphlet. "There's the sea," I began, "and behind it the Karst plateau. The climate is generally good, except in the winter when the wind blows. The Latin name was Tergestum, but the origin seems to be Slavic, Trg, which means a market square, because people traded there. Empress Maria Teresa of Austria was the one to make it so big. It was the only city in the Empire that faced the sea…

I went on like that for ten minutes or so, searching through the confused memories of my elementary school textbook. Meanwhile the cannelloni got cold in the plates, and she didn't stop looking at me. At a certain point she stretched out a hand, put it on top of mine.

"Those aren't your eyes," she whispered.

I felt the capillaries in my cheeks dilate like swollen rivers. My hands were cold, my head burning up.

"Well," I muttered, "that was a kind of introduction. I wanted to give you a point of reference."

Her hand was still on top of mine. I had the impression she was applying a stronger pressure. She sighed almost imperceptibly and said, "Why don't you talk to me about Rilke?"

So I started talking about the castle of the *Duino Elegies*, which wasn't at all far from my house. "By bicycle it would take thirty minutes, maybe less if you pedaled hard. Nearby is a White Bar, which is a place where all you can eat is cheese and all you can drink is milk. It's a perfect place for taking a rest."

The strange fact, which I confessed to her, was that for as long as I lived there I hadn't the foggiest idea of who Rilke was. I knew the White Bar but not the Elegies. I discovered those in Rome, when I was spending all my time in the library. First I'd read the *Notebooks of Malte Laurids Brigge* and literally fell in love with Malte Laurids Brigge. I could have even said, like Flaubert, "*Malte, c'est moi.*" After Malte I discovered the poetry. "Every angel is dread" became one of the cornerstones of my life. But I already knew poetry in general, not the verses themselves but the hidden soul of things. I believe it had begun to vibrate inside me, like the strings of a harp, from the moment I entered the world. I'd opened my eyes and felt different. I saw things no one else was able to see, but I still knew I wasn't crazy. Maybe one day I'd become that, you could never say.

I talked and talked, and in the meantime the béchamel on the cannelloni had taken on an opaque veil with fat floating all around it. She hadn't stopped listening, or interrupted, or been distracted. Whenever I stopped to take a breath, she said, "Go on."

182

I told her everything there was to tell. Not about my mother or the Formica kitchen or my drunk father, but about Hölderlin and my discovery of alcohol, about my schoolmate and his his eraser left in my bag, about the whirlwinds of emptiness that I saw appearing and disappearing in the midst of things, about the devil that no one knew but who existed. Maybe it was even him who, playing tricks on us, put on the good mask of God. I talked about the ghosts that had hounded me at night and those that followed me during the day, about my friendship with Andrea and how he had opened my eyes. I told her about the long lines of trucks packed with animals crossing the border and how they took them to the slaughterhouse. About the calls you could hardly listen to, the glances you couldn't endure.

By the end I practically shouted: "I grew up with those glances as background, those eyes staring at you. Understand? We're all inside there, in those trucks, in that innocent suffering! It's all a big comedy — you laugh, dance, pretend to be intelligent, and backstage the truck's waiting. You don't see it but it's there. It's hidden by the sets and curtains. It's waiting for us, engines running. It's always ready for departure. That's all there is, the trip from the stable to the slaughterhouse.... You know something?" I said, lowering my voice. "My only authentic sentiment is fury. Maybe I look like a tranquil sort on the outside, but it's not at all true. The fury of questions that don't have answers is the only sentiment I recognize as really mine."

"I know, Walter. It's clear from the first line. The life in flames is your life... ."

Just then a church bell rang the hour. It was four, and I felt confused as if I'd drunk and smoked at the same time. My head was spinning and I had a false perception of the distance between me and the objects around me. My ears felt like they must be white hot, my cheeks like embers, my eyes shining. I felt traces of fever. In the silence articulated by the tolling bell I regretted having talked too much. What the devil had come into my head, I asked myself. Now I'm like an armadillo without scales. A baby with a butter knife could wound me. I'd never talked for two hours straight completely unbridled.

When the echo of the bells had died, there was a great silence. Somewhere in the apartment a faucet was leaking.

"Look at that light," she said, going to the window.

I joined her. I was taller by a head. The light was truly beautiful. The Palatino was before us and above it all the shades of the sky, the deep blue of night in the west, the blue growing azure toward the east, an azure so white it seemed like ice, the ice then turning gold. A barely perceptible thread of orange streaked the horizon, an orange almost rose, and the rose reflected on the Forum. In front of the rock, two palms stood out, and above them was a small, tilted moon like that of the Turks. Beside the moon there was a large star. I pointed it out to my hostess, whose name I still did not know…"

"It's not a star, it's a planet," she said. "It's light giving Venus."

As she said this, she stepped back slightly and our bodies touched. She had an intense perfume on.

"Why light giving?" I asked, her hair in my mouth.

"The light's disappearing," she whispered. "We need to go to the bed. It's the only place you can see the end of the sunset from."

When I was a boy, my mother had a large stainless steel pressure cooker that was called "atomic." I never managed to figure out what its relation was to the notorious atomic war my father was always worried about. Maybe it was supposed to be hurled down from airplanes, or maybe millions of them would be buried underground. The only thing for sure was that the pot scared me. In the house's half-light it hissed like a train and was always on the brink of exploding. To make me less afraid, my mother one day had me touch the valve. "See," she said, "it's steam coming out little by little. Nothing's going to explode."

The atomic pot came back to me the moment I sat on the edge of the bed. I thought about correspondence courses and whether anyone really learned the things they were told they would. For example, does someone studying how to be a captain really learn how to bring a ship into a harbor? I asked myself this but nothing more.

I heard her repeating my name. Since I didn't know hers, I was silent. The telephone rang three or four times.

It was dark outside now, and we were still there together. The more time that passed, the more her eyes shone. She had a small beauty spot at the base of her neck that I hadn't seen until then. Before and after were erased. I was there. I'd be there forever.

But all at once she shook her head and got up. "I've got a cocktail party with my husband," she said, and disappeared into the bathroom.

VII

Someone must have poured poison into my veins. There wasn't fire anymore but some toxic substance. I couldn't sit still anywhere. I noticed it that night on my way home. I no longer wanted to stay cooped up.

I went out again despite the intense cold. The streets of this part of town were completely deserted. I saw a movie theater and went in. It was a Christmas movie with comedians in it. Everyone laughed all around me. I didn't even see the images on screen. I just thought and thought, but they weren't my usual thoughts, not evil and the infinite. There was only the nameless woman, her smell, her body.

I would have liked to spend the night with her, but she'd gone off for cocktails with her husband. Who knows if, at her party, she was thinking of me and my smell too. A sense of dismay descended upon these thoughts—in my haste I'd forgotten to ask for her number. I didn't know her name. I was at the mercy of her desires. I had no way of knowing when I might see her again, if I might see her again.

From that evening on the telephone became once again an instrument of torture for me. The anxiety with which I waited for this ring was much different from the one I'd waited for from the slave driver.

The next morning I went out early to do the shopping. I wanted to guarantee myself a long supply of food and tobacco. Then, the fridge full, I started waiting. I picked up the receiver every thirty minutes. The thing I was most afraid of was not having hung it up properly.

Andrea had told me women shouldn't be touched even with a flower. That didn't mean you weren't to strike them, it meant between us and them there should be a distance greater than the stem of a rose.

"Whoever has a precise plan," he'd said, "can't come near them without risking getting thrown off course. The senses, with all their voluptuous confusion, are a kind of drift for the hero. Just think of the Sirens and Ulysses. What did he do when he heard them singing? Did he jump into the water? Or did he have himself tied to a mast with strong ropes and put wax in his ears? Every time you hear that singing," he said, "think about those words."

Andrea had broken an open door. Even if I didn't really have any clear ideas about it, I still felt a kind of diffidence toward the relations that were supposed to take place between one sex and the other.

At the age when one usually starts experimenting, I was as alone as a bear in the taiga. There'd been two or three smiles from girl classmates at school, but instead of making me curious or excited, those had made me deeply uncomfortable. It wasn't that I didn't know how things went—the mating of mammals is always the same. What terrorized me wasn't the eventual act but all that went with it, her pimples too close to mine, her cold hand that I was supposed to hold with mine, pilfered clingy languors in the half-light of a street lamp, the jibes and jests of friends, and the best for last, maybe even lunch with her parents.

This ensemble of things had kept me from taking the first step. There was the appeal of the flesh, but the horror of victory I had to overcome was much more powerful. "If you want it done right, do it yourself," is an excellent saying for moving along.

After these initial flashes there was the period of poetry and alcohol, two adventures strong enough to cancel out everything else. My thoughts were always moving toward the absolute, flying at a high altitude. If there'd been a single human gender, neutral, that would have suited me just the same.

Toward sixteen, to be honest, I wavered a bit. Since my father always called me "pansy," I had a suspicion that inside me really was something of the execrated flower. But it was a short-lived fear. Bodies didn't interest me of either sex—period. I agreed with Andrea: friendship was the highest sentiment.

"In friendship," he said, "there aren't any mists, no false bottoms. The pleasure of the senses is far away. What's left is the pleasure of the mind, and the mind stretches toward the heights. One can die to save a friend, while, most often it's a lover who makes you die. She drains your energy and ideas, she wants pleasure, and after pleasure the security of social status, and after that come children inevitably and you're really finished. She never takes note of you as a person; you're just a ladder for climbing somewhere, the plain noise with which she fills the emptiness of her days."

I thought exactly the same. The horror I experienced toward the act that had brought me into the world was enough to push me toward renouncing that portion of life.

"After coitus you're assailed by sadness," Andrea said.

It cost me no effort at all to believe these words were true. The idea of a son who might look at me with the same consternation that I'd looked at my own parents with was more than valid motivation for my vowing perpetual chastity. More often than not, putting a child in the world means no more than continuing the chain of suffering. Really, I told myself, all this big sex obsessing was silliness. The ways of 666 were sneaky; it released the mist of confusion into the world. Who says all humans are supposed to be equal? That's fine for animals with instincts but not reason. And even the animals can't always manage. There's the season of love. Once that's done, they have to wait for the world to make its way around the sun. Only in man is luxury perpetual. Reason should give sense to things, but reason always loses out to instinct, and so the world goes on with its inevitable trail of misery and regrets.

189

"Here too," Andrea would say, "the pyramid helps us, because instinct is victorious in the bottom part. As one goes up, instinct is bridled; the falsehood that sex is good for one's health begins to crumble. There is no great vision, no greatness at all without distance from the flesh. It's not for nothing that religions are always prescribing chastity.

The energy that doesn't exit gives integrity and power. There are no veils before your eyes. The Siren's song leaves you indifferent. You're free. The eternal chain of attachment is no longer part of your life. The choice is yours. Either this or the muck of the pigsty."

The only possibility of avoiding this chaste solitude for Andrea was in meeting a woman who, through her natural gifts, had attained the highest point on the pyramid.

"It's something extremely rare," he said, "because women, by their physiology alone, tend to stay toward the bottom. The greater part of the feminine gender is imprisoned by their humors and lives between hormonal fits and primal desires. But when this doesn't happen and they're able to raise themselves, you can find extraordinary creatures, far superior to the majority of men. The difference between them and angels is minimal. They are feminine beings but imbued with masculine virtue. They know friendship, fidelity, purity, and all the highest sentiments. Only beside them can a man know the happiness of completion. Two wills united in a single project, like Dante and Beatrice, like Lancelot and Guinevere. That's the destiny of a superior love."

As for me, I had long before resigned myself to not being part of such an elect band. I knew around me people mumbled the same kinds of things they always mumble when they don't understand someone else's choices, that is, that you're a faggot or impotent or both at once. The conformism of sexuality is one of the hardest to overcome. But to me all that chatter meant nothing. It actually was the best way of getting yourself considered out of bounds. I'd been chaste to that moment and would have continued to be to the end of my days.

There seems to be a law that says a tiny, invisible thing, like a vibration, can destroy enormous buildings. If, for example, a platoon of soldiers bang their feet at the same instant, in less than a second a bridge can collapse. That law doesn't apply to bridges and arches alone but to an infinity of other things too. It also applies to hearts and the huge dikes erected to protect them.

I'd met the nameless woman, and inside me a note had sounded, vibrating softly amid the veins and organs. The effect was that of a shock, an acceleration. It was pleasurable, invigorating. It would have taken a lot more experience or a lot more imagination to understand the vibration was at just the right frequency to destroy just about anything.

I hadn't changed my mind about relations with women. My ideas were the same as when I'd been around Andrea. The catch was the thing about the "elect few." For me she was Beatrice, in fact I called her that during the long hours spent beside the phone, waiting for her signal.

191

Three days and nothing had happened. I was attached to the receiver, exhausted like a shipwreck victim. The phone had rung just once. It was a man who'd misdialed. On the fourth day I finished my cigarettes and went out on that mission, which took no more than ten minutes.

When I came back, the little light was blinking. In my rage I felt like dashing my head against the wall. Before pushing the button, I sat down on the bed and took a deep breath.

"Click" and her mellifluous voice immediately filled the room. "It's Orsa," she said. "Sorry I didn't call you sooner. I had to leave town with my husband. I'll be back at the studio all afternoon tomorrow. If you feel like it, come by. I'll be waiting."

Suddenly the nameless woman had acquired one, and it was the most extraordinary name I could have imagined. Orsa was the feminine version of orso, "bear," and since I'd always been one of those, it was a wondrous confirmation we were made for each other. I belonged to the top of the pyramid and so did she. Our love would be great and eternal like no other.

In the following weeks, the poison that had started to circulate in my veins gradually replaced my blood, feeding my lungs, heart, and stomach. I wasn't yet aware of its existence. Actually, I hadn't felt better in my whole life, so full of energy, vitality.

Suddenly my cynical gaze disappeared, and with it the absolute clarity with which I had looked at things. That more or less must be the state of monks who abandon the cowl—inexperience of the body renders them totally defenseless. One can discuss the spirit for days and then fall by means of a simple smile. Tearing the guts to pieces turns into child's play.

I didn't have the slightest inkling of all this then. I felt like I was sitting on a cloud, sliding in silence above everything else. I lived for her, for our meetings, for the hours and minutes we spent together. Even by myself I wasn't by myself at all. I was thinking back through our discussions, our moments of deepest intimacy. I talked in my room, and it was as if Orsa was there. I was convinced she too

was living the same communion, the same consuming desire when we were apart.

In addition to physical passion, the passion for literature united us. We experienced the same apprehension in
looking for words to express the world. More than anything
else she loved Mittleuropa. She was slightly jealous of the
fact that I'd been born within what remained of its borders.
She'd rented the studio four years before in order to have
the quiet she needed to write a book.

"To create," she said, "you can't stay imprisoned in the
day-to-day life of the house. There needs to be another
place that inspires you." And in fact, it was only in that
place that she was able to take her mind off things. Once,
when she was showing me the panorama of the Forum,
she'd said, "Any insult of modernity is excluded from here.
It's why the breath of the classical is spontaneous."

193

What she was working on, however, was a secret. Only
once did she let herself go a little, saying: "It will be something halfway between Proust's *Remembrance* and Musil's
Man Without Qualities...."

To give her time to write we would see each other every
other afternoon.

After a month we started taking weekend trips together
outside Rome. She drove and paid the bills. We went to
certain little rustic hotels in Tuscany or on the Amalfi coast.
Her husband was never named, as if he didn't exist. I worried a little, it didn't seem natural.

So once I asked, "What about your husband?"

She broke out laughing.

"What does my husband have to do with anything?" she

said. "It's normal. After a few years of marriage, you grant each other a little freedom."

I was won over by her confidence. One time he had even called on the intercom while we were in bed together. "I'll be there in a minute," she'd responded, dressing and going out as if nothing had happened. Who knows, I told myself, maybe he's got a studio somewhere too, and his life is the mirror image of hers. This was the only way I could justify to myself such indifference on his part. If I'd been in his place, I would have chopped her into pieces with a hatchet.

Still, one thing was certain, and that was that she had fun with me, not with him. Her husband was an important man, director of a newspaper, and her relation to him was limited to being a trophy.

But I was a bear, and she was my she-bear. The only fatigue that afflicted us was getting worn out completely. I started one day by saying, "That's how plantigrades do it," and from that moment on she'd demanded a different animal every time. I spent all my free moments frantically looking through books on the subject. From one week to the next we went through the whole zoological scale, from limpets to whales.

Never in all my life had I been so cheerful, every instant in some strange kind of euphoria. I was euphoric when we laughed and when we lay in silence beside each other. Near her my past, the dead weight of my past, was gone. I often felt like a baby that had just opened its eyes on the world. Everything was amazement, emotion. I existed in the eyes of another human being. In her glance there was no contempt or impatience, there was passion.

She lived for me, and I for her. There was the anticipation of meeting, and its fulfillment, a circular movement that seemed perfect, perfect and eternal. I was convinced it would last forever.

And so the weeks and months slipped by. One morning I woke up, and it was already summer.

It was June, the windows open. The twilight was firing the air in rose-orange shades. Martins flashed loudly among the ruins of the Forum and the roof tops.

For several days Orsa had been strange. I would talk to her, but her look was distant. It was the first time anything new had come between us. I thought maybe her husband had said something, or maybe she was at a particularly difficult place in her book.

"Do you know how spiders do it?" I asked to distract her. "The female sits in the middle of the web and the male has to get to her. It walks on the strings like a tightrope walker."

I had got on all fours and was already moving toward her when she passed a hand in front of her face, annoyed.

Without looking at me she said, "Leave me alone. Spiders make me sick."

Of all the things I had imagined about us the only one that had never entered my head was that our relationship might end. As I left through the entrance way, I justified her strangeness as a temporary indisposition. The next morning, I didn't hear from her. I called that afternoon but got her machine. Every once in a while she had to go out with her husband for some social event. She didn't always

195

remember to let me know beforehand, so I was still calm for a little while more.

We had decided to take a trip to Deauville at the beginning of July. I couldn't wait to be spending a long time by her side, and all my energies were turned toward the moment of our departure. That future project dispelled all shadows.

But days passed and the silence continued.

After a week anxiety woke me all of a sudden in the middle of the night.

I called at eight. I knew she wouldn't be there at that time because she always spent the night at Parioli, but I felt like hearing her voice. I tried again at nine, and ten, and eleven. Always the machine.

At twelve I was below her studio. The big window facing the Forum was visible from the street. The shutters and curtains were open. I went to the entrance and rang the intercom. My heart was beating hard, like on the first time. Nothing happened. I stayed down there the whole day, walking up to the door to check for signs of life every half hour.

Wandering around like that, I imagined the worst. She could have had a terrible accident. She might be in bed with some kind of infection. To find that out I'd have to call her at home, but my courage didn't reach that far. What would I say if her husband answered?

As evening fell I went home. I hadn't the slightest desire to stay cooped up inside there. I was nervous, agitated, but still thought she might need me. If she was sick or in the hospital, she'd be sad and disappointed to get my machine.

I smoked a whole pack of cigarettes that night and drank all the beer I had in the fridge. At eight the next

morning, I called the studio again, and again at nine. At ten
I rallied my courage and called her husband's house. After
four rings, the neutral voice of a Filipino answered. I didn't
say my name, only asked, "Is the Signora at home?"

"Signora's not here," he said.

"When can I find her at home?"

"I don't know."

That phrase increased my worry, and I asked, "She's not
in the hospital?"

There was a short silence on the other end.

"No hospital," said the Filipino. "Signora out."

I hung up without saying good-bye. I should have felt
calmer. At least one thing was certain, that she was okay.
But if she was in Rome and wasn't sick, how was it possible
she didn't want to see me anymore?

The sentiments of Othello were making their way inside
me. I knew I had no right to them. A jealous lover only ever
makes himself ridiculous. Sharing the beloved was in the
natural course of things, but, all the same, inside me I felt
anxiety turning into fury.

The anchor I kept latching onto was her work. Maybe
she'd been seized by some creative rapture. To be able to
write, she'd had to lock herself in the house and not answer
anyone. Basically the same thing had happened to me when
I wrote my book. They could have set fire to the building,
and I would have stayed put in my seat.

I called her in intervals of ten minutes. The greeting
hadn't changed. "I'm momentarily away. Leave a message
after the beep." In the end I decided, though as I spoke my
voice sounded uncertain to me.

197

I said: "Plantigrade speaking. I'm guessing the muses have come out to speak to you, so good luck with your work. But remember that in ten days the moon changes and with the full moon the bears are supposed to be together for dancing in the forest. Call me."

I left the message at eleven. By eleven ten, sitting on the unmade bed, I realized that without her I no longer knew what to do with my life.

It was a beautiful sunny day out. The house was in horrendous condition. For months on end I hadn't done the least bit of upkeep. Dust and all sorts of filth had formed into fat balls that flew about like desert brush with the rush of air whenever I opened the only door. A pile of washed but never ironed clothes stood in one corner. The window slits that gave onto the street were opaque. In the kitchen sink plates had been sitting for such a long time that the filth had determined not to be filth anymore and had transformed itself into a tapestry of mould.

Putting things in order, I thought, could be an excellent way of making the time pass. I went to the bathroom and took out everything needed for a radical cleansing. As I took the broom, I struck the fluorescent light that illuminated the apartment. The house went dark. In less than a second the spirit of home improvement turned to rage. I gave a kick to the bucket of water and tried to break the broom. After two or three failed attempts, I hurled it against the wall and left the apartment, cursing.

The meteorological state was exactly the opposite of what was going on inside me. The air was tepid and the people on the street were much more relaxed than usual. I took my scooter, which sputtered and coughed and sent out great clouds of smoke. I pedaled for a long time to get it started.

I have no destination, I told myself as I went through the streetlights of Via Tuscolana. Turning onto Appia Nuova, however, like an old faithful horse, the scooter took the route it had grown accustomed to over many months.

Meanwhile, as I jolted from one hole to the next something came to me. If from Orsa's place you could see the Forum, then naturally the contrary must be true too, that is, from the Forum you must be able to see her place. As the bed was right in front of the window, one time I had even said, "Wouldn't it be better to draw the curtains?"

She had shrugged and said, "What difference does it make to you? At worst, we'll make some tourist happy."

So it was clear that, in order to see her, all I had to do was pay for the entrance ticket and climb the hills on the front side. I locked my scooter on the Via dei Fori Imperiali and joined the long line of tourists. Inside I followed them for a little while, listening to the explanations of the guide as if I were one of them. They were in German and I didn't understand a word. Inside I was growing more and more agitated. I stopped to slow the movement of my heart.

After loitering a bit inside, I rallied my courage and went to the place from which everything was visible. Almost no one was there. Tourists were trailing from one place to another like flocks in seasonable migration. The grass was full of daisies and other yellow flowers, blackbirds scratching in their midst in search of worms to carry back to their consorts.

199

I took a deep breath. Everything is peace here, I told myself, and turned to face the baluster. The studio was right in front of me. I could see the rose-colored walls of the building and the windows of the top floor. The one by the dinner table was closed, the one in front of the bed, wide open. Orsa was there, stretched out, and beside her was the silhouette of a man.

Darkness. The end of everything.

A tree in the course of its life can be assailed by an enormous number of storms. Thunderstorms, blasts of wind, and blizzards bear down on it, beat it, knocking it from side to side without anything happening to it. When the sun comes back, it's always there in the middle of the field with its majestic branches. It's only fire it can't withstand. The flames run fast, but it has no legs of its own to move with. Everything crackles all around, every little piece of brush becoming a torch, licked and then swallowed. In the end the fire reaches its trunk. It caresses the bark and from the bark rises to the leafy branches, burning the insects and the nests, drying out the sap, setting the thick branches and leaves aflame. It took decades for the majestic form to come from a seed, and in a few hours everything's dead. The great bonfire lights up the night. There is heat and light all around and up above. After it comes white smoke. The column of clouds is visible from kilometers away. The next morning, in the midst of the clearing there's only a black stump.

The flames had come back to my life. I hadn't seen the blaze begin. Even if I had, it wouldn't have done any good because in all those years I'd forgotten I was a shrub. I'd thought I was made of cement, metal, asbestos, something that couldn't be touched by fire. At the moment I started to feel warm it was already too late. I was the pyre itself. Wherever I went I carried it with me.

I could have gone to her house and insulted her, picked a fist fight with the guy who'd usurped my place. I could have slashed the tires of her car and written slut in fluorescent paint on the hood. I could have threatened her in anonymous letters and silent phone calls until she got really scared. I could have used the "one nail drives out another" technique and found another woman on whom to vent my rage.

But I didn't do any of that. I left the Forum grounds and went to piazza Venezia. I went into a bar and ordered a whiskey.

VIII

Sometimes wild animals are lit up by a car's headlights on the street. The sudden flash leaves them stunned. For a moment they stagger, lose the rhythm of their step. That instant is often fatal. Where are they? What's happening, they wonder? And, an instant later, they lie dead on the ground.

That's how I felt at the end of the story with Orsa.

I couldn't manage to resign myself to it. I asked myself where I'd been wrong and found no answer. She'd replaced me at some point, like someone replaces a tire on a car. But the truth was I didn't feel worn out at all, or that our relationship had been worn out. She'd been the one to decide that. She had written the words "the end" without asking me if I wanted to write them too.

The emptiness took control of me again. Again I was the corpse of the pharaoh Tutankhamon making the rounds of the city from morning to night. I felt like a puppet or a scarecrow someone had forgotten to draw a smile on. I buzzed around the center of town and its outskirts on my scooter, getting off only to go into bars and put fuel in my body.

Day by day alcohol again became more necessary to me than oxygen. A fiery thirst crackled in the void but despite the fire I was always cold. It was July, then August, and I kept shivering. At night I would curl into a ball, but it wouldn't help. I'd wake up from a fitful sleep pale, bloated.

Instead of coffee, I drank aftershave for breakfast. There was an enemy inside, whose face I couldn't see, and without even knowing its name, I'd given into its desires. Every day it said, do this, do that, and I obeyed. Every one of its orders had a single goal: my destruction.

The city was hot, deserted. The asphalt melted beneath the shoe soles and gave off a strong smell of urine. Here and there marched columns of sweating tourists, white hats on heads, legs swollen. They pressed around the little fountains and when they found a bigger one put their feet in. With them, dogs abandoned by their masters wandered the streets. At night they gathered in dozens around the dumpsters and woke the few remaining inhabitants with the barking of their brawls.

None of the people I knew were in Rome. Even if someone had been around, it wouldn't have helped. I knew a lot of people but didn't have a single friend. It wasn't out of spite or negligence. I'd just done what everyone does. Everyone was "friends" with everyone else in Rome, but a real friend was as rare as a white tiger.

I wandered the streets even at the hottest times of day. Heat and alcohol were a deadly mix. The steam rising from the sidewalks blurred the outlines of things. Objects danced

203

instead of standing still, like a mirage of wells in the desert. Each thing might be or not be.

One day I saw my mother on Corso Vittorio. It was two in the afternoon. She was walking by the Church of Sant'Andrea della Valle. She had on a black coat with a fur collar, the same one she'd worn the only and last time she came to visit me. On her arm, a holiday purse. I was sure she'd seen me because she turned her head when I passed. Her expression was sad, resigned. Maybe she wanted to smile at me but didn't have the courage. I did an about face, but when I got to her she wasn't there anymore. Above me a kestrel sailed, its wings taut. It must have been young and inexperienced to be flying in the hour of the zenith. It repeated its call in the air as if it were searching for someone.

My mother wasn't there anymore, her void was. The same void as my classmate from school. Of her I didn't even have an eraser in my pocket. When she died the sorrow I'd experienced wasn't much different from an annoyance. Only that night at her tomb had I realized she was really dead. I would never see her face again or hear her light step roaming the house. I wouldn't be able to hug her or ask her forgiveness. The last image would always be of her leaving on the bus, waving her open palm at me, and of the astonished, cold embrace I'd given her just before saying good-bye. In truth she was the only person I'd had a minimum of communion with. For a part of my childhood we'd been a happy island, the two of us against the whole world. The world was my father. I was her consolation, her joy. I'd been that for such a brief time. She'd gone away and I hadn't even said good-bye.

I got off the scooter in front of the white steps of a church. The doors were open and inside it was very cool. I sat down on a bench and took my head in my hands.

"God, why do you let all this go on?"

I said it and immediately felt ashamed. My basic honesty hadn't disappeared. I knew it wasn't Him who let it go on but me, the faceless enemy inside me whose orders I took.

Besides me and an old sexton there was no one in the church. I raised my eyes to a large painting of a woman with a baby in her arms. They both had a relaxed, sweet expression. There was nothing unattainable in their faces. She was crushing a serpent with her foot. She didn't seem frightened or disgusted. She squashed it with serene certainty, as if it were an extinguished cigarette butt. She needed to protect her baby creature from the serpent, no more than that. My mother would have done the same, just as all the mothers of the world. Every mother thinks, "My love will protect you from evil," but it's a fragile thought, like a dry leaf. Evil enters by invisible paths, devastating every form of life. At a certain point, the son can become the serpent that used to be beneath her toes.

205

That night, at home, I destroyed everything there was to destroy. And when there wasn't anything more to break, I started banging my head against the wall.

Two days later, the persecution of the insects began. My whole body itched, and I knew they were causing it. There were tiny, quick black spiders. I saw them on my body and the floor of the apartment. I scratched wildly and in no time was covered with sores. I had stopped eating. I felt a fiery tube from one end of my inside to the other. It grew hot when I drank. When I didn't, it burned.

I wanted to die but didn't have the courage to make it happen. Instead of tying a rock around my neck and hurling myself into the water, I let myself be carried along, drifting on a raft. Out of cowardice or through some unconscious and frail sense of hope, I wanted to put a little time between death and me.

At the beginning of September the city went back to being populated by people and cars. For more than a month I'd been used to making my way around as if the streets were mine alone. I went to the right or the left without caring who might be behind me.

I saw the car get there and thought, "This is the end." The shock threw me from my seat. For some time, which seemed very long, I was flying across the tram rails and the asphalt.

Then came the dark. There were only voices around me.

"He came right at me. He must be on drugs."

"Don't move," said someone else. "Call an ambulance."

"What a bitch, right on his birthday…," added a third. He must have been holding my I.D.

I was in a coma for ten days.

I'd heard somewhere about people who came back to life after months, but they had always had a mother, a husband, an affectionate friend, someone who had held their hand and talked to them non stop and make them feel less alone.

That didn't happen to me. I was alone and remained

alone the whole time I was in the coma. There were machines with me, a heart monitor, a brain monitor. They went on slowly, like tired horses. The nurses changed in shifts. Some were nice, some brusque. They talked to one another about their love life or problems in the ward. I had a faint sense of what was going on around me, like when you have a high fever and drowse next to a radio.

One day I heard a nurse call out, "Number twelve!"

Number twelve was me. So something must be going wrong. And in fact, in the total blackness a thread suddenly appeared. It was thin and extremely bright. I couldn't see who was pulling. I only knew that it was about to break in the middle. "No! Not now!" I cried in the silence. My voice was weak and beseeching like a baby's. I was sobbing like it was a nightmare and said I'll be good, good forever. Then something very strange happened. Whoever was pulling the thread stopped, and in seconds the thread turned into a thick rope. It was gold, and in the darkness all around it shone bright like a ray of sunshine. It must be for going back down, I thought. I touched it and opened my eyes.

A nurse was before me, with locks of blond hair slipping out from under her green bonnet. She smiled at me.

I spent another three weeks in the hospital. In that time I never regretted being alive. I thought only that being dead would have been much more convenient. I was tired, tremendously tired. Once more I had my life in hand and no prospects, no hope for the future. I felt like a gardener who'd had his greenhouse destroyed by vandals during the night. There was debris everywhere, shards of glass, overturned, broken pots, uprooted plants. It was hard to imagine that in the midst of all that flowers had once grown.

But I knew they had, and I was the one who had planted their seeds one distant day. I needed to roll up my sleeves, clear away the rubble, piece together the pots, add fertilizer to the soil, and water it. Then wait patiently, and hope the sun would come out soon.

Going home was the hardest thing.

I opened the door to my basement room, and the horror appeared before my eyes. The destruction was the same as on the day of the accident. What am I doing here? I thought, falling onto the unmade bed. The answering machine light was blinking. I reached out a hand and let it start. The oldest was a call from Massimo, asking me to get back to him as soon as possible. Then there were two silent ones. The fourth was a voice I had trouble recognizing. I rewound the tape two or three times to identify it, then understood it was the neighbor from my parents' house. She said it had been months since my father had entered a hospital for the chronically ill. The apartment was falling apart, and they didn't know what to do. Was it possible I didn't have time to come up to take care of things?

So my father was still alive. The news didn't move or shake me. It just seemed strange to hear a distant voice after such a long time.

In the period I'd spent in the hospital, my thoughts had taken a slower course. I felt like an animal befuddled by lethargy. Every shadow that came into my field of view made me jump. It might be a rock or a predator come to put an end to my days. I wasn't in a position to tell them apart. I was an animal and also a baby taking its first steps. I didn't have any faith in my legs.

Escaping death is a little like being born a second time. A part of your existence has gone away. There's another before you in which to put yourself in play once more. I didn't yet know the rules of that play. I looked around at the broken objects on the floor and understood they belonged to the life that had just ended. I wouldn't have ever called Orio or shown up in front of Neno. As for Orsa, she didn't matter to me at all anymore.

I thought about my father and felt the desire not to see him had remained unchanged. But I felt like being again in the tidy bedroom of my childhood. I felt like getting up early in the morning and walking on the ridge of the Karst. I wanted to feel like a strong, vibrant animal. I wanted to run, tire myself out, throw myself flat out on the grass. I wanted to be there, breathing with the earth that breathed under me.

209

In all those years of confusion I'd lost sight of the truth, the one painful thing that made me feel alive. I looked back and couldn't understand how it had happened. Suddenly that way of looking must have separated from me, like a snake losing its old skin in the spring.

Without realizing it I'd entered someone else's life. The chosen life wasn't shining or comfortable, it was just surviving. For more than ten years I'd scraped along like a rat in an abandoned pantry. Once the food's gone, it starts in on the cork, after the cork the wood, after the wood the electric cords and anything made of plastic. In order to just go on it metabolizes anything it can.

I was a rat and all around there were other rats. The cats were Massimo, Orio, and others like them. They gave orders, saying squeak here, nibble there, and we squeaked and nibbled, convinced that one not too distant day from now we'd be promoted to cats.

Maybe all those years of confusion and pain had served one cause, which was to make me understand I wasn't an artist but just a person slightly more sensitive than others.

In less than fifteen years I'd been run over twice, the first time by a truck, the second by a car. The first time had convinced me I understood what I was. The second time made clear to me what I wasn't.

Could I have attained those things in less time, with less suffering? I asked myself this as I put my few things in a bag. I didn't have an answer.

210 Inexplicably, I was still alive. And that was enough.

WIND

1

The return home took place without fanfare. I wasn't a hero returning to his village but a failure without any place to welcome him.

Just off the train I lowered my eyes and kept them that way until I got to our small apartment. More than anything else I was afraid of someone recognizing me, the questions they'd have asked me. The neighbors didn't make a big deal of me, nor did I of them. They gave me the key and the address where my father had been sent. "Your apartment is a pigsty," they observed, accusing me with their eyes. "By now you can smell the stench all the way down here." They clearly thought I was a heartless being.

The apartment really had become disgusting. There was the pungent odor of an old person who'd stopped taking care of himself. My mother had been the anchor, my father the ship. Once the chain had broken, he'd been cast adrift. Without anyone to hurl his disdain at, he'd ended up turning it against himself.

I washed, swept, cleaned, and aired out his filth for

several days. Every evening I told myself the next morning I'd go visit him. Every morning I found a good reason not to. Cleaning up his mess didn't make me any tenderer toward him. On the contrary, I was horrified at the degradation and not just physically.

In his degradation I could see my own. While much younger, lately, after Orsa's abandonment I'd behaved the same way. "Blood is thicker than water," my mother liked to say. I had begrudgingly seen in those days the infuriating truth of the maxim. My attitude was the same as my father's.

The last thing I cleaned up were the drawers. Amid the old bills, waste paper, and used corks I found a letter addressed to me. It was still sealed and came from the area on the other side of the border. The postmark was still clear. It had been there for months, not years. I didn't wait to open it. There was only one person in the world who might have wanted to send me word of himself.

215

Dear Walter,

It's been raining for almost a week; a wall of water covers the landscape outside the window. There's no entertainment here, no television, no books, nothing. What do animals do when they're wounded? They look for a den, a place they'll be protected from the traps of predators. In the den nature decides: either it heals them, or they die. Do you remember the Leopardi poem about the nocturnal song of the shepherd wandering through Asia? I don't remember the exact words now, but I recall that at a certain point the shepherd envies the sheep for their lack of thought. The beasts don't know the future, that's what saves them from going mad. To them death is a thing like another, it comes when it comes, like rain, hail, wind, an utterly natural fact. They close their eyes and feel no remorse. They've lived according to the program nature gave them. Eating, sleeping, mating, rearing offspring, and then fertilizing the soil with their bodies.

With me here is a woman I often talk with late into the night. She says the hand of God is in nature. I say I've never seen that hand. Some animals are born programmed only for killing. I'm thinking of the jaws of a lion, a cheetah, jaws that can do nothing but crush vertebrae, dispensers of death that wander around a world made to their measure. I might still think about the hand of God if gazelles, for instance, had short legs that made them easy to overtake. But like all animals destined for being ripped to pieces, gazelles are agile and fleet. They can run for a long stretch without needing to rest. Their agility isn't a gift, it's a trap. Wherever they run the same unfailing destiny awaits them. The creator that made them able to escape can't be a God of good because their running just makes it possible for terror to be experienced. He could be rather a bored demiurge who, to pass the time, came up with this eternal spectacle. The demiurge or his antagonist forever hidden in the shadows. In a word, all choices come down to this in the end: being gazelles or cheetahs, chasing or being chased, ripping apart or being ripped apart.

What choice did you make? I don't know. I can't seem to imagine it. By natural instinct, you seemed more inclined to flight. There are tigers and there are house cats with their nails removed. I used up my nails but not on couches. One fine day I felt tired, and that was that. I picked out a den and stopped there. I'm here waiting for something to happen. Meanwhile the wretched monkey works; thoughts are like a drug, they're there, clinging to your back, confusing you. To the cruelty of the lion and the gazelle there's something else to add, which is that thoughts keep moving ahead, you can't

216

stop them. It's a powerful, uninterrupted noise, like a waterfall. You press your hands to your ears, but you hear it anyway. I've known for some time how it is that you go crazy. It's enough to be alone and unable to find the switch that turns off the din.

Then there's the great festival of regrets. We're all invited once we get to a certain age. There you are looking for a point at which everything might have been different, the point where things changed. You wonder: was there one? Or was there one and I didn't see it, didn't want to see it? You're the one who walked that path, not somebody else. All you had to do was take a step to get off it. It's an invisible line that holds you prisoner. You imagine it as high walls but it's barely a thread. You'd only have to lift your foot a little to step over.

It happened to me: there was a point but I didn't see it. I realized it had been there many years later, when it was too late to go back.

It happened in Africa, on the border of Chad, about ten years ago. I was standing watch at a checkpoint. There was desert all around. The wind was lifting the sand. It was a light breeze, not a storm. Boredom and thoughts were my only companions. Suddenly, close by a fennec was passing, the small Saharan fox. I took my rifle and told myself, "I'll kill it now. One precise shot is much better than the slow agony that's waiting for it sooner or later." It hadn't yet become aware of my presence, but continued to jog along with its big ears and its tail in the air. The instant before I pulled the trigger, something strange happened: it sat down and looked at me. I say it was strange because once it saw me it should have instinctively run away. I still would have hit it, but it would have performed its duty that way. Flight and terror for the spectacle of it. But no, it sat down and started looking at me. Its nose was small and black, its eyes shining. My sights were trained exactly on its forehead, a perfect target. I would have split it right in two.

They say animals aren't able to sustain the glance of a man. In those seconds I discovered rather the opposite is true. We're the ones who can't sustain it. In those black pupils there wasn't any panic, only a kind of painful wonder. Maybe it was the wind, the heat, the solitude, but all of a sudden I perceived its thoughts. "Not now," it said, "not like this. I'm not ready." All right, I thought, and lowered the rifle. He looked at me a little longer, then got up and disappeared, trotting lightly beyond the dunes.

Some delirium, eh? Afterward I was angry for letting a mirage scoff at me. I'd never missed a chance to take the shot. Humiliation, everything cancelled.

The festival of regrets came many years later. The scene was the same, but instead of a fox it was a human being before me. The desert was missing, the solitude, the wind. The shot was as precise as ever.

Why am I saying these things? Nothing's important anymore.
The fox's eyes made me remember the unsustainable glances of your lambs on their way to death. That's why I wrote you. I could have taken a step but didn't. Maybe staying on that path was a law of my destiny.

The woman I talk with always brings up grace. It gets on my nerves. What's that?! I shout at her. Where is it? I don't see it or feel it. I call but it won't come. Where's divine goodness if it chooses to show itself only to those whom it finds agreeable?

If you get this letter, if you can, if you want, come. The place isn't bad. The air's good, and nearby is a small lake for fishing. It's a den, I told you that, and it's big enough for two. Who knows, maybe you've accumulated your own wounds in all these years? It's probable, even very much so. Come. I'll be waiting.

Andrea

I read and re-read those lines several times over. In
places the writing was so agitated I had trouble making it
out. In the end I re-folded it and put it back in the envelope. I needed to breathe. It was cold out so I put on an old
thick jacket of my father's. It was drizzly and everything
was lusterless. Along the street people walked straight
without looking you in the face.

The light of the tavern where my father went to drink
was the same as when I was a kid. Inside probably there
were other fathers drinking and other kids waiting at the
door. Maybe I too, had I stayed here and taken up the same
project as everyone else, would have had the exact same end,
a wife and a house and a frightened son waiting outside.

I walked for a long time before going back, revisiting all
the places of my adolescence with the calm of a different
age. In some place not even that hidden inside myself I   219
hoped things might speak with the intensity of that time.
But it didn't happen. No emotion, no shock, no subversive
force. I saw my figure reflected in the shop windows of the
town, a rather large figure, with the same nose, the same
slow step as my father.

That night I had a nightmare. I dreamed I'd woken up
in bed and my pajamas had become a straightjacket. I didn't
realize it right away, only when a voice in the room said,
"Jump!" and I tried to raise myself. It was impossible. "How
do I do it?" I shouted, squirming like a netted fish. I couldn't
see the face of the person speaking but felt the presence
moving through the room. "How?" it said, laughing. "How?
You never jumped as a boy? Bend your knees and jump!" "I
can't!" I shouted. "I can't!" Meanwhile the pajamas were

crushing me. Then all of a sudden I wasn't in the pajamas anymore but was moving around the room, flying through the air like the voice had just before. There was a very old man laid out on the bed. His pajamas were the striped flannel ones of my father. The bed was mine. I didn't understand which of us it was. Age had eaten up the features so much that we looked almost identical. "Is he dying?" I asked, and my voice was the uncertain voice of a boy. In the air next to me was Andrea. Now I could see him clearly, offering me his hand as if there were a crevasse between us. He spoke in low tones. "Come on," he said. "Jump. Don't be afraid. It'll just be a second. It's like a strong wind hitting you in the face."

The next day I went to visit my father. Of the man who'd been my terror there was very little left, a slight outline, stiff beneath the covers. In the hospital the smell of urine caught in my throat.

"You should know," an orderly said on our way to him, "he's not all there anymore in his head."

Before me was a face almost completely anatomical. The skin, grayish yellow in color, adhered like a membrane to the structure below it. The nose and ears had grown enormous. Transparent lids half covered the eye balls. There was no peace in that kind of rest. The eyes rolled from one place to another, and the eyebrows contracted and released following the flow of thoughts. I had only ever seen the eyes of newborns move like that in their sleep.

I stood there looking at him. "It's useless for me to be

here," I told myself. "I'm going to take my coat now and go." I should have been moved, pained, but the only feeling I experienced was that of being uncomfortable. When he opened his eyes, I wondered, what would I call him? Papa, Father, Pop all seemed terribly false words to me.

Then he opened his eyes, and I called him Renzo. His glance wandered lost around the walls as if he'd never seen this place. Several times he turned his eyes on me. They came and went without ever stopping. The bed had smooth metal barriers, like those for babies. Slowly he stretched out a hand and took hold of a railing. The hand must have stabilized him because only then did he focus on me. I put my hand on the bar as well. They didn't touch; they were just near each other.

Two cars, down below on the street, stopped suddenly. I straightened up, expecting the collision, but it didn't come. One of his fingers touched mine. I don't think there was any intention in the gesture. Just after that he started moving his lips convulsively. Sounds came from his mouth, but I didn't understand.

"I can't hear you," I said.

He stretched his neck a little and said, "Can I play now?"

The voice wasn't the same anymore either. It was the voice of a little boy, two or three years old at most. It didn't thunder; it supplicated.

"Play?" I repeated. "What do you want to play?"

But he wasn't listening to me anymore. He was talking about a dog, the train. He needed to feed the chickens. Before he fell asleep again, he hummed ring-around-the-rosy to himself two or three times.

When I left it was evening. The self-sufficient patients were eating in the dining room.

I waited for the bus a long time. It was cold and it wasn't coming. Before me the darkness set off my father's ethereal pallor. I looked for the term to define the feeling I was experiencing but couldn't find it. Anger and fury were tempered. I searched for a memory, just one good memory, that might fill the emptiness with something similar to love or compassion. No matter how hard I tried, nothing came. Not a gesture, not a phrase, not a smile. Only his enormous shoes that I'd used as pirogues.

He had despised me. He'd wanted me to be different. With the years I'd understood that even if I had been different, he still would have despised me. I was wrong either way. Wrong was the fact of my coming into the world. But now he lay there defenseless. Instead of thundering, insulting, kicking everything that came his way, he was stuck in bed, asking — asking me — with a fearful voice, "Can I play?"

The disappearance of consciousness had dragged everything off with it. The only game left ahead of him was death.

To be born, like everyone, he'd left the obscurity. He'd made a long journey and then returned to the point of departure. He was eating baby food, using big diapers instead of little ones. Before long his heart would stop, his brain would become an inert sponge. Darkness was behind the door. Crossing the threshold was all it would take to be swallowed by nothingness.

It was only then I realized an extraordinary fact, which was that life was not a linear journey but a circle. You could move around however much you liked, but in the end you came back to exactly the same point. A crack opened to let you down, a crack opened to suck you back up.

If it really was like that, what was the importance of what came in the middle? What had the life of my father been? He'd been born in a simple family. He'd studied to have a trade he liked. He'd had ideals and for them he'd fought and run risks. He'd had a woman who loved him from the very first day and remained faithful to him all her life. Then there'd been the accident at the shipyard that left him disabled. He could have died but instead only lost a leg. The prosthesis was perfect, he walked almost as a normal man. After the accident he'd had a male child, healthy, moderately intelligent, probably no worse than many others. The son had grown up and gone away, the woman died, and he, suddenly grown old, would very soon be dead. That was it.

223

Listing the events of his life made it seem absolutely normal, even better than many others because for a brief period at least he'd believed in something. His mates from the tavern considered him a great man, almost a hero. Only my mother and I knew none of it was true. For all her life her husband and my father had been the sole creator of a tiny hell.

Where was the discrepancy, the point where things turned false?

My mother said up until the day of their wedding he'd been a wonderful man and only afterward had changed without apparent reason. Long before the accident he'd wake up gnashing his teeth and breaking everything. The reason was fairly easy to understand: he'd wanted to make an impression. The same thing happens with birds. During courtship they make a big show of their many-colored feathers. Afterward, once the copulation's done and their DNA has gone out in the world, everything goes back to how it was before.

Men do exactly the same. If they started showing how they really were from the very start, before long there probably wouldn't be many weddings anymore. But that didn't explain anything. The real question was why he'd had such contempt for life.

My father, and with him millions of others, could have had a happily normal life. The ingredients were all there. But he'd created a quick-sand marsh all around him. In that bog is where he'd grown old, where I'd taken my first steps. With his death it would all evaporate, and of all that grand universe of smells and insults nothing would remain.

As the bus made its way, slow and loud, up the slope that leads to the upper plain, I thought maybe the great muddle was all in a switching of verbs. From birth they teach you life is made for building, but it's not true. It's not true because whatever gets built sooner or later crumbles. No material is strong enough to last forever. Life isn't made for building but for seeding. In the wide ring-around-the-rosy, from the crack at the beginning to the one at the end, one passes and scatters seed. Maybe we won't ever see them born because, when they sprout, we won't be here anymore. That's not important at all. What's important is leaving something behind that's able to germinate and grow.

You build houses, families, careers, entire systems of

ideas. You accumulate estates for your children. All that noise of hammers and scrapers, all that rustling of banknotes reassures, cancels the perception of the void. Being always busy with something gets the most dangerous thoughts out of the way. Things grow and you watch them grow, satisfied. Whatever ends and crumbles needs to stay far from view. So my father had made a house and a family, but besides the money for those four sad walls and the spermatozoa he'd contributed to putting me in the world, he hadn't sown any other seeds. After his death, he'd leave behind only eighty square meters purchased with a mortgage and an orphan-born boy.

In the week I spent at his bedside, more than once I gave him liquid with a baby bottle, picked him up and pushed him from one place to another, so as not to irritate his bedsores. Immersed in sleep, he seemed innocent, and he was. Renzo the drunk had disappeared. Before me, in my arms there was just a defenseless being who needed help.

Something had cracked inside me. Maybe cracked isn't the right word, what's cracked is close to breaking. Re-assembled rather than cracked. I found myself thinking of those hours and days actually as a gift I'd been given. The gift of reconciling myself with the unhappy being to whom I owed life. I took care of him, fed him, did all the things he never did for me. The hatred had disappeared and the rage. In my gestures and thoughts there was only pity, pity for this man and for the insanity and uselessness of his brief existence. His brain now was just a sheet riddled with holes, one after the other of his zones of consciousness having disappeared, eaten up by senile dementia. It was a sheet and an ocean. An ocean in the midst of which there had once been a continent. The continent had been swallowed up. Two or three small islands remained, the oldest parts of his memory. That's what he was still attached to, the games of a three-year-old, the discoveries of a four-year-old. That world survived in the old man's body. I was convinced he'd pass away like that, calling loudly for his mother, fighting with his brother. But that's not how it was.

Friday evening, as I leafed through a magazine beside him, someone said my name. I looked up. There was no one else in the room, and I looked at the bed. He was there, his eyes open and shining. I saw his lips move to say "Walter...."

I jumped up.

"Yes...?" I said, uncertain, leaning over the bed. My back was covered in a cold sweat. His long white hands were racked.

"Walter," he said again.

"Yes, I'm here."

In the neighboring room the television was turned up high. They were showing a documentary on Russia. "Those nostalgic for communism are found mostly in the armed forces...." said the speaker.

My father grasped one of my hands, squeezed it, pulling it toward his chest. To help him I had to bend farther down. Now my hand was squeezed between his. His palms were icy. He held it like something precious.

"You need to drink?" I asked. "Are you hot? Cold?"

I felt I needed to fill the silence with something. He was looking at me with a strange fixity.

"Are you in pain?" I asked more brusquely.

226

Very slowly he brought my hand to his face. Fat tears were coming from his eyes, slipping straight down onto the pillow. He put it to his cheek, then started moving his lips, mumbling rather than speaking. Only on the third try did I make out his words.

Stammering, slobbering, he said, "Forgive me, Walter. Forgive."

I thought of responding, "What do you mean, forgive you for what?" but instead muttered, "Papà" and broke into sobs.

I cried with my head beside his on the pillow, his turned up, mine plunged down. Our tears had different temperatures. On the pillow case they formed a single blot. My breathing was labored, his was lighter.

The next day he died.

He passed from dozing into unconsciousness almost without notice. For just an instant he opened his eyes. They shone with a light they'd never had before. I don't know if he knew I was there, but, before closing them forever, he smiled sweetly.

Then I was the one to behave like a child. "Papà," I repeated, and didn't try at all to hold back my tears.

At one point, the daughter of another patient came up to me.

"You loved him a lot, didn't you?" she asked, trying to console me.

"No!" I shouted. "I hated him. "I always hated him. That's why I'm crying."

The wind came during the night and took the rain away. Toward three o'clock the shutters started banging. A gust came in through the window and filled the curtains. I couldn't sleep. I kept dozing off and waking up.

A little before daylight I got up and went to the kitchen for a glass of water. The door to my parents' room was half-closed. The shutters were wide open, and the orange light of the streetlamps was streaming in. The wind was jostling them, and the light shifted through the room, a warm, intense light curling like the flames of a fire. Everything was banging and creaking. The eighty square meters seemed like a lifeboat adrift. The waves lifted it and cast it down. There was no one at the wheel, and I was the only one aboard, sole survivor of the shipwreck.

The bedspread was perfectly smooth. On my mother's night table, in a shiny frame, was a picture from their wedding, two starry-eyed young people smiling at the photographer. On my father's there was a picture of him in the mountains during the war.

I looked around. Neither of them had a picture of me.

The fury came upon me from behind. I didn't realize it was coming and couldn't put up any resistance. I threw open the wardrobes and dresser drawers and cast everything inside onto the bed. My mother's clothes were exactly as she'd left them, folded in plastic sacks with fasteners on them and mothballs inside. My father's were merely tangles of dirty garments that gave off the stink of an old man. After the clothes, I threw shoes, pajamas, socks, underwear, two drawers of Christmas cards and bill receipts, my mother's sewing bag with all its colored threads and a piece of embroidery barely begun. I threw things and kept throwing. It looked like I was making a funeral pyre. When there was nothing left to throw, instead of a burning match I hurled myself onto the bed.

The odor of the stuffy wardrobe and my father's smoke permeated everything. I twisted around in it as if I'd been bitten by a tarantula, smelling first one thing then another. Some I kicked out, I don't know why or what I was looking for. I stopped only when from my mother's Aida fabric came the faint smell of violet. Parma Violet was the only perfume she ever wore. When she was young, she said she knew she smelled like an old woman but she didn't care because it was the only perfume she ever really liked.

I opened up the embroidery and saw it was an angel. Only the upper part of the body was visible. It was leaning on a cloud with its elbows, looking down. Its expression was ironic rather than serious or menacing. It smiled without malice at what was happening down there, in the confused world of men. It must have been her last piece. The angel itself had part of its head and a little of the wings. She was dying and sewing an angel. In the meantime I'd been in Rome and the thought of her had been only a nuisance.

I took the angel and launched it into the distance and did the same with everything else. I swung my arms like a child throwing a tantrum. I swept everything away like a ferocious hurricane. In the end I tried to tear off the bedspread, but it was resistant. I bit into it and felt my jaws creak under the strain.

Then, like a whirlwind that comes up quickly, destroys, and then departs, the fury left me, empty and inert among the bed linen of my parents, like a cadaver dropped on shore by the waves.

In that bed quite probably one day long ago I had been conceived. In that bed, at that instant, I would have liked to die. But death never comes when you'd like it to, and dying alone I knew now was no longer possible.

For thirty years I'd been moving in one direction. The direction was distance from my parents. I'd behaved like one of Pavlov's dogs responding to a bell: the conditioned reflex always made me do the opposite. In all that flight I hadn't made anything. Neither made nor seeded. I squeezed my fists and found them empty. Now I no longer had any reason to squeeze them because the reason for my opposition had disappeared. My father and mother had died according to the natural order of things. The counter impulse no longer had any meaning. Around me there was just a great and sudden emptiness. An impulse toward something ought to have come into being, but toward what? I was too tired to even think about it. It was the empty fatigue of someone who has accomplished nothing, someone who's walked and walked and remained in one place.

At seven the street lights went off, and the cold light of a winter dawn filtered into the room. I put the coffee on and went to wash my face. My eyes were swollen like those of a toad.

When I went out onto the street, all you could hear was the sound of the wind making everything jingle. The fury of just before had turned into energy, movement. It had been more than a decade since I'd walked in the forest. I left the town behind and went into the hills, toward the black pines, the red earth, and the little oaks.

The air was cold. It went straight into my lungs like a single blade. Whoever knows the wind knows there's no way to defend yourself against its harshness, you just have to forget about it. At every step I looked around and asked myself, "How could I have lived without this for so long?"

For years and years I'd lived like a plastic clone, forgotten the smell of the earth and its seasons, the sound of steps on the frozen ground. I'd forgotten the briefest instant in which you feel joy, being a thing among other created things, breathing among the breath around you.

The sumacs up in the hills had already turned completely red. At every puff of wind the dry leaves rustled in different tones like some strange instrument. The dog-rose berries were the beautiful vermillion of their ripest maturity. Their showy tint invited the birds to feed. At that moment none were flying. The wind was too strong for their fragile wings to hold up against it. Even I had trouble going forward at times. The struggle, rather than wearing me down, made me euphoric. According to some strange law, I hoped the fury of the air would carry off the shadow left in me by so many dark years.

I had given up truth to live in illusion. From everything that had come to me I'd been content with the exterior. I'd acted like the great majority of people. I'd chosen rhetoric instead of persuasion. Now I knew what had happened the very moment I had dreamed of glory, the moment I'd wanted difference to become an external marker, the moment I'd believed that different and superior were one and the same.

Looking back, I was astounded at how easy and sudden the transformation had been. A few intense thoughts and a little flattery had been enough. I wasn't immersed in truth. It wasn't an unrenouncable part of my being, only a handhold on a bus: the moment holding on was the least bit uncomfortable, I'd let go and grabbed onto something else.

I walked and walked and walking tried to connect the fragments. I needed to recompose more than ten years. What I was piecing together wasn't a journey but a process of slow degradation. Instead of building or sowing, I had dissipated. From the taut lucidity of poetry I'd landed in the bed of a bored socialite. I'd let myself be used by her and everyone else. I'd thought I was important, but I was just a jester. With my ingenuousness and desire for compensation I'd become the ideal puppet in their hands. For their entertainment I'd been a step away from death.

232

My circle was on the point of shattering long before it would bring me back to the point of departure. I was close to leaving everything in disorder, like in the room of a hotel. By some happy chance I had turned back.

There must be a why in these feet still on the earth, in this pulsing heart, in these eyes able to grasp every nuance of light. Maybe ahead of me there would again be a handhold. I needed to look around me, find it, reach out my hand to grasp it.

I'd reached the summit meanwhile. For three hundred sixty degrees in all directions there wasn't a cloud. The heights of Nanos were covered with snow.

Wind - I

Above me were two sparrow hawks. They seemed to be playing at letting themselves be pulled away by the wind.

I too wanted to feel lighter. I collected dry leaves and on the back of each wrote in pen the name of a person I knew. I wrote Neno, Federico, Orio, Massimo, Orsa. Then, with a stronger gust, I let them go one after another in the wind. They disappeared, swirling toward the sea.

On the last leaf I wrote Andrea and put it in the inside pocket of my jacket, next to my heart.

II

I had nothing else to keep me in town. I'd buried my father and taken care of the necessary formalities. I could finally accept Andrea's invitation.

As the train pulled out of the station, it occurred to me this was the second time I was leaving my city. The first had been flight. This time I was in search of a friend.

Beyond Postumia the sleet became actual snow, the black pines gave way to firs. What I saw out the window no longer resembled the Karst but a kind of sleepy mountain plain. I got off the train in Ljubjlana and took a bus. It was slower and its shocks were in bad shape. I got to the town Andrea had indicated with my stomach inside out.

It was already dark. Here the snow hadn't fallen. There was just one restaurant. I showed the address to a woman, and she said it was another two-hour walk away. I was tired, so I ate dinner there and spent the night in a room on the floor above.

More than fatigue it was accumulated tension. I wanted to sleep, but my eyelids had no intention of closing. I looked into the dark and kept thinking. Among all my thoughts, the most obsessive was the uselessness of looking for Andrea. An insistent voice kept telling me he too was just a dream, a ghost I'd created for the purposes of my own survival. Andrea served, had served, to justify all the things I wasn't able to bear on my own. In our encounter, said the voice, there was never any real friendship. Andrea was the maple and I was the mistletoe clinging above it. We each had our own leaves and breathed on our own account. But his roots reached deep into the ground while mine barely penetrated his branches. I was superficially attached, sucking water and minerals. Not even a meter long, I enjoyed the panoramic view from on high.

The long separation hadn't changed the relationship. At just the moment I found myself estranged from my life, he had come to my aid. I was pretending to run to save him because I wanted to save myself from the sudden emptiness that had opened up before me.

235

No matter what system I tried to get myself to sleep, from counting sheep to deep breathing, I didn't even feel drowsy. Somewhere in the room a woodworm was chewing. The voice kept talking and talking even when I covered my ears, maybe because it was right. What the hell kind friendship is it when you don't send even a letter in ten years? A friendship where you never feel like finding out what's happening with the other person, telling him about some joy or discovery or emotion? It talked and all I could do was feel guilty. If he's got to this point, I told myself, the fault is really mine too. In all those years I'd never given him even a sign of life, while he, even if it was ten years late, had taken up a pen and paper and written me a letter.

Night is terrifying because it makes everything big. A woodworm becomes a jack-hammer, breaking your thoughts up, enlarging them, repeating them back to you enough to make you crazy. I tried to marshal my fragile forces, to use greater reason and silence the worries this journey was provoking.

At the moment Andrea and I met, we weren't two human beings but two communicating vessels filled with white-hot liquid. There was magma inside, and the glass walls were fragile. Our friendship had been a decanting of furious humors. Once the osmosis had taken place, we separated from each other. The pressure had reached its maximum in each. Just one atmosphere more and we would have exploded, bursting into flame before returning our energy to the world.

Perhaps that was why we needed to put so much distance between us. Once we were far away, we transformed into tightrope walkers, traversing a steel wire suspended over the void. We were the ones who had pulled it tight. We were the ones who'd wanted that walk across the chasm, which was why we couldn't be distracted or look around. The day we left each other, we'd climbed onto that wire. As in a duel, our departure took place back to back. "When it wants, destiny creates meetings." This was Andrea's good-bye, his mysterious promise of our seeing each other again.

After a very long time I'd fallen off the wire. Or maybe I'd fallen off from the very start and just didn't realize it. If I didn't destroy myself it was only because something had broken my fall. I'd fallen and lacked the courage to tell him. The great difference between us was only this, that as soon as he'd felt the wire reeling beneath his feet, he'd taken up a pen and paper and written to me.

When I fell asleep it was almost dawn. A little before seven a rooster in the courtyard woke me up.

The room was frozen. I got dressed without washing, paid the bill, and had the owner of the restaurant explain the right road to get to where Andrea was.

I passed the few houses of the town. All their windows were already lit. From there the white road rose into the mountains.

The cart path passed through some meadow valleys and into a forest of firs and spruces. In the woods was the silence of winter. Only from the tops of the trees could I hear the plaintive peep of crossbills intent on opening pine cones. As I went up I kept asking myself questions, running back over Andrea's letter. There were too many things I didn't know how or didn't want to respond to.

Why had he found himself that day in the middle of the desert with a rifle in his hands? While I was feverishly writing *A Life in Flames*, he'd been there deciding whether to shoot or not. Before the fox's stare he had lowered his weapon and around that apparently simple target-shooting gesture his remorse had pivoted. What had his life been? What had he done in all those years? How had he lived?

I was afraid of finding a person completely different from the Andrea I'd known. It had happened to me not long before, when I was going through the paperwork for

237

my father in one of the city offices. A bald, slightly over-weight city employee had knocked on the glass. I thought he was calling me about some bureaucratic mistake and went up. "Hey, Walter! Long time no see!" he had cried into the microphone that connected him to the world. I smiled without knowing who the aging gentleman calling me by name was. "It's Paciotti! Don't you remember? Sophomore year." Suddenly from the fog of a distant past, the face of a thin boy emerged, sitting at the third desk, with a passion for model war planes. Paciotti was the boy and the man with the shiny head waving behind the glass. "Paciotti," I exclaimed, "Of course I remember." And I opened my hand and placed it on the glace opposite his. "What are you doing? Shall we get a coffee?" he asked. "Not today. I'm in a hurry. Maybe another time…."

That's how I'd answered Paciotti. I couldn't have done the same with Andrea. It's one thing to meet someone in an office or on the street but something else when you go look-ing for him. If Andrea wasn't Andrea anymore, if he irritat-ed or disappointed me somehow, if he merely bored me, how would I have hid my anger, my irritation, my disap-pointment? How could I have said, "Not today, I'm in a hurry. Maybe another time?"

I didn't understand how he could end up in this place. This was the land of his sworn enemies, the reds who had destroyed his father. It was true there weren't any reds any-more, they had disappeared from this place and about ev-erywhere else in the world, but it still seemed a bizarre choice. Blood had been spilt in this land. Blood that soaks the soil evaporates much more slowly than rain water.

238

Maybe, I told myself as I went up, he too at a certain point had decided to follow the example of the leaves. Having no more energy, instead of resisting and giving orders, he'd had himself docilely transported by the wind. Or maybe he too, despite all countermeasures, had been caught in the coils of a woman, the same as what had happened to me with Orsa. He was bewildered, reduced to nothing, ready to follow her to the end of the world. In his letter he had said there was a woman beside him, his sole companion.

By degrees all these thoughts slowed my progress. The idea of turning back grew more pressing with every step. I had set out in the wake of an emotional breakdown due to the death of my father. Now that I felt less fragile, I understood I'd made a mistake. It wouldn't take much to about face toward the valley.

After about two hours of walking, I saw a clearing. There was the odor of burnt wood. The house must not be far.

239

I felt a hand squeezing my heart and lungs. It was hard to breath. At the end was a building. I went slowly forward. Maybe he'd seen me already. I knew by now that everything I had discovered about Andrea, I would discover about myself.

The structure was of wood and stone. From outside it didn't look like a shelter, and it wasn't; it was a convent. The only sign of life was the thread of smoke coming from the chimney. All my fear left me when I was before the door. I was happy, that was all, content with the surprise I would give to Andrea. There was a kind of antique bell. I pulled it two or three times. Several minutes passed before the door opened.

I was ready to shout, "Andrea!" but before me stood a nun. She was old and bent forward slightly. Surprise had frozen the words in my throat. She stood there, her hand on the door, looking at me without speaking. Finally I managed to mutter, "Hello. I'm a friend of Andrea. I've come to see him."

Then the sister opened the door. As we went through a kind of courtyard, she asked where I'd come from.

"From Trieste," I said. "We're childhood friends." I had the impression she was deaf or didn't understand my words well. So I lowered my head toward her ear and shouted, "Andrea! Andrea! Is he here?"

She nodded, lowering her head. "Yes, yes. Come. Follow me."

She led me through a long, closed room. At the end was a wooden door that creaked on its hinges. Beyond the door there was a small meadow surrounded by a white wall. The sister stopped on the threshold, gestured with her hand.

"Andrea is there," she said.

In the middle of the meadow was a cross made of wood.

I didn't shout or cry. Of all the hypotheses the only one that hadn't ever occurred to me was this. There wasn't any name or date on the cross. But the earth seemed to have been dug recently.

There are some wasps that paralyze their prey with their sting. The poison doesn't kill, it just inhibits movement. Later, when the insect is hungry, it comes back to eat. Its food doesn't go bad that way. It stays fresh and flavorful. Andrea was the one who'd told me about them. He liked everything that exalted the mercilessness of life. He'd read the story in a biography of Darwin. After discovering the ways of those insects, Darwin himself was supposed to have lost his faith in a beneficent all-powerful God.

I stood there in front of that mound and was the hunted larva. The horror, surprise and sudden emptiness had paralyzed the tissues of my body. I was a thin shell with something heavy inside. Andrea had gone away. That was the last sting he'd punctured me with. He liked to astonish, turn things upside down. He'd succeeded yet again in this. All that I had imagined, the long evenings spent recounting our lives in the dark, none of that would be. Andrea wouldn't be my mirror. Before me was just earth, opaque, reflecting nothing.

I felt betrayed and blameworthy at the same time.

He'd written me at a moment of distress, and I hadn't responded. He must have mistaken that silence, that absence for indifference. He must have thought, as I had, that our relationship had existed only in his head. He couldn't bear that absolute solitude and for that reason went away. Not for a moment did I consider, among all the sensations and hypotheses, the possibility that his death might have been due to natural causes.

I had confirmation after a bit, when the sister reappeared.

"It was his choice," she said quietly.

"I know," I answered, while a veil fell before my eyes.

Later it started raining, fat, angry drops that rang metallic on the tiles and stones. The sister was taciturn. She led me into the room with the stove.

"There were five of us here once," she said, adding wood. "Now I'm alone. Soon there won't be anyone."

241

I felt rage toward this woman. She'd had Andrea beside her for months and hadn't succeeded in saving him. Neither fatigue nor respect for her age held me back from showing it.

"Why didn't you do anything?" I shouted at her back. "You, you're supposed to be able do that kind of thing, aren't you?"

She turned, "You who?"

"You! Priests, nuns, the Church, you know, people who believe…. It's impossible that in all those months you couldn't find the arguments to make him change his mind."

"We're human beings like everyone else. We're all equally powerless."

"No, you're just better than others at easing your own conscience."

She got up. The light from the stove illuminated her face. How old could she have been? Maybe eighty, maybe less than that. Her features didn't have that placid obtuseness that's usually attributed to nuns. The eyes were very dark and bright at the same time. They shone in the room like little embers.

"Come. I'll take you to your room."

She led me to a little room with a cot and a table. There was a closed knapsack in one corner, and next to it two muddy rubber boots. From the window all that was visible was the dark green of the woods.

"He stayed here too," she said at the door, then as she was leaving added, "Pray if you can. Andrea needs it very much."

Left alone I lifted the chair and threw it against the floor. Then I did the same with the table.

"There's my prayers!" I shouted. "That's them!"

I shouted and cursed. In a sense I hoped she could hear. The rage went to my head. I kicked my pack and his, hurling his boots against the walls. They fell and I picked them up to do it again. Then I attacked the bed. At the fourth or fifth kick I slipped and struck my lower leg hard against the metal. I collapsed on the floor in pain, holding my leg and cried, repeating Andrea's name. From tears to sleep I passed almost without noticing.

When I opened my eyes it was dark out. Beneath me the pavement was extremely cold. I got up with difficulty and dropped onto the bed. There wasn't any bed linen, only two military blankets folded atop the mattress. I opened them up and wrapped myself in them.

243

I had a dream. I was walking in the Karst. Here and there the sky was veiled by banks of clouds. I thought I was by myself, but Andrea was before me. His back was to me, he walked at a slow pace. I started running. I wanted to catch up to him. I ran and ran, and the distance was always the same. He walked on lazily, looking ahead. Then I stopped and shouted with all the air I had in my lungs, "Andrea!" Without stopping, he turned toward me. His face was motionless and neutral like certain Japanese masks. He extended a hand back like a relay runner. "Wait," I shouted and in that instant, the soil under my feet started crackling. Then I saw it wasn't earth but water, the wide surface of a frozen river. The sheet was breaking, being pulled downstream by the swift current.

Meanwhile Andrea had disappeared into the fog and I, shouting his name, slipped farther and farther back.

At dawn I opened my eyes. Daylight was coming feebly into the room. My body hurt everywhere, and I felt terribly far from my life. On the floor were our two packs over-turned in the fury of the night before. I picked his up, opened it, and slowly took everything out, putting it all carefully on the bed. They were mostly personal effects, undershirts, socks, a pair of binoculars, sweats. Only near the bottom did I find a date book from the previous year and a school notepad. The date book was tan, plastic. On the cover of the notepad, in capital letters, was written "Walter," and my name was underlined three times.

Dear Walter,

I'm not sick, at least I don't think so. I just feel terribly cold in-side. For the past two weeks my teeth have been chattering even though it's the end of August.

I wrote you a letter a couple of months ago. I don't know if it ever arrived or, if so, if you took it into consideration. I was going through a moment of distress. You, the memory of our relationship, had seemed the only grip I could latch onto. Remember the question of the pyramid, the various levels that different people's conscious-ness was divided into?

One day, not long before we parted ways, we attributed to each level a meteorological state. Fog characterized the lowest levels. Whoever was there wandered from one place to another without any precise idea. After fog came pounding rain, after pounding rain, drizzle, and then veiled sunlight. At that point, by natural logic what should have followed was the splendor of full sunlight, but logic

doesn't follow human destiny with the same precision of changing
meteorological conditions. So we'd wanted to put storms after veiled
sunlight. Hail, sleet, and blizzards pounded on the next highest rung
without rest.

The summits of high mountains are often hidden in clouds. From
below all one sees are the heights. To reach the top one must cross
through this uncertain zone. Not everyone has the courage to clam-
ber up the rock walls. In the last part there is cold and solitude and
fear of death. Natural selection applies to souls too, and it couldn't
be otherwise because the power of the light makes everything shine.
Not everyone has the strength to withstand its reflection.

Why am I saying this? Maybe to justify myself for the fact that
in all these years I never felt like looking for you. It wasn't out of lack
of interest that I didn't look but because all my energies were taken up
with trying to overcome the next to last level. Only here, in this long
solitude, far from time's wrinkles, did the ghosts begin to come out.
They didn't all come out at once, like evil from Pandora's Box, but one
at a time. One by one they rose up and knocked at my door.

I say ghosts and not memories because they don't have the clear
precision of things that happened in the past. They're not photos but
fleeting, toxic fumes, fumes I myself created through the actions of
my body. As I told you in my earlier letter, with me here is only one
old woman, a nun, and I often have long conversations with her. A
couple of times at the end of these arguments of ours I had the distinct impression that something inside me was coming untied. Somewhere very far away a torch was burning. I felt it and also sensed
that there was the direction I should set out in. But it was an almost
imperceptible sense, so fleeting that I couldn't ever grab hold of it. It
was and remained the memory of a happy dream that disappeared
upon waking.

In the other letter I think I told you about the fox too, and how an act of will on my part had saved it from death, and how that act had been the sole moment of my life about which I'd felt regret. It was right there I could have begun a new paragraph, flipped over the hourglass.

Maybe the big black hole of our friendship, a black hole I only now see, was that I only ever talked to you about my ideas and never about myself, as if ideas were born from some neutral world and not from the gaze and the pain of a life.

There's something you don't know and maybe don't even suspect. Before Andrea the eagle you knew there'd been Andrea the chick, a chick that could have also become a duck, a rooster, a calm courtyard animal, ready to conceal itself at the appearance of a mere shadow. I couldn't say when exactly the change came. When I try to see my past, I discern not one but many Andreas, closed one inside another like so many Russian nesting dolls. My mother had one she inherited from her grandmother. She used it for darning socks. It was so worn you couldn't make out the face any longer, and the color was almost all gone. Sitting at the foot of the armchair, I used to spend hours and hours taking it apart and putting it back together. I wasn't able to get used to the idea that the last one wouldn't open. I hoped to break the spell, that sooner or later even the tiniest doll, through some kind of magic, would open too. I was convinced some secret lay inside there and wanted to find out what it was. I had the natural attitude of trying to discover whatever was hidden: any kind of wall or barrier made me stubborn. I couldn't think about anything else until I'd knocked it down.

My mother was an affectionate, patient woman. A thousand times she explained to me that the doll with just one color really was the last one and that it was so small because it was for darning the

246

tiny socks of newborns. "At the end," she said, "they get so small you can't divide them anymore." As a young woman she'd studied chemistry, and from her studies she'd drawn the conviction that everything has some causal or necessary connection to something else. From a certain standpoint, this way of making everything reasonable could have been reassuring, and, for a time it was. For years she wove a web of responses to my questions. With sweetness and determination she'd managed to make even the craziest ones plain. "This happens because earlier that other thing happened," she'd say. "There's the stimulus, here's the response," and so on like that.

I never had any reason to blame her. This attention of hers was the most natural way of expressing her love. The explanations she gave corresponded to her vision of the world. Despite the great quantity of clues to the contrary, to the end of her days she continued to believe that a logical course was concealed behind every occurrence.

But one thing had escaped the thread of her understanding. That thing was me, her son, flesh of her flesh, the being she and my father had given life.

If the law of existence really was that of the consequentiality of events, if you could always know the results by knowing the premises, then I should have been the exact opposite from what I grew up to be.

With a pedagogy long before its time, my mother always treated me with great respect. She put into my hands all the means, all the keys to solving problems on my own. I should have been a little wise accountant, a scientist immersed in his vials. But very quickly I started to become something else. The only light inside me was the one kept alive artificially by her speeches. All around it was pitch blackness. Something would flare up in that blackness from time to time. It wasn't the sun but the fiery darts of a luminescence. There were jaws down there, and teeth and icy glares. I wasn't alone. With me were the heartless figures of fish in the depths.

It's not true that babies at birth are just blank sheets, fabrics on which it's possible to write in dark ink, depending on your intent, words of good or bad. When I think back on my first steps in the world of consciousness, I'm almost certain that inside me there was already something, and the something was quite different from what my mother wanted. No matter how hard she tried, my glance was almost completely turned to the darkness that surrounds things.

I was born with a heavy piece of baggage. I don't know at what point it was lifted onto my shoulders. It certainly doesn't have anything to do with an absence of love or any of those absurdities psychologists talk about. If they were right, scoundrels and murderers would never come from good families, but it happens. As does the opposite—people who've grown up in hardship and violence then turn out to be capable of great love. It's not the rule, but it happens. The fact that it does makes the clever system of justifications crumble. I was wanted by both my parents, I was an only child, I had every kind of attention possible, without excess or affectation.

I never told you anything about my father and probably not by chance. They say DNA hands down the color of the eyes and hair, the length of the nose and legs. They say that in the boundless number of its threads, it also passes on some part of the character. But they don't say whether it's possible to pass on feelings in one's genes, not the feeling of life but the stronger, more ineffable one, that takes life to its limit. Do terror, anxiety, the desire to destroy come down to us together with the color of our eyes?

My father was a mild person. When a fly was buzzing around the room, he'd capture it with a glass, then open a window and let it

248

go. But he was the one to whom my dark side could be traced. Now you're going to think he was like Doctor Jekyll and Mister Hyde or like your father, fun-loving at the pub but raging at home. Nothing of the kind, his behavior was consistent. It would have always been that way if, at a certain moment, his history hadn't become intertwined with the bigger one, the History that moves countries and fills textbooks. Try looking around. Look behind you. What's there? Listen, what do you hear? Behind us, in front, all around in this century that's about to end there is only horror. It walks along dripping blood like Macbeth. It doesn't speak. It shouts, groans, cries. We came into the world of the Moloch century, the bone-shredder.

If you listen to people talk in bars or on the street, you'll hear them say people have become bad, that before there was never so much cruelty. Do you know what that is? Nothing but a lie, a sugared sleeping pill for easing the conscience.

Man is bad from the moment he comes into the world. His mark has always been soaked in blood. With time he has merely perfected the technique. Now it's possible to kill a lot more people with much less effort. The achievement is called progress. Progress is in the service of ideas. And ideas, do you know what those are? The purest kind of poison. Suddenly someone's convinced he knows better than anyone else how the world's supposed to go. Why wait for death in order to see paradise? With a little effort, the celestial garden can be realized on earth. The word effort contains the whole essence of the slaughterhouse. "Effort" means eliminating everyone opposed to the dream. With "effort" everyone comes to think the same way. That's what great ideas result in. The spontaneous response would be that you need to eliminate ideas. But what kind of life would it be without them? A life that doesn't imagine anything better, that doesn't place a goal to strive for up ahead? What is existence reduced to when you take away the project? Mere reproduction.

This is the other side of the coin. Anyone who offers, asks questions. Anyone who keeps inside the germ of a conscience can't help but recognize the great inequality that surrounds us. It's the healthy point from which insanity sets out. You feel called to provide some remedy. Somewhere hidden inside us sits a sense of guilt brooding, or justice, two names for the same thing.

This is the weak point that all great ideas appeal to. I think the wisest thing to do would be to recognize the problem and not do anything. There is injustice: I see it and it leaves me indifferent. But maybe it's only the Indians who are capable of this. They live in eternal detachment, and in the depths of their culture there's no Adam or Eve, or the apple and serpent. There is no regret for the lost earthly paradise. Who could have wisped the nostalgia for such a state into our heads?

I say there's the paw of the great adversary in this. The 666 has been active since before the world's creation. Only a superior mind, dedicated to pure evil, could have instilled in men's minds the nostalgia for something perfect because perfection would never be within our reach.

At their birth all human beings cry. If they don't, it means they're dead. Pain exists even before consciousness. Dogs, cats, cows, horses all are born in silence. At most they make a little call to let their mothers know they've been born in good health. They say the labor pain of human birth comes from the disproportionate largeness of the head, which is clearly a pathetic fantasy. Horses and elephants are born with their enormous heads, but the landing is painless. At the moment of giving birth, women scream with all the air they have in their bodies, while cats purr. This is where the abyss that renders us unhappy comes into being.

250

Wind - II

I've taken a long time to say just one thing really. My father was a man of noble sentiments, and from his nobility he believed it was right to commit to creating a better world. I say noble out of the affection of memory. Maybe it would be more correct to say "ingenuous." He was ingenuous like the greater part of his generation, those born in and around 1920. How could he not have been? I too, if I'd been born then, would have probably fallen into the trap. The great technological bloodbaths hadn't taken place yet. Rather convincing ideas about the possibility of creating a more just world were in the air. The future was radiant and just there. All you had to do was reach out your hand to touch it. From good intentions, it was thought, evil could not be the result. But a monster was born: rather than a beneficent sun, a blast furnace it was dangerous to get close to.

My father loved literature, poetry, and all that was beautiful. Right after he graduated, he'd been called up to arms. On the eighth of September he was in the mountains of Croatia with a group of companions. He'd thrown the fascist uniform into the bushes and joined the partisans. He hadn't been a communist before. The horrors of an idiotic war lost from the beginning had brought things to that point. If I have to fight, he must have thought, at least I'll be doing it for a just cause. He was already engaged to my mother, and the years apart, rather than wearing out their relationship, had made it stronger. At the end of the war, he'd returned to Italy and asked her to marry him. After the wedding they'd gone back to Fiume, which was where my father had decided to live. He'd fought for that land and felt it was his. She put her degree in a drawer, and he became headmaster of a small middle-school.

A normal couple, a normal life, with a breath only slightly deeper for having been inserted into the dynamics of History.

I'm boring you, I know. You're reading and wondering, why's he recounting such a banal story? There were thousands of such stories in those years. Maybe you've noticed I've never written, "My father said, my father responded…" Do you know why? For the simple fact that my father was mute, he didn't speak. From when I was born to when he died, I only ever saw him motionless in the arm chair, silent, looking at the void.

He was mute but not deaf. If I talked to him, once in a while he would move his head in my direction and smile feebly. This was the only rapport between us for fourteen years. He looked much older than his years. When you told me about the look of lambs being led to their death, I understood it was his look too. There was a painful astonishment and innocence in those eyes, the eyes of a young boy in the body of an old man.

Everything I knew about him, everything I know, was told to me by my mother. Not everything and not all at once, but the great majority I learned after his death. For many years the story was there'd been an accident. Some people get run over by a car and lose their legs, others, no one knows why, go mute. I had to content myself with that.

"Papa's not an invalid," my mother told me toward the age of five or six. "He's got a tongue, a uvula, and everything else. A big fright got hold of him is all."

"So will he get better?" I'd asked.

My mother had smiled and said, "Maybe."

I started watching him. In some comic I'd read the story of the magic glance, which could pass through objects and perform extraordinary deeds: decimate enemies, heal friends. I was convinced I possessed it too. I'd sit down close by and stare at him. Sooner or later something was bound to happen. I waited and waited, and

252

nothing ever did. Or better, something did but it had nothing to do with the miracle of the word. Even if I hid, behind or next to the armchair, he'd feel my presence. I don't know how but at a certain point I'd see his hand searching for my head. He had big, beautiful hands, and sometimes he'd rest them on me. With the armchair between us, we looked like a master and his dog. I liked playing the puppy and would sit beside the arm rest and bark a couple of times, putting a paw on his knee.

With time I noticed this happened on sunny days. On rainy days, rather than putting his hand on my head he'd lift me in his arms. I didn't like that. I hated playing the cat-son. But he'd hold me tight. I wanted to go play but had to stay there. Even in the middle of the summer his body gave off a sort of frozen halo. He was cold and trembled imperceptibly. The moment I got down I would feel cold too and had the impression he was some kind of vampire, a vampire-father who'd given me life one day and, through his embraces, was slowly taking it back.

253

At this point it would be easy to think, voilà the usual story of childhood unhappiness. It was lack of communication with the father that unleashed the disaster and all the rest of it. Any person stuffed with the stupidity of our times would confirm it. I'm the only one who knows that's not it at all. My anomalous state of being depended on my father, yes, but not in the manner it's usually believed. Inside him was a great black lake, the kind of underground lake that forms inside caverns and beneath the mountains. It was black because of the darkness and because the liquid that filled it came from much deeper strata. It wasn't water but oil, thick, viscous, leaden.

If a flame falls into the water, it's extinguished. But if it touches oil, everything erupts instantaneously.

His was the lake of the mountains, mine the lake of the valley. They were connected by a tiny outlet.

The dark blot I'd always felt inside me wasn't original sin but the dark shadow of my father. I was still a boy. A stubborn part of me tried to be like all the others. I ran, jumped, played. But it was enough for me to stop for a moment, stretch out my ear in the night to feel the little blot growing, becoming a puddle, a lake, an ocean, an expanse capable of swallowing everything. And it was. With the calm of one who's got the victory in hand, the dark halo conquered ever more territory. It wasn't in a hurry at all. It swallowed the light in the manner of a black hole in space.

Why my father was always silent, why he almost always sat like that I understood much later. He was like a puppet stuffed with TNT. Even the tiniest mistake could have made him blow up. When did I understand? Too late. The combustion inside me had already been set in motion.

254

There's the great contradiction, the point at which it becomes difficult to believe me. I said my father was a mild man and then claimed the opposite, that he was burdened with an explosive, ready to burst into flame. How is that possible, you ask? Let me turn the question around and ask what would happen to a mild, innocent man who ended up in hell by mistake? Hell presupposes fault, but that's only true for the hell created from the heavens. If the hell's created by men, who determines what the fault is? Against what weight is judgment measured? The relativity of values permits no certainty. What for one person is called fault for another might be loyalty or distraction: in short, it has another face, and that face doesn't contain evil inside it.

So we come back to the point I was discussing before, the point where men, having lost the thought of a governor of all, decided to create a reign of perpetual happiness on earth. From this we come to the idea that whoever opposes it must necessarily end up in hell, a hell without flames but with pits, dogs, and barbed wire.

I had long discussions with the sister about this.

"How is it possible," I asked her, "that man could be so zealous as to construct hells even more perfect than the one made by the devil himself? God is dead," I said, "and couldn't be otherwise. If not, how could you ever explain the fact that the actions that are victorious on this earth are always those of his adversary? Good only triumphs in edifying books. In the concreteness of every day it's always defeated. It would be moving and nice to discover suddenly that, as it says in the Gospels, meekness defeats force and forgiveness kills violence, but that doesn't ever happen and never has. Christ was murdered, and so was Gandhi, and that closes the circle. The final word was written in that blood. How can anyone be so dishonest as to deny it?"

She would always take her time in answering me. At first I thought she was deaf. Then I understood she'd been accustomed to solitude for too long. My words aren't questions but a raging, swollen river. Listening to me, trying to find the way out, is hard for her. When she finally answers, it's always with just a few words.

"Man is lazy," she said to me that time. "If he needs to go somewhere, he always chooses the shortest path. To get to evil all you have to do is reach out a hand. To do good it takes effort. Too often we forget that we're the ones who have to decide. Evil is more evident, good less so. But that's not a good reason to take a short cut."

"Choose? What difference does it make?" I answered. "The short cut is always victorious. And all those tall tales you fill the heads of children with, hell and paradise and the craziness of limbo, that doesn't mean anything to anyone anymore. Now's no longer the time for acts of mortification and classification lists, sickly sweet deeds for an improbable future. I've always hated how people collect prize coupons. The more you've got the bigger your prize.... ."

"I've always hated those too," she said, getting up, and left the room.

This way of behaving of hers makes me crazy. Suddenly in the middle of a discussion she gets up and leaves. I thought she didn't have any more answers and was escaping for that reason. I thought she was very arrogant to not want to lose an argument.

So one day, as she got up, I shouted, "You commit the sin of arrogance, of pride!"

"Yes, it's true," she said, turning. "I sin out of arrogance and pride, but I sin out of reflex. You ask me questions and demand answers. That's where we both fall."

"What then? Do we just stay silent, not speak at all?"

256   Do you know what she answered?

"You have to trust."

I don't know why I got off track. I was telling you about my father and then started describing my disputes about the nothing that oversees the heavens. The sensation pervading me these days is like that of a beast surrounded by fire. At first it looked like a far-off blaze, something I'd be able to escape from one way or another. I had managed to get here, exhausted, convinced this place was a den. It's only been lately that I've understood the blaze has followed me. It's not a linear front but a circle, shrinking from hour to hour with me in the middle. For that reason I get distracted from time to time. It's not fear that blocks my view but smoke.

My father and History. In 1948 Tito breaks his pact with Stalin, leaves the Comintern, choosing an independent route for the construction of socialism. As a consequence, from one day to the next former allies turn into sworn enemies. *The Italian Communist Party under Palmiro Togliatti remains allied with the USSR.* In a very short time the land around the Italians grows white hot. They're no longer comrades in the battle for liberation but spies, traitors, filth. They start to disappear, one after another, no one knows where or why. One day my father disappears too. He doesn't come back from school. His crime? Having in his home the Russian classics: Dostoevsky, Gogol, Chekhov. They were all there, lined up on his book shelves. Someone had informed on him. The system didn't work by equality and solidarity but by betrayal and denunciation. When honest people became aware of what was happening, it was too late. The great bone-shredding machine had already been set in motion.

I was born a good many years later. It had been some time since my family had managed to return to Italy. I came into the world and grew up without knowing anything. The truth came to light only with my father's death. I was fourteen, and my restlessness was beginning to overflow. Maybe for that reason my mother took me aside and said, "I need to speak with you." In her universe of thought everything needed to be clear. If she'd remained silent until that moment it was only out of respect for my father's pain. She started the story from a distance. "At a certain point in his life," she said, "your father was forced to act against his moral principles."

"Did he steal?" I asked.

"No, he killed."

The phrase remained suspended between us. Meanwhile I thought: theft would have bothered me more. Then I spoke. I said, "Of course. He was in the war."

My mother lowered her glance. "This happened much later. It was his best friend. 'Kill him,' they said, 'or we'll kill you.' He chose to live. Other people told me the story. When he came back home, he *didn't talk anymore. I knew the man too. Years later I met his wife. She didn't hate your father or want revenge. She hugged me and said, 'I feel pain for you. For me the pain was one thing. For you the cross will last all your life. Your husband made the harder choice."*

We were in the kitchen as I listened to my mother. I felt suspended. What kind of a sentiment should I have felt toward my father? Within the limits of a relationship without words, I had loved him. I would continue to love him in my memory too. What fault of his was it if he'd come up against a wall? Almost everyone would have done the same. The instinct of self-preservation always pushes one toward the death of the other. Most people then would have gone on living, put it behind them and gone forward. He was different, sensitive, good. He'd punished himself by choosing silence. He was alive but it was as if he wasn't. He didn't participate, didn't share. Maybe it was his way of remaining close to his friend.

"You don't have anything to say?" my mother asked, interrupting the train of my thoughts.

"What should I say? What happened happened."

I think she was quite satisfied with my calm, mature reaction. I was too.

I remained so until I noticed the calm was only apparent. My father's pain was already all inside me. It had been a part of my being from the very instant his semen had united with the egg. There it had combined in equal parts with the rational faith of my mother. An explosive mix. From one side the desire to understand, from the other the impossibility of doing so. After that revelation I spent a week immersed in a kind of trance. The two opposing forces were colliding. Neither was able to defeat the other. The encounter generated friction. One day I changed position and a part of me blew up.

I've already told you about my mother's rational faith. If it had been just slightly less deep-rooted, she probably would have never talked to me. But that's the way she was. She went around everywhere with a torch in hand. The moment anything unclear appeared, she held it up. She wanted light everywhere. There was something pathetic in that desire of hers. The light she carried around was artificial. It could do nothing against the deepest shadows.

Should one always tell the truth at any cost? I don't know. I can't judge her way of acting. She was consistent with herself, and that's enough for me not to condemn her. I can't and don't want to imagine my road without this confession.

One day the plug came out. I left home and didn't go back. I wasn't intending to run away or leave my mother in anxiety. I only went out for a walk. As I walked I lost my way, couldn't remember where I was, who I was, why I was living. They found me three days later in a completely confused state. I spent one month in the neurology ward of the hospital. When I was released, I was convinced my mother had lied to me. I kept pestering her with questions, where, how, why? When she finally answered me, I shouted, "Liar!"

According to her it had all happened on Goli Otok, a desert island transformed into a gulag, a few kilometers off the Dalmatian coast. It was the place where "traitors" were re-educated. Re-education consisted of removing every vestige of humanity from men. The detainees tortured each other. Respect, dignity, the force of the most intimate ties, everything was cancelled out. Fathers killed sons and vice versa. Murdering your neighbor was the only way possible to live a little longer. There were no more faces, only gasping, death rattles, blood masks.

"There are moments," she had said, "when the usual rules are no longer valid. You can't condemn. You have to try and understand."

Anima Mundi

"You're inventing all this!" I'd shouted in her face. "That place never existed. It's not in any books."

"One day it will be," she had said, while I kept shouting into the middle of the night, shouting until fatigue shot me down like a wild animal.

Then one morning, suddenly and without my understanding why, I woke up calm. In all those nights of shouting and pain, some metamorphosis must have taken place. The parts inside me had battled and battled, and in the end one had taken control. Lucidity had won, the clear reason of my mother, but it was a rationality as parasitic as a tick: the host from which it drew its nourishment was my father's suffering, repressed, insane. From my mother's universe the idea of a Someone who had forged the world had always been excluded. The world had created itself, she said, and it was for the perfection of its own laws that it continued on. She was staunchly, serenely atheist. When I was younger, she'd said, "Imagine a train. That is the world. It runs forward in space and time."

I liked that image, that little round, colorful train carrying us calmly forward. As the years went by, the only thing we didn't agree about was the conductor. She maintained that the lead engine was empty. I, on the other hand, that someone was driving, and that some-one was God's antagonist. Not goats or witches' rites or hooves or pitch forks, not bloody hosts or rustling hoods. No spectacle or inverted ritu-als. Only the second law of thermodynamics applied to hearts.

What is wisdom? Living in harmony with the laws of nature. The law that dominates nature is entropy: live and destroy, and you're wise.

For some time now I've felt like shouting again. I'm speaking and suddenly my voice escapes my control, grows louder.

One day the sister noted it to me.

260

"You don't have to shout so loud if I'm the only one who needs to hear you."

"And who else is supposed to hear me?" I shouted.

Instead of responding, she left the room.

I recounted the story of my father to her too. Why? Out of stupidity, the desire to annoy. She listened in silence. Was she suffering? Was she upset? I couldn't figure it out. When I finished, there was a long silence.

"So," I asked her after a bit, "don't you have anything to say?"

"What am I supposed to say?" she said.

"I don't know. You're the specialists in consolation. If you want, you can even absolve him, can't you? Or can't you because you're a woman?"

Instead of being offended she smiled. "I can't do it," she said, "not because I'm a woman but because I'm a human being."

"Well then say something edifying, you know, the moral of the story."

261

"You know something," she said. "I don't know if anyone's ever told you but you have a great defect... ."

"And that is?"

"Generalization. You don't do anything but make judgments and in making them you put categories to use. Since I wear a certain kind of clothing, a religious habit, you feel you have the right to attribute a whole series of ready made sentiments that you've got in your head. I'm supposed to drip with honey sweet phrases and have the rapt expression of certain pictures. To you I'm not a person, a human being who's taken her own journey, with mistakes and suffering like everybody else. To you I'm just an icon, an icon you decided to spit on from the start. You say you don't have any scruples about looking right at things, but a profound look doesn't ever use little moulds. *The life of the Spirit is very different from the anti-religious chatter you've filled your head with. You judge and rebel, but in reality you don't have the slightest idea about the object of your judgment and your opposition. I can't absolve your father and can't judge him. His story is a story of great pain, and the only feeling I can express is deep compassion. Compassion for his destiny, for the moment when he might have made a different choice but didn't have the strength.*"

"*What choice are you talking about?*"

"*Not to kill.*"

"*Then he would have died!*" *I shouted.*

"*Exactly.*"

With that response the letter broke off temporarily. There were several pages covered with scribbling to make them illegible, then others torn out abruptly. I needed air, room to breathe.

I closed the notebook. Before facing the last part, I went out to stretch my legs.

III

Dear Walter, these days I've been feeling like a tarantist. I can't find rest anywhere. When I came here, I told you, I was a wounded beast looking for a den where I might take possession of my health again. This nearly abandoned convent seemed a fitting place. I'd seen it on the map.

"Who lives there?" I asked in the village below.

"Only a nun," they'd answered.

I'd reached it in haste. To heal, I thought, one must huddle up, get proper care. Not even for an instant did it occur to me the cure might at times be more painful than the illness. I believed I'd found a den of leaves, but inside there turned out to be barbed wire.

But I don't have the strength to leave. These days, besides the unusual agitation, I've been feeling a great fatigue. I've never felt so worn out and restless in all my life. Sometimes during the day I doze off. I'm in a daze rather than asleep. I close my eyes, and horrible images immediately appear. The sister says I yell in my sleep and, it's true, sometimes my own voice wakes me. You know, it's hard to be in here without any other sound but the birds singing. I've come to despise them in the end. Every morning I wish I had a gun to shoot them all with one by one. I look in the sky and wonder, "What the devil do they have to sing about?"

Yesterday at dawn I threw open the window and shouted, "Enough! Enough already!" Then without any reason I started striking my head.

If I think of all those idiots who sing the praises of country life, the crazies who think of finding peace among the quiet of the woods! It's obvious they're incapable of seeing even a little beyond their own noses! Nature is a mirror, a litmus paper oozing out poison. Being here is like being in a room with white walls. Sensorial deprivations and nature are exactly the same thing. In different ways both bring you to insanity sooner or later. I don't know how to decipher the images that appear just as I fall asleep. There actually isn't even one that's distinct. It's a mixed up kaleidoscope of different forms.

The other day I opened my eyes and thought, "That's how it must have been at the beginning of the world." Light pierces the shadows, and the shadows try to regain the upper hand. Except that, instead of it being the universe, it's my body that's the battle ground. Who will win? Which will put the other to flight?

Yesterday I woke up, and the sister was beside me.

"Do you need help?" she asked, putting a hand on my forehead. I said, "No" and turned the other way. She stayed a little more. I could hear her breathing behind me. She breathed quietly. Only once in a while she'd take a deeper breath as if she suddenly had great need of air.

Later I found her in the big kitchen, stirring one of her usual tasteless soups.

"My father killed for love!" I shouted in her face.

"For love?" she repeated like an echo.

"Yes, for love. You don't understand? That man was his best friend. If he hadn't been, everything would have happened differently. He killed him because he knew what would have happened to him. He killed him because he didn't want to make him suffer. How do you put it? He took up his cross."

"You're not well," she answered. "So I'm going to pretend I didn't hear you."

I lost control, hurled myself at her and started shaking her by the shoulders. The ladle she had in her hand fell to the floor.

"Pretend?!" I shouted, "Pretend!? What does that mean? It's convenient, too convenient to be here looking at the birds, pretending everything's okay! But doesn't your life make you sick? Aren't you ashamed? You're all champions of egoism. You should win the Olympics of don't give a damn. You're protected from everything, and sitting in your chair on high you say, 'This is good, that's bad.' Then, with your starched, rustling skirt, you kneel and there you've done your duty, everything in its place, you can go to bed tranquil. The angels will watch over your hypocritical dreams. But outside meanwhile, the world goes to the dogs, everyone slaughtering everyone else like pigs, and you don't care at all, not at all. Too convenient," I said, shaking her, "too convenient!"

Exhausted, I fell onto a chair.

She was unmoved. She picked the ladle from the floor and asked, "Who's the world?"

I made an angry gesture in the air as if to say, "Everything all around."

"Your eternal defect," she said. "You generalize. The world is you, it's me. The world is the journey of our consciousnesses. I don't judge you, but you judge me. You don't know my life, but you judge me all the same. You've never felt the desire to ask me anything. You

265

don't want to know what brought me here or what was in my past. It doesn't interest you. The only thing you want from me is for me to respond to your worries with certain answers. I don't do it, or don't do it the way you want me to, and for that reason you shout and are so angry. Haven't you realized that? With every day that passes you shout louder. It's not really from me that you want an answer but from Someone higher up. That's why you shout so much."

She paused for a moment and then continued.

"But I can give you an answer too. The first one to kill was Cain, and he didn't do it out of love but out of envy. He was afraid of not being loved enough. With all your intelligence, all your knowledge and speculation, you will never be able to create even a single blade of grass. We're not the ones who give life. We're not the ones able to take it away. Faced with an extreme situation, we can only accept that life may be taken from us. It isn't easy, it isn't natural or desirable, but it's the way it is. The most profound law of Being obliges us to negate violence. It may be that your father was moved by pity and not by the desire to save himself. In the insanity of his pain he might even have thought this. The greatest delusion may appear on a low horizon, the illusion of believing oneself the arbiter of another's life. In the absence of fear of God, anything can happen."

"But life is violence," I answered, exhausted.

"It is," she answered, "until we make a choice."

Cain! How many times he has come into my head lately. I always imagine him as pervaded by astonishment. "Is it so simple?" he must have thought, just after the act. "Is that all there is? Is that what taking a life is?" Killing doesn't require any more strength than lifting a suitcase. The effort is minimal, the effect great. Thinking about all the different ways there are to go to the next world can make your

266

head spin. *The deaths hidden in the banality of daily life are almost more fearful than those caused by accidents or natural disasters. No one's bewildered if you smash up a car and don't come out of it alive, or if you step on a mine and get blasted into the air. But if you die munching on a grape during a picnic, or a vase falls on your head while you're on your way to buy cigarettes? It's the ease of it, see? If you step on a berry, at most the soul of your shoe gets a little wet. But if that same berry slips into your trachea you suffocate. Facility and fragility. It's not playing with words, it's the point where everything becomes critical. How long does it take for a human being to get big? How much time and food and care and effort? And how much time does it take to become a cadaver? Isn't the disproportion enormous? A couple of decades and one second? Who enjoys himself by playing such games? The same one who made the gazelles able to run almost as fast as the cheetahs? But for the cheetah too, it's actually more complicated than that. It has to be in excellent form. It has to be lucky enough to find gazelles in worse form and also less alert than others. It has to lie in wait and then run. And even then, it's never really certain of the result of its run. It's not the same for us. All we need to do is lift up a rock and hurl it at whoever's nearby.*

Herein lies all the folly of life, so much effort and then nothing. Already as kids people like to kill. They kill ants, chicks in the nest. If they can they kill kittens too. Why in the world should they stop as adults? Why were we given the possibility not of giving life but of taking it away? We can't create anything. Maybe destroying things is the outlet for such impotence. Cain was seized with guilt almost immediately. "What have you done?" asked a Voice. He looked around and was horrified at what he'd done. I don't know if it was luck or misfortune. But above him was that Voice. The Voice spoke, and in speaking it imposed contrition. Why did it go mute after him? It should have been an unrepeatable act. But in the millennia to follow it's become most common. Neither civilization nor the various faiths have ever managed to stop it. In fact faith and civilization have often served as the vehicles for spreading it even faster.

Do you remember what I told you the day we parted ways? That your life was that of art and mine was that of action. I was fed up with books and with reasoning about everything. I'd already understood the most powerful law governing life and that opposing it or running away was a ridiculous waste of time. In all these years only once did a voice talk to me. It was the fox's, not God's. I can't get it out of my head. What stupidity, what delirium! No one's ever seen a fox that talks. If it was God talking through him, why didn't he do it anymore? He could have easily appeared an infinity of other times to thunder, "What are you doing?" But he was silent.

268

There's oxygen in the sky, and hydrogen, helium, water vapor, and clouds. In small parts there are even the rarest gases. Up farther, on high, there are satellites and space ships, then the other planets and the sun. Between the sun and planets, wandering here and there are meteorites and comets, remainders of the instant when the universe was created. Besides this, there's nothing else. Above our heads the sky's just an immense stretched out blanket. There's always been the dark, acting out of inertia. I said as much to the sister: "What you genuflect toward is a great emptiness. Nobody there is directing our actions. No one guides us or loves us." Do you know what she said?

"Delegation, that's the most common error. Two thousand years have passed since Christ came down to the earth, and still we all act like babies, waiting to be fed. If the food doesn't come, we immediately think we've been forsaken. But whoever said God was supposed to act in our place? He gave us the possibility of choosing. With this he showed the loving power of creation. Good and evil are in our hands. In this sense, you're right. There's no one there preparing our gruel. Our existence isn't like that of babes in arms. It might be nice, yes, but what meaning would we give to our lives if everything was fixed from the beginning?"

At that point I told her it could very well be that way. God could also not give a damn about our fate; he could not be good but still, at least, be just. There are those born with Grace and those who chase after it all their lives without ever finding it. Maybe there were top grade products, run of the mill ones, and cast offs, likes and dislikes? Classifications of merits? What was hidden behind this great injustice? "Why is it," I shouted at the end, "that it talks to you with the familiarity of a neighbor but never to me?"

"Are you sure?" she asked.

"Absolutely," I said.

269

"You want to know the reason, the real reason?"

"Yes."

"Because you've never lowered your weapons. That's why you haven't heard it."

I started kicking things. "What weapons are you talk about?!" I shouted, beside myself. "What the hell kind of weapons?!"

She came close and tried to touch me.

"Leave me alone!" I yelled, moving aside. "Don't you know I could murder you?"

Again she took my hand and said, "Yes."

One thing I hate is the way she takes care of the garden. Growing plants for eating is fine, but she's put flowers in the midst of the ones for food. She takes care of them, looks at them for hours as if they

were there to tell her something. I can't put up with this kind of ego-
ism anymore, this paying attention to things of no value.

The other day I watched her from the window. I leaned out and
said, "What use are flowers in the middle of the chard?"

She broke out laughing. I hadn't ever heard her laugh like that.

"What use are they? None!" she shouted from the other end of
the garden.

Last night I didn't sleep at all. Sleepless nights have become the
rule of my life. I thought of all that wasted love and was filled with
rage. I closed my eyes and ground my teeth. It's impossible, I told
myself, that things keep going on in this idiotic manner. It's stupid, I
know, but I felt extremely jealous. The sister said that envy is the
fear of not being loved enough. At that moment it was true. In the
solitude of the dark, the flowers had become my enemies, the flowers
and all other beings, creatures simply alive. I hated the triumph of
life, that overpowering, blind growth. I could no longer tolerate that
waste of energy that sooner or later would become death. At the
change of seasons the flowers wither. To kill a human being not even
a single terrestrial rotation is needed. It's extremely easy. A blow
right between the nose and mouth is enough, or on the neck. Killing
means inserting an element of disturbance in the great complexity
of order.

At three I got up and went out. The moon was high in the sky
and lit up the things all around as if it were day. I went into the gar-
den and started destroying. I ripped out the flowers with savage
fury, as if they were nails in my heart. When there wasn't even a
corolla intact anymore, I wiped my hands on my trousers and, in
silence, reached the sister's room.

IV

These were the last words in Andrea's diary. The writing stopped at that point. Below, there were a few confused words, and the handwriting was very different from what was on the preceding pages. With some difficulty I managed to decipher "you will never come" underlined twice and then below that in infantile block letters "FOR-GIVE, FORGIVE."

I opened the window. It had stopped raining. The earth was giving off steam. Fog was rising up and looked like breath. The drops collected on the leaves were dropping to the soil. I looked up. In the sky fat white clouds were being driven off by the wind. In the breaks between one and another the sky was limpid, punctuated by stars.

I stayed there until, in the east, the vault of heaven began to be tinged by a more intense light. Then I closed the window and went to bed. Apparently I didn't feel anything, neither rebellion nor restlessness. Inside me was the empty calm that follows overly strong emotions.

Before falling asleep a tiny thought occurred to me. "My

father," I thought, "was one of the ruins of my life, and before dying he'd asked for my forgiveness. I always considered Andrea my friend-teacher, and at the moment of departure he'd said exactly the same thing, 'Forgive.'"

I woke up in the middle of the night. For an instant I was seized by panic. I'd gone to sleep at dawn and it was still dark. The clock had stopped. The dogs were barking like crazy. Could the sun have suddenly decided not to come out? I was too afraid to get up, so I stayed in bed shutting and opening my eyes, waiting for the light. And in the end the light came. The window was covered with frozen vapor. The clear weather must have brought the cold with it. I wandered through the empty halls before finding the sister. She was in the kitchen sitting by the little fire place, mending something.

"Finally," she said. "I was beginning to think I'd taken in a marmot."

"Why?" I asked.

"Because you slept for two whole days."

"I was tired," I said.

She'd made me something to eat. As she moved about the kitchen, I watched her in silence. I was having difficulty matching the person before me with all that Andrea had written in his diary.

When she held out the cup with milk to me, I asked, "Could you have saved him?"

I no longer felt hatred toward her, only a kind of mournful curiosity.

She took a seat beside me.

"For several days," she said, "I had the impression I'd done it. My mistake was believing in appearances."

"After that night with the garden?"

She was taken aback. "How did you know?"

"From his notebook. He wrote it all down."

"Yes, after that night. It was the lowest point, do you understand? When you get down that low, you have to come back up. You can't stay still. That night he freed himself of his dead-weight. He felt lighter. Maybe it was that lightness that threw off his equilibrium completely. He wasn't used to walking without weight. The only explanation I can give is that he was afraid."

"He wanted to kill you?"

"Yes, I believe he came into my cell with that intention."

"But you're still alive. What happened?"

We kept talking there for a long time before the fire. She got up every now and then to stoke it with another log.

That night, she told me, there'd been a full moon. She'd heard him come in. She'd always slept lightly. His eyes shone like ice. He was breathing heavily. They looked at each other for a time that seemed to her like forever. Then he'd reached out his hands toward her neck. Instead of crying out or trying to defend herself, she had placed her hands on top of the young, strong hands of Andrea.

"You feel like crying. Cry."

And Andrea had broken into sobs. He cried like a baby left alone for too long. The sister had sat up in bed, and he, crushed at her feet, had placed his head on her knees.

"I am a murderer," he'd confessed.

The morning light found them exactly as before, Andrea's large body entrusted to the minute, fragile body of the old woman.

273

In those hours he told her everything, everything he'd kept sealed up inside him until that moment. A little after our separation, he'd entered the Foreign Legion and gone to fight in Chad and Guyana. Then, after his discharge, he'd gone over to the free profession.

He'd called it that exactly, "the free profession of murderer."

So for more than ten years he'd been a mercenary. Back in Africa when the war in Yugoslavia erupted, he'd immediately come back to Europe.

The thing that had so shaken him took place in the same mountains where, fifty years before, his father had fought. The father for an idea, Andrea for money. He couldn't say how many times he had already pulled the trigger at a live target. He did his job and that was that. He didn't overdo anything. He was valued for his coldness.

274

There was just one thing that upset him — people who were afraid. "They got on my nerves," was the way he put it to the sister.

During one round-up, they'd "gotten on his nerves" in front of a young woman. She was the sole survivor of an entire village, and they didn't want to waist ammunition on her.

"Get rid of her outside," Andrea had said to a kid. The kid and the girl must have been about the same age. His beard was just beginning to grow. They stood there in front of each other without either of them moving.

Andrea had got impatient, picked up a fat stick and killed her.

At that point, the sister said, the story became choppy. Andrea's words came out confused, incoherent. He kept repeating, "Matgrass... never went away... it was like matgrass.... Looked at me, shouldn't have looked.... I raised the stick and heard the fox's voice, the fox's voice. You understand?"

Now the sister seemed to be speaking with the same agitation as Andrea had. The story must have been stamped in her memory.

"'Thousands of kilometers away,' Andrea had said, 'in the middle of the woods, that woman was looking at me and the strident little voice was repeating, 'Not now. I'm not ready.' I couldn't stand to hear that hiss. To not hear it I beat and beat, and when I was done I was completely wet. It was winter and I was sweating ice. I looked down. Nearby was a baby. I hadn't seen him before. I don't know why I hadn't seen him. I don't know, but he couldn't have been more than two. He had pajamas on still and no shoes. He was sitting in the mud. Instead of crying or shrieking he was looking straight at me. There in front was the body of his mother without eyes or smile. If he had cried I would have finished my work immediately. Crying gets on my nerves too. Far off there was only the sound of a truck. Nearby men were walking into the houses. In reality I felt nothing. Him and me in a capsule, his eyes motionless, the pupils fixed, not a bat from the lids. The two of us and all the rest suspended. Those eyes, you know, made me completely naked. No one had ever done that to me before. It was the exact same expression I'd had in one of my baby pictures. The age was the same too, the age when my vampire-father used to take me in his arms. Now I understood he'd been a vampire in reverse. He hadn't sapped my energy. Rather his frozen halo had given me something. It had

275

given me horror. For more than thirty years I'd just been going around. The whole road I'd followed wasn't a circle but a spiral. The embraces of the vampire. The horror, followed by a long flight. When I realized the flight was merely a return, I'd arrived at my destination. They say the sins of the fathers fall on their children. That's not true. They don't fall, they mould. The sins of the fathers shape their children."

After telling this story, the sister said, Andrea had fallen into a deep sleep. He slept huddled up like a baby before it comes into the world. He had an expression on his face she hadn't ever seen before in all those months. When he woke up he was a different person. Even the tone of his voice was lower. He spoke softly, as if he was afraid of being heard. He was kind, attentive. He followed her through the corridors like a dog following its master.

"That was what misled me," she said. "It was silly and superficial of me to believe those were the symptoms of a change of course. He had changed. He helped me in my chores. He'd started painting the walls of the church on his own initiative. He'd been the one to point out to me how sad they were all chipped away. One day as I was in the garden I heard him singing. His voice rang out clear from inside the door of the church. I put my tools down and said, 'Thank you, God, thank you for bringing the light into his heart.' The next week, he took me by the hand and led me inside to see the results. He looked around and said, it still needs this and that. 'If you like,' I answered, 'you take care of it. I'm too old.'

"We'd begun to address each other less formally, and in

a way I thought of him as a son. Then we sat down and remained beside each other for a long time in silence. Between us at that instant was a great fullness. Any word or gesture would have been superfluous. In the evening after supper, he asked me to show him the place in the Gospel with the parable of the prodigal son. He read it several times in front of me and then said, 'But it's not right.' 'What isn't?' I asked. 'That children who've behaved well are ignored and that the return of the delinquent is cause for a great celebration. Why don't they rise up? Why don't they send him packing back where he came from? What does it mean? That the best thing is to behave badly?'

"'The logic of love,' I answered, 'is a kind of non-logic. It often follows routes that are hard for our intellect to grasp. There's giving freely in love. That's what we have trouble accepting. In the normal logic everything has a weight and counterweight, action and reaction. Between one and the other there's always a known relationship. The love of God is different. It's an excessive love. Instead of settling things, most often it subverts them. That's what staggers us, makes us afraid. But it's also what permits the wayward son to return home and be received with joy rather than resentment. He made mistakes, he was troubled, maybe he performed evil too, but then he comes home. He doesn't come home by accident. He chooses to. He chooses to come home to the abode of his Father.'

"I concluded by saying: 'The door is always open, you see? It means that too.'"

"Andrea was lost in thought for some time. Then he got up and wished me good night.

"The next morning, up to a certain point I wasn't worried. Andrea often appeared around ten o'clock. The anxiety took hold around noon. I knocked at his door, but there was no answer. I went in. The cell was empty. On the bed was a notebook and pencil, on the floor his boots all muddy. At that point anxiety turned to panic. I opened all the cell doors one by one then ran outside toward the tool shed. As I crossed the courtyard, through the window of the storeroom I saw his legs hanging from the ceiling. There was a pile of dirt a little ways from the door. Before committing suicide he had dug a grave for himself."

A long silence followed.

"It was awful," she began again, "awful. Andrea was a seedling that had just begun to sprout. The hail came and took him away. I came to think actually that all the serenity he'd displayed in those days was due only to the fact that he'd already decided. It was death, the end of pain, that had made him cheerful. But maybe that's not it, I'm mistaken, his light was the real light, and for that reason he became afraid. He committed the error of judging himself with his human yardstick. He wasn't capable of pity for himself. He couldn't have it. A soul that goes away like that is a defeated soul. Its own defeat and ours. Now more than ever Andrea needs help. That's why I asked you to pray that first evening, to help him overcome the weight of his act."

"I don't know how to pray," I told her.

She looked at me. Her glance became clear again.

"No one does. To learn you first have to put aside your pride."

V

There was one bus per day from the village down to Lju-
bljiana. Every morning I packed the few things I had, intent
on leaving. Every evening I was still there, before the fire
with the sister. After ten days I emptied my bag and tossed
it onto the top of the armoire. In the frozen, solitary nights
I understood that leaving would have just been continuing
to behave as I always had.

You run when something's chasing you. At my back all I had
were ghosts. Whoever runs from ghosts runs toward insanity.

There were four crosses behind me, my mother's, my
father's, Andrea's, and my ambition's. They were all buried
beneath a thin layer of earth. I no longer had any need of
acting in order to show anything to anyone, not even to
me. By now I understood all my actions had been mere reactions. All my movements had been undertaken in opposition to other people's wills. Inside me now there wasn't
motion anymore but inertia. I was inert and defenseless. I
was the age of a man but in the condition of a baby just into
the world. I felt as if all those years had left incrustations on

me. I was a boat left too long in the water without care. I could decide to break free of my moorings and be cast adrift forever, or lift my hull into dry dock, scrape and refinish it, and make it fit to navigate the open seas once more.

No one waited for me at home. My life existed in me and in the heart of no one else. If I were dead, nobody would have mourned me. I had no work or goal. Around me was the kind of desert that often follows an irrational exploitation of the earth.

From time to time as I worked in the garden or mended a fence, scenes from my life in Rome would pass before my eyes. I'd see Orsa stretched out on the bed and Neno seated on his couch, his legs crossed. I'd see life as it is said that people see it when they're on the verge of death. Now I was the spectator, and that was all.

Both had replaced me. In Orsa's bed there was surely someone else, and beside Neno a new poor fool pervaded with my same craving for success. From up here all events seemed to me only a great wheel. The wheel turned, its spokes turning. I thought about the ecological niches Andrea had told me so much about. I'd left an empty one down there, and someone else had immediately filled it. That someone else wouldn't escape what had been my destiny: contempt and despair lay waiting around the corner. He believed he was important, but actually he was a clown, jumping and singing and turning somersaults among skeletons sitting in the desert.

I couldn't get death out of my head. Not Andrea's or mine but that which struck down people who thought they were omnipotent.

One day Federico too would be dead, along with his sleek-thighed assistants, and Orio, collapsed atop his ottomans stuffed with money. The panther glance of Orsa too would be subject to the veil of cataracts and then that of death. We would all find the same bed in the end, the cold slab of a mortuary. Dissolution was the woolen yarn we were all rushing toward. The winners rushed, and the failures rushed. You could see it clearly at the end of the line. But the majority continued to act as if it weren't true. They kept feeling young, healthy, and powerful, certain they would always be that way.

It was as if I suddenly found myself before a mountain. It had always been there, I'd just never been able to see it. But it was there all the time, ever since the day my bench mate from school had died and I'd felt the void all around. There was that mountain, that volcano, that iceberg, and on its slopes life took place. It was impossible to understand its mystery without getting to its peak. Maybe tossing out the bait to get me to come to this convent had been the only act of love Andrea had ever performed in his whole life.

In the evening I often talked with the sister in front of the fire. I was surprised at how the words had a different weight up here. Until then without really knowing it I'd been immersed in continual chatter. Words, words, and more words had escaped from my mouth and other people's. Those words were none other than the ink that squids emit to cloud the water. You could barely see a thing, but that wasn't important. It was convenient to live inside it.

I often thought back on the "forgive me" my father had pronounced and Andrea had repeated.

I asked the sister, "Why did they both say the same thing on the point of dying?"

"Often," she said, "it's only the end of a journey that tells what was in it. The emergency makes actions appear in a different light. You're suddenly aware you made a mistake. It's too late to change things. So you ask for forgiveness. I'll ask for it too," she added. "So will you. No one can help it. Not doing so would be presumptuous, because life after all is a course marked by mistakes. Very few know the Light from the beginning. All the others proceed blindly. Even when someone arrives at an intuition of the Spirit, he makes mistakes. We all make mistakes for the simple fact of being human, because our eyes can only see so far. They can't see through objects or climb over horizons. There's always a dark corner one can't make out. Slipping is often easier than moving forward."

We talked a lot about the conversations Andrea and I had had as boys, too. About how I'd been fascinated by his words, and my recognition of him as a kind of teacher, how his speeches had become the program of my life.

It still made her feel terrible to talk about Andrea, of course. As soon as I mentioned his name, the luminous joy of her expression would be clouded for a moment. But she didn't avoid talking about him.

"Andrea's great prison," she told me one evening, "was his extreme intelligence. That was what constructed the cage around him. It constructed it through deception, by seducing its owner. For too long it made him believe it was a powerful binoculars, or perhaps even a telescope. With those lenses he could rove from the earth's abysses to the distant light of the stars. He could trace trajectories and determine the points of falling. The acuteness of his thought made him feel omnipotent. He was convinced he saw things that were concealed from the majority. Maybe in a way he was right. But with the habit of keeping his eyes glued to that instrument, he didn't realize that before him only a miniscule segment of reality was open. Binoculars make a limited angle of vision larger and closer. There are twenty degrees there in front and then another three hundred forty all around. When he moved his eyes away in the end, he couldn't bear looking at the whole. It was too much for him."

"Do we need to be stupid?"

"No," she answered, "humble."

"You see," she went on, looking me in the eyes, "the mistake is believing we deserve credit for our own intelligence. The more intelligent one is the more one tends to think that. Intelligence nurtures inside it the germ of superiority. But over what? Over whom? We're not the ones who make intelligence. It's a gift, a kind of little treasure we must take proper care of. It's entrusted to us and we need to respect it, have faith in it. No one can decide to be intelligent, do you understand? No one can expect it, just as no one can decide 'how much' intelligence to have. You only have to linger a little over this to bar the path to pride.

283

"But one day we'll be asked to give an account of how we've used it. You probably know the parable of talent. The great confusion is in mixing up knowledge and power, thinking intelligence alone can be used to dominate things, possess and shape them. Things and people. Without humility, without compassion intelligence is just a wretched parody of itself. You think it sets you free, but actually it keeps you prisoner. It's invisible and patient, and it builds a cage around you. You're inside thinking your breathing space is vast. When you realize that's not the case, it's often too late. You're afraid of going out, like animals who've lived too long in a cage.

"I'm old enough to have seen the better part of a century slip by. I can say now this is the evil of our time. Proud intelligence nourished on itself alone. At a certain point, fear of God was set aside, actions became empty, uprooted from a larger project. Where there is emptiness there's the Irrational. It glides in everywhere quickly, scattering its insanity everywhere. What has been — what is — depends on this. Without respect, without love, man is just a big monkey running around the world with bloody hands."

"Who is the Irrational?" I asked.

"You can call it how you like. It has a lot of names, but its activity is one."

"Which is?"

"Destroying destinies. By spreading darkness, it estranges man from himself."

In the months we spent together, I learned to understand her frailty and strength, the frailty of her old being, the timeless strength of her thinking. I often thought back on the sense of irritation I'd experienced on first seeing her.

Like Andrea and everyone else, I too had in my head only the cliché of a nun. I had judged the habit rather than seeing the person. I thought of sickeningly sweet consolation. But before me was a human being who spoke with a clarity and knowledge I hadn't found in anyone else.

So in the end I gathered my courage and asked her the question that had always tormented me, the hinge on which my life had turned.

"What about evil? Why does evil exist?"

It was an afternoon in March. We were planting chard in the garden. She rose to her feet and stood in the middle of a furrow, the seeds in her hand.

"Do you really want an answer?"

"Yes."

"The answer is there isn't any answer. Some people say they know, they talk about rewards and punishments. They're lying. When a baby dies, what can you say? Nothing. You can curse heaven or accept the mystery of it. Evil is a surprise and a scandal. You can only fight against the smaller kind, the one that comes from our actions. With a word, a gesture, you can add to the evil in the world or diminish it. Deciding one or the other depends only on us.

"Look at these chard seeds," she said. "Look how awkward, even ugly they are. If you didn't know what they were, you might easily think they were the droppings of some rodent. But actually here, in these few cubic millimeters of matter, there's everything. There's energy gathered up and the project of growth. The great green leaves that will shade the garden in June are already here inside. Many people are moved by large open spaces, the mountains or the sea. It's only there that they feel in communion with the breath of the universe. To me the opposite has always

285

been the case. It's the little things that make me giddy over the infinite.

"A pumpkin seed, for instance, you can eat it or put it in the earth. In the first case nothing happens, but in the second, at the end of a few months, an enormous plant grows, its leaves invading the whole garden. It seems almost a magic plant, and among the leaves pumpkins appear. They're round, shiny. If you open them, the color inside is that of the setting sun. Then you stop and ask yourself, where did all this come from? It's very hard to go back to the tiny seeds. But the project was there, you know? The task of that tiny entity was to become that orange light closed up inside the rind.

"We're all seeds thrown onto the earth. That's what we forget too often."

I knew little about her life. She was rather reticent to talk about herself and only answered when I asked her questions. She would only add things about herself to help me on the road of understanding.

She told me about studying mathematics before entering the convent. Her intelligence had thirsted for perfection, which was why she'd turned to that kind of study. For a long time she'd been convinced that theorems and calculations could find a name and a law for every thing.

She'd been teaching in a lyceum for years when her family was wiped out by the Ustashe. She was saved because she'd gone down to the cellar for the wine.

In the face of the violent eruption, she'd understood

how tiny was the knowledge she'd believed was enormous. She gave herself no peace for having survived her family.

"For years after the slaughter I lived with my heart gripped in a vice of thorns. I would have preferred blades since they kill, while thorns only make every breath painful.

"I wandered around Europe for years like a wild dog. No place, no relationship was able to provide me with any state other than bewilderment. The light that irradiated every morning was the light of hatred. I hated those who had killed. I hated my father and his principles for getting him killed. I hated my great learning that was as useless as a fish net with torn meshes.

"For a long time," she said, "my sky was lit up only with the glare of flames, which were carried from one place to another by the wind. They lapped and scorched everything without stopping or asking permission."

She stopped for a moment as if catching her breath, then went on in a low voice.

"Then one day, traveling by train, I found a set of the Gospels someone had left on the seat next to me. I had nothing to read, so I picked it up. It was springtime, and the train proceeded slowly. From the window came the intense smell of acacias in bloom. I opened it randomly, and my eyes happened to fall on a line. It was written: *'Peace I leave to you. My peace I give to you. Not as the world gives, do I give it to you.'*

"Those words immediately entered inside me. Once inside they turned into a nail, a drill. They opened a tiny hole in the darkness that had been wrapped around my days for too long. Light came into the hole, at first barely a sliver, coming and going. It was and wasn't there. Sometimes as I went to sleep at night I would turn to someone whose face I didn't yet know. 'Please,' I would say, 'make this light not disappear. Make it be here tomorrow.'

"I was like someone extremely thirsty who finds a drop of water on a rock. I knew my salvation depended on it. What I didn't yet know was whether there was a whole watery stratum below it or this was merely a dewdrop. I'd been walking for a long time in a stone desert. Walking and walking, I'd been convinced the whole world was the same. Parched, harsh, without any form of life, without light except for the fire that I carried with me as I walked. Then, ahead of me, there was suddenly an oasis. There were palms, flowers, birds singing, fruit, and the constant gurgle of a spring. It might or might not have been a mirage. How could I know? Only as I approached nearer was I able to see that the shadow was real, the water was real. As it descended fresh into my body, something strange suddenly happened. My sight changed. The opaque veil that had covered it for so long disappeared. My eyes were the same. What I saw was different."

"Different how?" I asked.

"In its joy."

It was late evening. We talked for a little while longer. She told me about how she'd gone into the convent and the long years she'd spent caring for the sick in India.

"You wanted to punish yourself?" I asked her as we were getting up.

She smiled as one does at the question of a child.

"Punish myself?" she said "What for?"

Then, with a light step, she disappeared down the hall.

288

VI

Sister Irene died on December 2 the following winter.

She died of that long surrender that afflicts very old, healthy people. In summer she started having difficulty walking. In October she took to her bed. She didn't want me to call a doctor or take her to a hospital.

So I started carrying her. Who knows why I thought she would be heavy, but she was extremely light.

The first times she seemed a little embarrassed. She'd been taking care of others for too many years. She wasn't ready for the opposite.

But after a few days, she began to entrust herself to me. Instead of keeping her head high, she laid it against my chest. From a curious little bird that tries to see out of its nest she had become a tired little bird. I felt her long, cold fingers on my neck.

At other times that contact would have irritated me. But something had changed inside me. I thought about my mother and her solitary anguish and felt myself giving off more warmth. Caring for her, I was caring for those who had passed by me and died without my being able to touch them, scratch the surface of their solitude, their suffering.

Her voice followed the decline of her body, growing feebler from day to day. Only her thoughts remained unchanged. The clarity and precision of her words were the same as ever. So as not to leave her alone, I made up little beds throughout the convent. Wherever I went she went.

"We're like a hermit crab and an anemone," she said one day. "You walk and I follow. Even if I don't want to I have to anyway."

The sudden intimacy had led us to say *tu* to each other, and with *tu* our relationship entered another dimension. We no longer shouted things to each other like a couple of mountain climbers spanning two peaks. Our phrases ended up seeming more and more like whispers.

290   One day, as we crossed the cloister, she said:

"I came here to die alone. I wanted to leave discretely, without bothering anyone. But then you came and now everything revolves around me. I have to be carried about from morning to night like a Grand Vizier."

Sometimes she was sadder, and complained that I was caring for her too much.

"It's not worth the effort," she would say. "Go for a walk, go have some fun. You're young. You have so much energy in your body."

"There's nothing I want to do besides this."

"To punish yourself?" she'd asked.

"No, to mortify your sense of pride."

My joke made her smile.

"You're right. Pride gets worse with age."

What she'd said about the varieties of joy continued to torment me through all those months. I'd learned to get up with the light. As I woke, ever more frequently I happened to feel a new sensation. I felt cheerful. There wasn't any precise motive or idea. The tiniest thing made me smile. In my vision there was wonder, nothing else. It was as if some part of me had begun to expand, to breathe differently. I thought often about the tiny hole into which the light had entered in Sister Irene's story.

One morning, while I kneeled on the garden soil, planting cabbages, I suddenly asked, "Grace is joy?"

She was very tired. Instead of answering, she lowered her eyelids as a sign of affirmation.

Stupidly I added, "Why?"

She slowly raised her arm. I followed her gesture with my eyes. Above us was a chestnut tree weighed down with fruit and then the wide luminous silence of the sky.

291

She was lucid until her final days. I never left her in those hours.

When she took my hand in hers and murmured, "Forgive," the rain was beating against the window pane.

She stopped breathing a little before dawn.

I combed her hair, washed her, and lay her on the bed. Beside her I placed two lit white candles.

Then I put on my wind breaker and went out for a walk.

The sky was still dark, but it had stopped raining. I started up the narrow path that leads from the convent to the mountain summit. I felt extraordinarily light. There was pain inside, but also a sense of a different freedom.

As I walked I thought about the long year we'd spent together, about her hand filled with seeds, her joy and toughness. I thought of the chance that had brought out lives together, and the fact that, perhaps, from the moment of my birth I'd been destined to arrive at this place.

Behind me were the long years of confusion, all the pain I'd felt and made others feel. I needed to go back very far to get to a point where it was possible to put myself back together. A point before the chatter, before the vanity of ambition. In that year all the incrustations had slowly disappeared. I no longer had blinkers or little moulds for seeing things. Intelligence was softening into something else.

I hadn't yet given a name to the something else. But I knew I'd met it at least once before, when I was a boy, caressing the lambs on their way to die. It was barely a flash, which had lit up a different kind of understanding. At sixteen I had confused it with art. Now I understood it was merely the feeling of compassion.

Suddenly before me appeared the image of a baby coming into the world. It was my father. He wasn't alone. Behind him was my mother, and then Andrea, Neno, Federico, Orio, Orsa. It was them and the tiny wrinkled body of Sister Irene. And after Sister Irene, my body. One day long before, we'd all been naked, helpless, frail and bewildered. We'd all had the same expression that day, an expression devoid of prejudice, bright with joy. There was something that made you melt in the image, something that burned me inside. Ultimately, I thought as I clambered up the mountain, seeing people in this way would be enough to stop hating.

If I'd remembered my father as a newborn, rather than a drunk, any resentment would have disappeared. The only feeling possible would have been the tenderness. The exact same tenderness I'd felt beside his death bed.

Tenderness and compassion.

Tenderness for his nakedness, compassion for his fragility. The same tenderness and compassion I now felt for all the existences that moved ahead unknown to themselves, those smothered, crushed, maimed, burst asunder, those that slipped away like sand between a child's fingers. Compassion for the enormous garland of lives intertwined one with another without distinction, estranged from the mystery of first sight, confused in the crossing, frightened at the final instant.

Growing doesn't mean forgetting that state but reacquiring it, finding our sight again.

When I got to the top of the mountain, the wind began to blow, the temperature dropped. There was no other sound but its whistling as I stood there, the same sound that had filled my childhood nightmares.

As I stood there I knew she was dead. I knew this and knew she was alive too. I had an almost physical perception of her presence beside me.

Up there I understood death no longer frightened me because death and life were two forms of existence. I stood there and understood, too, that there was no more space inside me for the void and the void exists only until one assimilates death.

I stood there happy for that wind. For the wind and the earth and rain that falls and makes the plants grow.

I stood and was no longer me but the breath of the whales sleeping in the depths of the sea. I was a lion walking in the savanna and the gazelle drinking deep from the river. I was the seed and the plant and the young colt staggering on its hooves, the horse, the plant, the dying elephant, its enormous, wise body collapsing exhausted.

I was this universe of breath and growth, all this and also a man, and it was this being man that made me weep, because he lives amid the greatness and magnificence of the universe without ever being fully aware of it. He destroys, consumes, subdues all the immense intelligent beauty that was given him as a gift.

I stood there sobbing. At a certain point the wind died down and the snow began to fall, not sleet but fat flakes that melted as they fell onto me, covering the landscape all around.

And so I set out on the way back. The path was white, and my steps resounded on it differently.

A little before the convent I came upon a buck with enormous antlers. It was rubbing its neck and snout against the bark of a tree. The snow coated its body evenly.

I thought it would run away when it saw me, but it stood still. It had extraordinarily black, lucid eyes, with long frozen lashes. It wasn't afraid. There was neither judgment nor challenge in its glance. It watched me, that was all.

Sister Irene had once said to me, "Men like to kill animals because they envy their natural grace."

When the deer moved, I thought she'd been right. There

was a Grace of the living world, and man did everything he could to be excluded from it.

When I entered the cell, the candles were about to go out. I licked my fingers and extinguished them, then put new ones in their place.

I stayed beside Sister Irene all afternoon and all night. More than once as I looked at her in the uncertain light of the flames, I had the impression she was smiling.

"Now you've understood," she said to me on one of the last days.

"Is that a question?"

"No, an affirmation."

"Understood what?"

"The simplest thing. What love is."

"And what is it?"

"Attention."

The next morning, according to her wishes, I wrapped her body in a white cloth. There were big dense, motionless clouds.

I had to shovel away a lot of snow before getting to the earth and a lot of earth before managing to bury her.

Around her were all her dead sisters and the restless body of Andrea.

She'd given me a sheet of paper to read. It was the simple prayer of San Francis.

When I had read, "Forgiving one is forgiven, dying one awakens to eternal life," from the sky the snow began to fall again.